POINT OF TRANSMISSION

A Post-Apocalyptic Epidemic Survival - The Morgan
Strain Series Book 1

MAX LOCKWOOD

Illustrated by
HRISTO KOVATLIEV

Edited by
VALORIE CLIFTON

Contents

Acknowledgments v

Chapter 1 1
Chapter 2 11
Chapter 3 21
Chapter 4 33
Chapter 5 43
Chapter 6 53
Chapter 7 65
Chapter 8 71
Chapter 9 81
Chapter 10 91
Chapter 11 101
Chapter 12 111
Chapter 13 121
Chapter 14 131
Chapter 15 141
Chapter 16 151
Chapter 17 161
Chapter 18 171
Chapter 19 177
Chapter 20 191
Chapter 21 201
Chapter 22 211
Chapter 23 223
Chapter 24 233
Chapter 25 245
Chapter 26 255
Chapter 27 265
Chapter 28 275

Chapter 29   285
Chapter 30   297

About Max Lockwood   303
Also by Max Lockwood   305

Excerpt From It Began

Chapter 1   309
Chapter 2   319
Chapter 3   325

Acknowledgments

I want to thank the following people in helping me with this new series, in one way or another. L.L. Akers, Boyd Craven III, Alison Ryan, Jenn Falls, and L.G. Davis. I am glad to have the support and encouragement from all of you that helps me write what I write for all my readers and fans! Definitely recommend reading their books when you get a chance as well!

Chapter One

The cold mist fell in tiny specks on the diner's windows, forming tiny rivers as they fell down the glass. Elaina breathed hot air on the pane and traced doodles in the condensation. To the average eye, it looked like geometric nonsense—just hexagons with straight lines shooting off into other shapes. Only Elaina understood the intricacies of the chemical formulas she designed.

When it comes to art, most people appreciate paintings, literature, or music. Though culture frequently shifts, people tend to find beauty in works created by others. No one catches a cold and marvels at the nasty little virus that causes their suffering. No one except, perhaps, for Elaina Morgan.

After a particularly bad stomach virus at the age of three, a precocious Elaina asked her mom why she was sick. At that age, all children are full of questions, but they never think too much about the answers. When her mom explained that tiny creatures had entered her body and made her sick, this small nugget of knowledge didn't disappear like other childhood musings. Instead, she begged her parents to buy her books about viruses.

Already used to her strange requests at this age, her parents read her short sections of completely age-inappropriate books every night. As a middle school English teacher and a mechanical engineer, her father and mother knew little of the subject matter as they read to their daughter. Within a few years, their services were no longer needed, and a bike ride to the library took Elaina to a new world of discoveries.

It was no surprise, then, that by the age of fifteen, Elaina had completed her high school courses while she took college prerequisites at the local community college at night. When most students wrote their college application essay on why they wanted to attend their school of choice, Elaina attached a copy of her study on the Ebola virus to her Princeton application. She was awarded a full scholarship the very next day.

Elaina nervously tapped her fingertips on the slightly sticky table as she waited for her coffee refill to arrive. She picked at a cheese Danish, knowing that she should eat but not really tasting anything. Sleep hadn't come easily for Elaina in the past few days. She had never been a particularly good sleeper. There was always too much work to be done, too many ideas floating around her head. But, recent events had made it impossible to quiet her mind for long enough to make it through a few REM cycles.

"Thank you," Elaina muttered as the waitress came

around with the steaming hot carafe of coffee for the second time. During her high school years, Elaina had frequented that diner, becoming a bit of a regular. Now, with her very own office, she didn't have to leave the privacy of her laboratory to get her fix. When she arrived, she was mildly concerned that an old waitress or cook would remember one of their most loyal patrons, but in a college town, she was just one face out of many.

She greedily gulped down her coffee after stirring a splash of milk and an artificial sweetener into the cup of dark liquid. In a few minutes, she would have to pack up her things and go, but she knew to savor the moment in the warm café.

Drops of rainwater dripped from her baseball cap onto the counter, leaving small puddles that she wiped away with the sleeve of her baggy sweatshirt. Never much of a sports fan, she still loved to wear her old Mariners hat that her dad bought her years ago. She wore it like camouflage, blending in with the other caffeine addicts in the diner.

Elaina made tight fists, trying to stop her hands from shaking. Too little food and too many stimulants made her heart race and her extremities quiver. A grandfatherly man two seats away offered her a small smile.

"When you're old like me," he said in his pack-a-day voice, "just half a cup will do that to you. You're too young to be so tired," he said, noticing the dark circles around the eyes she tried to hide from the public. "I'm sure whatever you're staying awake for isn't as important as you think it is. I remember when my son was in college. He'd stay up all night studying for tests, only to fall asleep halfway through."

She nodded, covering her face with her cup. Appearing unfriendly was never really a concern of hers. Making friends with old men was very low on her list of current priorities. In fact, making friends was never on any list of priorities.

"Can you believe it?" he muttered, nodding at the old television mounted on the wall.

She turned to look and gritted her teeth at what she saw.

Elaina had watched more news broadcasts in the past week than she had in all twenty-three years of her life. The information it presented never really had much to do with her life or her own concerns. Therefore, any time consuming that kind of information would be a waste, in the scheme of things. Time was best spent working on new discoveries in her field.

"We've now received reports from the CDC that the virus is beginning to mutate as more people become infected," an anchorwoman spoke in an unnatural rhythm that Elaina found grating.

"It's scary, that," the man said, pointing at the screen, speaking to no one in particular. "I'm just lucky I live alone and don't go out much. I heard they had to close down every school in the county to keep this thing from spreading."

"Hmm," Elaina hummed, hoping he'd change the subject.

"New guidelines for avoiding the spread of this infection have been put into place and are being strongly enforced at all government agencies. The Morgan Virus is spread through the contact of bodily fluids, which can even include sneezes and coughs if the microscopic droplets enter the body."

"I heard there were a few cases being treated in the hospital on Maple Street," a cook said from the other side of the counter. "It's scary to think of how close it is to us. You just never know, one of these customers might be a few hours away from losing their minds and infecting someone. It's like people are turning into zombies out there."

Elaina sighed, louder than she intended. This was how misinformation was spread. The fear of the unknown always opened up opportunities for rumors to fly. If any of these people had just a working knowledge of how viruses worked, this wouldn't even be news.

This strain, the Morgan Strain, was an impressive little virus. In its purest state, it had the power to cure the most troubling diseases in the world. But, released on the world in an uncontrolled manner, it caused great destruction.

The zombie comparison was a bit of an exaggeration, but still not too far from reality. The sickness caused the patient to become agitated and more likely to act out in anger against others, but only in later stages. Most patients didn't survive that long.

"If you or someone you know is experiencing headaches, high fever, chills, and oozing sores that are slow to heal, call the emergency hotline on the bottom of the screen. Do not enter a hospital if you suspect you have been infected without being directed to your nearest Morgan virus center first. It is important for the doctors and nurses treating you to be properly prepared."

Elaina rolled her eyes. It didn't help that the media was spreading the panic about the virus. It was a sad fact that average humans didn't know how to keep their germs to themselves. However, Elaina knew that viruses like this were nature's way of keeping the population in check. Unfortunately, when human sentiment becomes involved, people forget that sickness and death are perils of life.

Of course, she understood the mind's own attempts at self-preservation. She herself took measures every day in the lab to make sure she didn't accidentally infect herself. She was not afraid of death in the same way most people were. She knew firsthand that it took the best people without any reason or discrimination. She knew the suffering it caused others. In her career, she strived to make new discoveries out of her own personal curiosity, but if it made it so others didn't have to feel the pain she knew too well, that was just one of the perks of the job.

"Do you think it can be spread through kissing?" a young, wide-eyed waitress asked. "Not even tongue-kissing—just a peck on the lips?"

"I don't think so, honey," the older waitress replied. "The news never said anything about any kind of intimate contact."

Wrong, Elaina thought to herself. Apparently, it was too obscene for the news to talk about sex, which was one of the most common ways of transmitting the disease. Knowing the risks of the virus, she wouldn't chance it herself. Although, she was probably the only one in the world who was better equipped to cure it or at least vaccinate against it.

"We wouldn't even have this problem if it weren't for the idiot scientists who created this thing in the lab," the cook behind the counter grunted.

"But how did it possibly get out into the public?" the man sitting next to Elaina asked. "Isn't that stuff under lock and key?"

"My guess is that it's either a government conspiracy or just plain stupidity and carelessness. But it's gotten out of control now. It's mutating and becoming impossible to predict. It's so much worse than we could have ever imagined."

Elaina clenched her teeth. She wanted to speak up, but she knew that she couldn't. If they only knew the good that the Morgan virus could do in its intended state, they would never talk about it in that manner. There was only one expert in the entire diner, and she was sitting with her head bowed, hoping the conversation would shift with the next news story.

"Police are currently looking for a person of interest in the initial spread of the virus. Elaina Morgan, age twenty-three, was last seen outside her laboratory on September fourth. She is wanted by the state for reckless endangerment. If anyone has information on Elaina's whereabouts, police would appreciate any leads they can get," the news reporter droned on before shifting the news to the weather.

Elaina quickly grabbed a handful of crumpled bills

from her front pocket and set them on the table. She felt as though she was about to be sick, but she kept her focus.

Her car was approximately fifty-seven steps away from the diner counter. If she could keep an even pace, she wouldn't appear suspicious. Once in her car, she would leave the city and get as far away as she could. The next few minutes were important, though, and she could not afford to make a mistake.

Elaina made it about three steps before the man next to her stood up.

"Wait," he said. "Isn't that her?"

He pointed at the television screen, flashing a smiling photo of her from her undergraduate graduation ceremony. It was a rare moment for her to smile in any photo, but she was just so pleased to go on to the next step in her career that she didn't even mind that her mom was catching such a rare moment.

Everyone at the counter turned to look, thrilled to have the opportunity to catch a real-life criminal on the run. If they called her in, there was no doubt that they would earn a television interview on the news station they watched all day. The fifteen minutes of fame would leave quickly, but it would be so satisfying in the moment.

Composure flew out the window. Elaina took a running start for her car, hoping that she would at least be able to outrun the police when they showed up at the diner. With her shoes slipping on the wet pavement, she made her way to her vehicle.

Keys in hand, she lunged for the door when

someone got in her way. Her body halted in front of a tall, sturdy man dressed in a blue uniform. Elaina's stomach dropped.

"I'm sorry," she said to the police officer she ran into. "I have to get home. I think my mom is sick," she tried.

He stared at her, his eyes black and beady. His mouth was drawn into a scowl.

This was it. She was caught just weeks after the first outbreak. No jury in the world would be able to acquit her because by the time she got a trial, everyone would have lost a loved one to the virus. Also, as quickly as it spread, she probably wouldn't survive prison. One infected person showing minimal symptoms could kill off an entire prison population. Plus, judging by the strange symptoms that appeared as it mutated, it would not be pretty.

"Can I get to my car, please?" she asked politely, pointing to the car that the officer's body was blocking.

He was silent. Upon closer inspection, Elaina realized that his skin was a mottled grey color. His pupils were dilated as if he were in the sun, but it was an overcast day. Also, they extended far beyond normal pupil dilation.

Without any warning, the man lunged at Elaina, wrapping his big hands around her biceps. Taken aback, she stumbled a few steps backward, coming loose from his grip. She ran to the passenger side door and quickly slid into the seat before he could follow.

She managed to slam the door behind her, but not without catching the man's fingertips in the car. He howled an unnatural sound as the very ends of his fingertips fell to the dusty floor mat.

Elaina locked the doors and slid into the driver's seat, reversing out of the parking lot as quickly as possible. With a skid, she shifted her car into drive and didn't look back at the possessed policeman who was staggering toward the diner.

Chapter Two

An empty beer bottle rolled off the table, but Alec caught it before it hit the ground. Even after six drinks, his reflexes were still relatively sharp. His motions were fluid. He'd often react to outside stimuli before he even had a chance to think about what his body was doing. Usually, his quick reactions served him well.

Alec set the bottle upright on the coffee table and reached for another lukewarm brew. He was drinking purposefully, so it didn't matter if he didn't enjoy the warm beer. After five or so, they didn't taste the same anyway.

Outside his small, two-bedroom home, he heard noises in the street. Given his meager income, his home wasn't in a great neighborhood. If he weren't a cop, he would have been more afraid of the characters who roamed in and out of the neighborhood.

Perhaps being an officer of the law put him at a

bigger risk. He didn't go out of his way to patrol the streets where he lived, but he always wondered if he would be ambushed at his home if he pulled over the wrong person. Luckily, he spent most of his time directing traffic. It was hard to get into trouble doing that.

Still, he managed to see his fair share of action every now and again. His very first day on the job, he was sent to a home to check on a noise complaint. Typically, these calls involved telling homeowners that their nosy neighbors didn't like the music they were blasting late at night. It just so happened that this particular home was the holding cell of two kidnapped kids. Once he was labeled a "hero", he was allowed to go on more important calls when an extra body was needed.

Alec flipped through television channels, looking for something worth watching, or at the very least, something worth falling asleep to. At one in the afternoon, there weren't a lot of choices. He settled on a game show and tossed the remote on the ground. A short nap would pass the time well before he started drinking again.

He only managed to slumber for a couple of hours when he woke up to the shrill sounds of his cellphone.

"Hello?" he answered groggily, the rest of his buzz wearing off.

"Lawrence," the sheriff growled. "It sounds like you're sleeping."

"No, I'm awake," he lied, blinking his eyes rapidly. "What's up?"

"What's up?" the sheriff echoed. "Do you have any idea what's happening outside as we speak?"

"Uh, no," Alec admitted. He avoided the outside world whenever he could.

"The riots are getting worse. They're not even looting anymore. No, they're destroying everything just to be destructive. It's absolute madness. Anyway, I need everyone I can get. I know you're on probation, but you need to get your ass down to the station as soon as possible."

"Now?" he asked, looking at the beer bottles surrounding him. He wasn't exactly in working condition.

"Now," the sheriff answered. "I don't care if you have to walk downtown. We need everyone we can get. Do you understand me?"

"Do I get my gun back?" he asked.

The sheriff paused. "You'll be outfitted with the usual riot gear. If the situation changes, we'll adapt."

That was a no. Alec didn't blame him though. Everyone knew that he was quick with a gun. With riots going on, it was sometimes hard to tell which people were dangerous and which were innocent bystanders.

Once he got off the phone with his superior, Alec brewed a strong pot of coffee and chugged a steaming cup. Then, he poured the rest into a travel mug for his trip to the station. He hoped that between his nap, the coffee, and the convenience store sandwich he pulled out of the fridge, he would be alert enough to work.

He knew he shouldn't have been driving, but he got into his old patrol car anyway and slowly drove into work, being extra-cautious. He could feel himself sobering up as the hangover came on in full force. Luckily for Alec, he was used to this routine. Unfortunately, he couldn't stave it off with another drink at this moment. With any luck, this riot would be over soon and he could find his spot back on the couch.

On his way, he noticed a lot of people wandering around the streets—many more than usual. The strangest part was that it didn't look like they were walking with purpose, just kind of mindlessly following the others. A few times, he had to stop quickly while they crossed in the middle of the road, not caring that they were crossing two lanes of traffic in the middle of a freeway.

Finally, he carefully parked in a spot as far away from the building as he could. He couldn't risk hitting a car in the parking lot of a police station. As he walked inside, he noticed that the station was eerily empty, strange for a supposedly busy day.

"Nice to see you," Officer Hardwick said to Alec when he walked in. "How's it been?"

"It could be worse," Alec replied.

"I'm afraid we're about to find out how bad things can be," Hardwick said, frowning.

"What's going on?" Alec asked. "Davidson called me in and told me that there were riots going on. I get that it has something to do with the virus. Is everyone panicking because they're worried about supply shortages?"

"You would think that, but it's not exactly that rational. In past cases, panic over an epidemic probably would spur some overexcited people into stockpiling goods in case things got bad. But you know, things never escalate that far."

"Then what's going on now?" Alec asked.

Hardwick grimaced. "I don't want to over exaggerate, especially when everybody is going crazy over this thing, but it might actually be that bad. Even the station has ordered a bunch of goods in case we have to stay holed up in here. The Washington National Guard has already been called in."

Alec suspected that he had a drinking problem, but he knew for sure when his first concern about the madness was that he wouldn't be able to stockpile enough alcohol before things really got out of hand. He made a mental note to stop at the store whenever he was relieved of his daily duties.

"You missed the briefing earlier, so I should probably fill you in," Hardwick continued. "It's believed that a lot of people out on the streets right now already have the virus. There are probably some crazies who don't have it yet, but if they stay out there too long, they're bound to catch it. Not only do we need to go out there and break up the crowds, but we need to try to determine who's infected and who's just a little too riled up about this disease."

Alec scoffed. He knew this game too well. "How the hell are we supposed to do that? We're not trained doctors. I can't perform a blood test on every person who looks a little crazy. That's just about everybody."

"I know," Hardwick said softly. "All I know is that I just want to get the streets cleared as quickly as possible without getting hurt. My family has been stuck inside for days, and the last thing I want is for something to happen to me. Or worse," he said grimly, "I don't want to be the one bringing the virus into our home."

Alec nodded, but he wondered if anyone would really miss him if he were gone. He was single, and his family lived out of the state. Plus, things weren't great at work, and he wasn't sure if he'd ever have the chance to rise through the ranks again. If he caught the virus, would anyone even care? Would he just quietly ride out the symptoms at home and pass on?

He shook the thoughts out of his head. He had just read an article that described the psychological effects the virus had on the body. Catching the disease meant that he would probably put others in harm's way. That was the last thing he wanted.

The reason he became a cop in the first place was because he truly cared about the safety and wellbeing of everyone—those he knew, and those he didn't know. While traffic stops and busting teen parties were just an annoying part of the job, he really cared about the big stuff. He wanted to rescue children from abusive homes, stop violent offenders from hurting or killing citizens, and maybe even save the odd cat stuck in a tree. He wanted to do good in a world that so badly needed it.

Alec was walking to the breakroom for one final cup of coffee before going out when the memory of the last time he went out on patrol hit him. He slumped into the chair, the memory of what happened overwhelming his senses.

Before the virus became well-known, he had been

sent out on a call about a belligerent woman causing all sorts of problems. Being newly promoted, he was eager to scope out the situation. He drove out to a shopping center to find a crowd gathering outside. In the middle of the commotion, a teenage girl wielded a steak knife at strangers in the crowd.

Chaos ensued. Even though people were running from the scene, it seemed as though just as many were running to watch. Something about violence really drew a crowd. When he saw what was happening, he immediately called for backup.

The first thing he tried to do was clear the entrance of the mall. Alec shouted for everyone to back away and go home, but there were still gawkers standing around with their phones out, ready to take a video of the young attacker.

The thin, blonde girl in her school's cheerleading uniform was covered in blood. Alec wasn't sure if it was hers or someone else's. He called out to her to get her to stop, but she didn't listen. It was as if she could hear that he was making noises, but she had no idea what he was saying.

After a few attempts at telling her to drop her weapon, the young officer approached her. She was pretty small and starting to get tired, so Alec knew that if he lunged at her, he could tackle her and hold her down for long enough to get handcuffs on her.

After one final plea for her to drop her weapon, he strode toward her, gaining speed with each step. Instead of carrying on in her dozy manner, she suddenly became enraged, as if she were possessed by a demon.

She screamed a high-pitched howl and raced toward him, the blade of the knife aimed straight for his neck.

What happened in that next split second was still hazy for Alec. He remembered seeing her coming toward him, but he couldn't remember any thoughts or memories he had before he drew his gun and pulled the trigger. The witnesses said that he was completely silent as he took one perfect shot to her chest.

Alec's body camera and all of the witnesses with cellphones painted a perfectly clear picture of what happened. He was well within his right to use deadly force as she was running straight toward him with a weapon in an attempt to seriously wound or kill him. Legally, he did nothing wrong.

However, there was some controversy surrounding his case. Many argued that he could have stopped her with a non-lethal weapon or simply shot her in the leg. The girl was so small that a lot of people figured a man of his stature could stop her with a takedown maneuver.

But, as the autopsy report proved, the girl was suffering from an early mutation of the virus. She was perhaps the first that mania was associated with. Her brain had become so addled by the disease that the honor student went into a rage. First, she cut herself to release the pathogens in her body, then she tried to attack others so they would become infected. By stopping her from cutting anyone, Alec had saved a large crowd of people from becoming infected. That didn't make him feel any better about it though.

The police department decided to put Alec on leave for a little bit. He was allowed to do paperwork and write reports, but he couldn't go out into the field again until the police chief deemed him ready.

That was fine with Alec. He was really shaken up about it and had no interest in getting himself back into a position like that. He told the chief that he'd take one week at home and then he'd come in to do administrative work. But two weeks had passed, and it wasn't looking like he would return anytime soon.

So, it was apparent to Alec that something had gone terribly wrong if they wanted him to work. He tried to push the incident with the girl into the back of his head and focus on the fact that his city needed his protection.

"Good to see you, Lawrence," Officer Davidson said. "I wasn't sure you'd come."

"You were the one who called me in," he replied.

Davidson looked him up and down as if he could tell his mental state from a cursory glance. "I wouldn't have called you if I didn't think it was absolutely necessary. If you get into any trouble, I want you to come straight back here and we can deal with it, okay?"

Alec furrowed his brow. "I'm not sure what kind of trouble I'm going to get into when I don't even have a gun."

Davidson blinked slowly and sighed. "I think I've changed my mind on my previous stance."

He handed Alec the key to the gun safe.

"Understand that we want as little violence as possible today, but you need to protect yourself if you find yourself in extreme danger. Especially," he added, "since many of those causing this problem might not have much time to live as it is."

Chapter Three

Dr. Bretton Vincent sat tensely in his leather armchair in his home office. Today, like every other day for the past few weeks, he sat with a cup of coffee—or scotch, depending on his mood—and watched the news.

He watched to get a good sense about what was going on in the world without actually going out there to see it himself. Plus, he was occasionally mentioned, and he liked that celebrity status. Furthermore, he needed to ensure the stories that involved him suited his best interests. He needed the truth to be heard. Elaina Morgan, his associate, had created a dangerous virus strain which was causing complete pandemonium in Seattle. In no time, it would spread across the world.

When he really thought about it, he couldn't stand Elaina. Thirteen years her senior, he was on equal footing with her when it came to their careers. He worked his ass off and earned his doctorate while trying to raise a daughter with his ex-wife. He was just starting out in his dream job, beginning to get noticed, when this girl strolled into his lab.

She was fresh off her dissertation and thought she ruled the field. What she had accomplished was impressive, but when Bretton considered the facts, it made sense why she had done so much in such a short amount of time.

Throughout his academic years, he lived a very well-rounded life. He was active in extracurricular activities in his undergraduate years. Then, he met his wife, married her, had a child, and divorced her within ten years. All of this happened while studying for his doctorate.

Elaina, on the other hand, had few life experiences. From what he gathered, she had all the personality of an empty Petri dish. From childhood, she did nothing but study. She had no friends, no family, and no romantic partners. When you replace everything that makes life interesting with academia, you're bound to impress people. But at what cost? If Bretton didn't despise her so much, he might have felt sorry for Elaina.

But it was hard to feel pity for someone who annoyed him day in and day out. Although he felt sick and could hardly sleep about what had happened in his lab, it made him feel a little better to know that she was getting all the heat for it. For once, it paid to be a supporting character in the cast. His time was coming, though. He had waited in the shadows long enough. Soon, he would be a star.

Bretton Vincent knew something that very few

people knew to be true—while he didn't create the Morgan Strain, he was solely responsible for releasing it into the outside world.

Perfect little Elaina Morgan had created the strain in an attempt to introduce a virus that was capable of attacking cancer cells without causing harm to the patient. In early tests in mice and rats, it appeared that her plan was working exactly how she wanted it to.

This was too much for Bretton. It was already too much for him to bear that some young girl took over his lab, but for her to discover something that could potentially cure cancer would kill him. If she succeeded, he would forever be a lowly assistant for some savant freak.

In early tests, the virus killed cancer in rodents, but not without leaving them with horrible boils. These lesions eventually went away, but it turned them into disgusting little critters. He figured if he could infect a few healthy people, they would believe that what she was doing was harmful and shut down her strain.

In the meantime, it was Bretton's plan to work on a way to create a virus with all of the same benefits while removing all side effects. Once he figured out how to do that, the Vincent Virus would probably win a Nobel Peace Prize. He would be more rich and famous than he ever thought a scientist could be.

But, he got too greedy after launching his plan. He started working on his new strain immediately. He managed to fix whatever was causing the sores, but somewhere along the line, he went terribly wrong. Focused on the wrong aspects of the virus, he didn't account for any other side effects. He ran a few quick trials on rodents, realized that they weren't showing outward signs of illness, and decided that he was finished. His plan was moving a lot faster than he thought it could.

With two tiny vials of the virus, he decided to run his own human trials. Not fully confident in his work, he found two interns new to the lab and infected their lunches in the breakroom fridge. As far as he knew, they were both perfectly healthy, so the virus shouldn't have shown any side effects.

Unfortunately, he was dead wrong. The interns showed no visible signs of illness in the first two days, so Bretton thought he was home free. He even started writing his research proposal after making casual small talk with them to ensure they were okay.

Then the symptoms developed.

Coincidentally, both interns called in sick on the third day. Lab management didn't think anything of it. College kids spread diseases like kindergarteners.

But after the second day of their absence from the lab, Dr. Vincent made a personal call to them. Trying not to give away the nature of his call, he asked the students how they were feeling. They both reported high fevers, chills, stomach cramps, and strangely enough, mood swings. He wished them well, told them to get rest, and promised to check up on them later. He assured them that they'd just caught the influenza virus that was going around and if things got worse, he'd personally bring them a week's dose of antiviral medication.

Being inexperienced with viruses, they didn't realize

that antiviral medication only worked when taken at the first sign of symptoms. But, since an expert was telling them that he would take care of them, they listened.

Instead, Bretton used them as his own human guinea pigs. He charted their symptoms for about a week before giving them a medication to help with their symptoms.

Within two weeks, the interns were feeling much better and had returned to work. But, as most busy college students can attest, just because they are allowed to stay home from their internship, it doesn't mean that they stayed at home. The University of Washington's student health records showed that shortly after the interns became ill, one hundred and thirty-five students were treated for flu-like symptoms.

Bretton was in deep trouble, and he knew it. If anyone realized that he was the one behind the virus, he would surely get fired and wouldn't be able to work in another lab ever again. He either needed the virus to stop spreading, or he needed someone to pin it on.

In the end, only one option would work. As the epidemic took over the city, he leaked to the newspapers that Elaina Morgan's experiment had gone terribly wrong and was causing people to become very sick. With no better information to go on, they took his story and ran with it. Eventually, Elaina had to go into hiding because the press and the general public were after her.

Bretton, on the other hand, was in pretty good shape. With Elaina gone, he could appear to be the hero in the department. Then, he would have all of his assistants at his disposal, helping him work on a cure or a vaccine. When it was ready, everyone would recover and the disease could be eradicated.

"Dad?" Bretton's eighteen-year-old daughter, Natalia, asked him as she peeked her head into the study. "Are you busy?"

He took off his glasses and rubbed his temples. "Nope. What's up?"

"One of my friend's cars was broken into last night. It was weird, because nothing was stolen from it. All of the windows were smashed and the paint is all scratched up."

"That sucks," Bretton said. "Did your friend call the police?"

"Yeah, but they told her that they have so many of those reports that they probably can't send an officer over until next week. Can you believe that? What's going on out there? I used to think Seattle was safe."

Bretton pursed his lips. Even though he only saw his daughter a few times a week, he still felt like he did a pretty good job raising her. She would be attending the University of Washington in the fall and had already decided that she was going to pursue a future in nursing.

She still spent most of her time with her mother, who was always a little more nurturing. Bretton tried, but he was never quite sure how to interact with a teenage girl. He found that she liked his money, so he often replaced human interaction with material gifts.

"I know things are a little crazy right now, but I'm sure everything will settle down soon. This is a good city with good people. There's always the riffraff that hang in the shadows, but the police will put them back where they belong. Don't worry about that."

"I don't know," she replied. "I've seen the news. It's not just poor people out there looting stores. I've seen footage of women and men in business suits throwing bricks through storefronts. They say it has to do with the virus that's going around. How could a virus cause people to act like that?"

He shook his head. "Whatever Elaina Morgan created was an act against nature. She created a madness in otherwise healthy people. But you don't have to worry about catching it. All you have to do is avoid crowded places and wash your hands well after being with other people. No spending time with boys, do you understand?"

She rolled her eyes. "I've hardly left the house in the past week. I don't think that's going to be a concern."

He smiled and turned back to the television. There was a new story about riots. The mayor was now urging all residents to stay at home and only go to work if absolutely necessary. He stressed that evacuation would not be necessary.

The color drained from Bretton's face.

If the government was trying to downplay the scope of the virus and discouraging people from leaving the city, then he knew that it must be bad. He knew that the city would soon become a quarantine chamber and the virus would spread and kill everyone off before they had a chance to run.

"Pack a bag, Natalia," he said flatly, turning off the

television. "We're going to your grandmother's house for a little while."

"But the news just said that everyone should just stay in the city."

"I know more about this than you do," Bretton argued. "Pack your suitcase. We're leaving in an hour."

"How long are we staying?" she asked.

"Just for a few days," he lied, not sure how long it would take for everything to blow over. He wasn't even sure if they'd ever make it back to Seattle. He could try to work on a cure from any lab in the world. All he needed were good colleagues who could put in a lot of long hours.

After Natalia stomped out of the study, he retreated to his own bedroom and hastily stuffed clothing into his suitcase. He packed dress clothes in case he had an opportunity to work right away. He even packed his favorite lab coat that he'd snagged and sterilized before the lab was shut down.

He would miss the home that he had built in Seattle, no doubt, but being away from the danger within the city would be a big relief. Plus, if he stayed out of the limelight for the moment, he would not come into questioning about what happened at the lab.

About thirty minutes later, Natalia dropped her suitcase at the door with a dramatic thud.

"You have everything you need?" Bretton asked.

"Most of my things are at Mom's house, but she picked a very convenient time to be on vacation."

"Well, whatever you need, we can buy when we get to Grandma's," he said, plastering a bright smile onto his face. "Go ahead and get in the car. I'll take your suit-case out."

Hands full of their most prized possessions, Bretton Vincent looked back at the home where he had spent so many years of his life. It was hard to say goodbye, but he knew he wouldn't survive the city if he stayed.

"I called your grandmother earlier, and she said she's going to make her famous baked ziti for you," he said, trying to cheer up his sullen daughter.

"Cool," she said dryly, looking out the window.

Just blocks away from their wealthy neighborhood, there were people forming crowds. Bretton was relieved, as he had a sneaking suspicion that the people he saw were infected and looking to become violent.

They rolled up to a stoplight at the edge of town, just before the highway. Just a few more minutes, and they would be out of town. They could leave this madness behind.

A group of disheveled looking people swarmed Bretton's car, expressionless faces peering into the windows.

"Dad," Natalia called, looking at her father in fear. It didn't take an expert to know that there was something terribly wrong with those people.

Bretton clutched the steering wheel until his knuckles turned white. There were now people standing directly in front of his car, blocking his passage to the outside world.

He laid on the horn, hoping to startle the people in front of them. This did nothing to scare them away, but instead infuriated them. They pounded on the car as if they had predetermined their actions.

"Just drive," Natalia screamed.

Bretton hesitated. If he drove on, he would certainly kill people. He had already done enough damage to his city. He didn't want to see the blood on his hands. It was easier to pretend it didn't exist.

Suddenly, a baseball bat shattered the passenger's side window and grey hands of all sizes reached for his daughter, yanking her from her seat. Natalia let out a blood curdling scream, freezing Bretton in his tracks.

When his mind finally caught up to his surroundings, he reached for her foot, but she was already nearly out of the car. It was one against twenty at this point. The road ahead of him was now clear, and with the bat-wielding maniac making his way toward the driver's side window, Bretton had a choice to make.

With tears in his eyes, he pressed down on the gas pedal, leaving his daughter in the midst of the swarm.

As he drove, he reasoned that if he had been infected, there would be no one left to create a remedy. He was gutted that he had to watch his daughter go, but she was collateral damage in the war between humans and the virus. He knew that there was still a chance she'd survive the attack, and then he could come back for her to deliver the first cure to her. He just needed a little more time.

If anyone asked, he would say that he hadn't seen his daughter in days. Or, he'd explain that she had become infected and there was nothing he could do. They would understand.

He wondered how long the guilt would eat at him, tearing him apart from the inside, just as his laboratory creation was currently doing to hundreds or even thousands of people.

Bretton's first priority was to find a safe place. Then, and only then, would he begin to work on a cure. He knew that it was only a matter of time before he was infected by his own invention. He just needed to create the solution to his problem before it was the death of him.

Chapter Four

E laina took the exit to head into a small suburb not far from the city. She wanted to go farther down the road, but she figured that the police would be looking for her at all major research facilities in the country. If she got brought in for questioning, she would be set so far back in her progress that there would be no chance of curing the disease.

Besides, she had few supplies with her besides the lab equipment she took before it was shut down. There wasn't a lot, but she had the necessary items she couldn't find anywhere else. This included special beakers and flasks that she had designed herself. They also contained a few test tubes that contained the specimens she had been working with.

She looked at her options. There was a community college about sixty miles away, or she could break into a high school lab in the little suburb. By the looks of the town, the majority of the residents had left for their vacation homes when the virus hit.

If there weren't a lot of people wandering around, then she figured she had a good chance of squatting somewhere without being noticed. She pulled off the entrance ramp and into the town.

Elaina had been to Lakeshore once in her life for a high school science competition. It only took a few minutes to drive through, but it contained all the supplies she would need to survive a short stay. For everything else, she would have to make due.

Her first stop was the grocery store. Luckily, it hadn't been completely emptied by panicked citizens and loot-ers. Though rations were scarce, she grabbed a few boxes of cereal, frozen pizzas, and store brand canned fruits and vegetables. She ate worse in her daily life, but now, she didn't feel the mild shame involved in loading a cart up with junk food.

When she got to the checkout, the store employee gave her an apologetic shrug. Elaina nodded half-heart-edly in response, not exactly sure how to act around other people in this situation. She didn't want to draw attention to herself in any way, either by being too friendly or too standoffish.

"Do you live here, or are you just passing through?" the plump middle-aged woman in the surgical mask asked Elaina. "We've had so many people come through here who are just stocking up on their way out of Seattle."

"Passing through," Elaina answered, neither choice

of answer quite accurate. "Has Lakeshore seen any outbreaks yet?"

"Oh, maybe a few cases. But a lot of people can afford to pack up everything and move somewhere safer. I'm not so lucky. But, if I don't survive this thing, then that's one mortgage I don't have to pay."

Elaina couldn't comprehend the woman's crinkle-eyed smile under her mask. She seemed so calm compared to everyone in Seattle.

"Oh, dear," the woman said, "I suppose I shouldn't be joking about something so serious. Does anyone you know have the virus?"

"No one close to me," Elaina answered.

"That's good. Stay safe out there, dear. The world can be a scary place when people aren't willing to help one another. Take care of yourself first, but take care of others when you can."

"I will," Elaina answered, gathering her bags. "Thank you."

"Anytime. It's nice to have people around to talk to. This city is a ghost town."

After Elaina went back to her car, she stuffed the groceries in the back of her car, along with a few items of clothing and her lab equipment. If she couldn't find a place to crash, she would be sleeping back there too.

When she was sure she had all of her necessities covered, Elaina drove to Lakeshore High School. The school district was wealthy enough, so they would at least have one decent centrifuge for Elaina to use.

Besides, a school was a safe place to go, since all

learning institutions in Washington had been closed down in the past week. Disease spread like wildfire amongst kids, so just one infected student could cause mass destruction in a matter of days.

Though she was prepared to break a window to gain access to the building, the first door she checked was unlocked. Perhaps an oversight when the virus struck, this little mistake made Elaina feel much better about breaking and entering.

She made a beeline toward the chemistry lab and turned on a few lights. The dim lighting illuminated her new work station for the next few weeks as she worked on reversing all the damage her lab had created in the first place.

Being in the room brought her back to her high school days. Being the youngest student was tough, but the classroom was a nice respite from the stares and whispers she got when she walked down the hall. It wasn't that the kids were mean to her, they just didn't know how to deal with the fact that Elaina Morgan was different from the rest of them.

She had a few friends to talk to during the day, but they were also sort of loners themselves. But if any of the cliques in her high school could welcome her, it was the nerds. While some resented her smarts and drive, others looked up to her and admired her academic passions.

Plus, if her friends ever needed help in their advanced science classes, Elaina was their go-to girl. By learning how to break down difficult concepts for the high school crowd, she became a favorite amongst teaching assistants in college. This practice helped her when it came time to explain her work to newspapers and scholarly journals. On the inside, she abhorred being interviewed, but being the head woman in charge made her a natural candidate. It also didn't hurt that she was pretty.

Her soft, hazel eyes rarely lit up at anything besides her work and her family corgi, Bagel, but when they did, she was enchanting. Her long auburn hair was usually wound tight into a bun to stay safe from the lab. Her porcelain face was dotted with a few freckles across the bridge of her nose. She always wondered if her entire face would erupt into freckles if she ever managed to spend enough time in the sunlight.

Elaina's hands floated over the clean test tubes, neatly in their drying racks. She traced a fingernail over the assortment of different sized beakers, listening to the clinking sound they made.

The stockroom was neatly kept, but it lacked the scope of chemicals she would have preferred to have. It was no problem, though. She could make due. Elaina admired the care the chemistry teacher had put into keeping a good lab. There was a place for everything here.

At her old high school lab, everything was a scattered mess. Her teacher, while a smart and engaging man, was a bit scatterbrained and unorganized at times. During her free period, Elaina would visit Mr. Ryan and help him identify and label glass bottles filled with mysterious liquids. By the time she graduated, her school's lab storage room looked as neat and orderly as Lakeshore's. Elaina wondered how her old sanctuary looked now.

She gathered everything she needed and placed it on the largest table in the room. She worked methodically, as if she were a master baker and making a batch of her famous red velvet cupcakes. Instead, her work was with dangerous viruses that had the potential to wipe out entire populations.

Finally, she placed two very important vials on the table, both labeled in her meticulous handwriting —*Morgan Strain* and *LILY*.

First, she wanted to know why her virus was having such strange effects in people. In lab tests, side effects were only cosmetic and went away with other drugs that were already on the market.

A quick trip to the animal science room provided her with everything else that she needed to run trials. Snakes slithered in glass enclosures, hungry birds cheeped behind wire cages, and fat guinea pigs squeaked in giant plastic bins.

Feeling sorry for the abandoned animals, she quickly made sure every critter had a few days' supply of food and water. Once that was taken care of, she plucked the chubbiest guinea pig from the container and pushed it into a smaller wire cage.

"I'm sorry about this," she muttered to the guinea pig who was used to being handled by strangers. It didn't expect to be tested on, much less by one of the biggest names in virology. Instead, it happily munched on dried alfalfa in its new home for the length of the newest trial.

One drop of the virus went directly into the guinea pig's tiny mouth from the vial. Elaina would have to wait a day to look at the blood samples under the microscope to see what was going on. Having a hunch that something terrible had happened to her sample, she cleaned up a dusty microscope from the biology lab and looked at her creation for the thousandth time.

Everything about the virus was the same as the day she'd started working on it. Every flagellum was in its place and there weren't any mutations. She knew this virus inside and out. Why was she suddenly having problems?

Elaina returned to the lab and grabbed a little spotted guinea pig from the container. This one was more mild-mannered than the other and sat patiently in the crook of her arm as she walked back to the lab. This guinea pig would be the first recipient of LILY. Once the guinea pig was symptom-free, it would then receive a tiny dose of the Morgan Strain. After that, time would tell if the critter would carry the virus or if it would be immune.

If her untested vaccine worked, she might have a chance to reenter the world for human trials. Since there was such a dire need for a vaccine, she assumed she'd be allowed to work on it. Afterward, maybe she would be charged and put on trial. Any sane and logical jury would realize that what happened wasn't her fault in any way, but not all juries were sane and logical. She couldn't think about that too much, though. Any fear of the future would only hold her back.

Just as she opened the bottle of LILY, she heard a noise. She held her breath, in hopes that her paranoia would soon subside after realizing there was nothing there.

Then, footsteps echoed down the tile floors. She was not alone in the high school.

Men's voices chuckled and jeered, probably opportunistic looters. From what she heard on the news, the mutation caused sufferers to be in a nearly comatose-like state. These men sounded like they were full of life.

Elaina pocketed her vials and tiptoed back to the store cupboard. She pushed a lab stool out of the way and crawled into the crevice it opened along the lab table. Carefully, she replaced the stool directly in front of her. Unless someone was specifically looking for her, she would be perfectly hidden.

She closed her eyes, trying to slow her breathing and heart rate. Clutching her stomach, she wished she had eaten some of her rations, as her stomach was gurgling conspiratorially. Elaina listened carefully as the footsteps came closer but ultimately passed the science classrooms and continued on. With any luck, the men would realize that they had no business in an abandoned school and leave her alone. However, she was already mentally preparing herself for a long night crouched down behind a stool.

Once she thought the immediate danger had passed, Elaina heard a shriek. It was unmistakably the scream of a young woman, clearly in danger. She froze in her tracks, weighing her options.

If she investigated the scream, she would be putting herself in harm's way. Not only would she expose herself to whatever danger the girl was in, but also to having her makeshift lab shutdown. If the men realized she was a wanted woman, she would end up at the nearest police station, with no work to back up her theories on the vaccine.

But if she stayed silent, something terrible would happen to the woman. She was sure of it.

She had a choice to make, and she needed to make it soon.

The girl screamed again, this time with more panic in her voice. It was the chilling noise of someone who was desperately looking for help but knowing there was little chance of being saved.

Elaina remembered what the woman at the grocery store told her. Elaina felt partially responsible for some of the bad that was occurring in the world and felt like she owed it to her community to correct a few wrongs, no matter how isolated or specific they were. She might not be able to cure the virus taking hold of the country, but she could save one girl from whatever danger she was in.

Checking to make sure her vials were secure in her pocket, she grabbed a scalpel from the lab and quietly ran out the door.

Elaina would never categorize herself as being particularly brave, but she also thought of herself as a generally good person. In the middle of an epidemic centered around her work, she felt it necessary to make sure she made it through with some of her morals still intact.

With one last deep, wavering breath, she stood up straight and ran directly toward the source of danger, ready to fight.

Chapter Five

_____

Bretton had driven for about an hour without his daughter. A few times, he thought about turning around and going back to look for her, but he had to stop himself. He knew deep down that she was already infected and would likely pass the virus on to him.

He couldn't go to his mother's house now after letting his daughter be dragged away by strange men. She was perhaps the only person in the world who could see past his lies. One look into her eyes, and his story would be blown. He would call her later to tell her of their change in plans.

She'd be concerned about them, but he'd reassure her that wherever they were going was especially safe. He'd maybe even tell her to come visit them once it was safe to travel. Of course, the virus would continue to spread for some time, so he had a good cover. Then, he'd provide everyone with the cure, and the country would be so grateful that no one would ever question his past actions. No, he would be akin to a saint.

While getting his doctorate in virology, he had worked closely with medical doctors to help them to create new vaccines to improve upon old technology. He'd even done a little pharmacological work on antiviral medication. He wasn't an absolute expert, by any means, but he had a good enough working knowledge that he figured he could make a rough product. Then, when he had more help, he could hire people to refine his work and make it salable on the market.

Not only would he be saving the world, but the sale of his drug patent to a pharmaceutical company would garner him millions. He wondered if he would have any say on how much the drug would sell for. In a few weeks, perhaps tens of thousands would become infected, and anyone who could afford the cure would be sure to buy it. He imagined that it could sell for a few hundred dollars a dose, and the recipients of it would be thankful that it was available at all.

Then, when the vaccine was available, everyone in the world would want it. Everyone would go to their doctor's office and ask for it by name. He'd see to it that whatever it was called would include his name in some variation. Between an antiviral and a vaccine, he'd probably be featured on a postage stamp some day.

Bretton was so caught up in his daydream that he had momentarily forgotten all about his missing daughter. In fact, he was so wrapped up in his fantasy that he didn't seem to notice that the stoplight in front of him had turned red.

His SUV slammed into the side of a compact car, crushing it like an aluminum can. He spun around twice, completely out of control.

When his car stopped, he looked to see what he'd hit. Pushed onto the opposite sidewalk lay a little blue car, tipped over on its side. Bretton couldn't tell how many people were inside, but he heard signs of life.

A cold sweat washed over him. This was the last thing he needed at the moment. Not only had his daughter been snatched right from underneath his nose, but he had just gotten into a serious car accident, the fault, no doubt, his own.

"Shit," he cursed under his breath. He looked around. There were a few people starting to poke their heads out of their houses, but besides that, there were few bystanders. He hoped there weren't any witnesses and it would just be his word against the other driver's. He couldn't afford to get himself into any trouble right now.

As he neared the car, he could hear calls for help become increasingly louder. When he looked into the window, he gasped.

A young woman lay tipped over with blood covering her entire face. He could hardly make out facial features underneath all the red.

"I'm stuck," she cried, straining to free herself from the crushed metal.

"I'll call for an ambulance," Bretton said. "Are you badly hurt?"

"I'm not sure," she said. "I can feel a few cuts, and my legs are killing me, but otherwise, just a little sore all over."

"So no neck or head trauma?" Bretton asked, trying to get a good feel for the situation.

"Not that I know of," she replied. "I just can't move because I'm completely trapped in here."

"My phone's in the car. Give me one minute and I'll be right back."

"Please hurry," she called.

Bretton jogged to his car to grab his cellphone. He dialed 911 and requested an ambulance for the corner of 13th and Vine.

"Listen," he said to the operator. "I can discuss the specifics of the accident with the officers when they arrive. I just need to quickly let you know that she's in need of medical attention so I can go back there and help. Just send help," he said shortly.

"I'm sorry, sir," the operator responded in a calm but firm voice. "It could be quite some time until somebody can get there. A lot of our city employees have been ordered to go into the city to help. Everyone left here is busy with calls about illness and looting. I'm going to need you to stay on the line so I can give you first aid instructions if needed."

Bretton sighed and threw his one free hand up in the air. "I'm going to hang up now."

"Wait," the operator quickly interjected. "I need to ask you one last question. Are there people swarming the injured motorist?"

"Excuse me?" Bretton asked, confused.

"For the safety of our first responders," he said nervously, "I need to know if there are any people swarming the car in an unusual way."

"Unusual, how?" Bretton asked, raising his voice.

"Like the infected act," the operator said, getting to the point.

Bretton whipped around and looked at the little blue car. Sure enough, a few people had come out of their homes. But Bretton couldn't tell if they were infected or just bystanders looking to help.

"I—I don't know," he stuttered. "There are a few more people now, but I can't tell if they're infected or just trying to help."

"Try to take a closer look. Are they helping like normal people would, or are their movements erratic?"

Bretton took a few steps closer. Out of the corner of his eye, he watched a woman run down the street, snarling. Two others followed her.

"Shit," Bretton hissed, hanging up the phone. He heard the woman in the car calling for help, but he ignored her, jumping into the driver's seat of his car.

Turning the keys in the ignition, he muttered to himself, pleading for the car to start. Just when he thought he heard the sound of the engine turning over, it would groan to a stop. He had damaged the vehicle too much in the crash. It was not functional enough to take him away from the danger.

He knew that if he sat in his car, eventually, someone would come by and drag him out of the window like they did with his daughter. Not a particularly strong man, he didn't think he would be able to fight off more than one infected person.

With no other options, he grabbed his wallet and phone and jumped out of his car, running like hell in the opposite direction of the crash. In the span of an hour, he'd watched a kidnapping and committed a hit and run, and he didn't even look back. He knew that they had entered into a time of lawlessness, and if he didn't watch out for himself, no one would.

As he ran, he heard the calls for help turn into screams. The screams became louder and shriller the further he got. Bretton focused on the sound of his breathing so he didn't have to hear the woman yell. When that didn't work, he made a low humming noise to quiet the deafening screams he heard. He ran so far away that he wasn't entirely sure whether he was hearing the woman or just unable to shake the sound.

Finally, they stopped.

It was eerily silent. When Bretton surveyed the scene, he was in the middle of a dirt road, surrounded by empty fields. He couldn't see or hear anyone. The only sounds came from the wind and the crunch of the gravel underneath his shoes.

He wiped the thin layer of sweat from his forehead on the back of his hand. The sun was starting to retreat back into the horizon. If he didn't see shelter by nightfall, he had no chance of sleeping. From everything he'd experienced in the last twenty-four hours, he was certain that if he weren't careful, he would be attacked next.

Bretton continued down the road, panting. He

couldn't see the next town, but he hoped it would be a safe haven for him. Once he caught his breath, he planned on picking up the pace until he reached civilization.

In the distance, he heard a car drive in his direction. Not confident that the person inside would be useful to him, he crouched down into a ditch to let it pass. If he could catch a tiny glimpse of the driver and determine that he or she was safe, he would flag them down. If there were anything suspicious about them, he would lie down and play dead. From what he saw on the news, the infected were only interested in the living.

As the vehicle came up over the hill, Bretton realized that the car wasn't civilian at all. The bulky military vehicle slowed as it reached Bretton's hiding place.

"Stand up and put your hands on your head," a female voice boomed from the armored car.

Bretton jumped up and waved his hands above his head, in hopes that the occupants would realize that he was not infected and in need of help.

In response to his movements, three different firearms aimed directly at his head and torso.

"No, don't shoot," Bretton screamed. "I'm not infected. I was chased out here by a group of infected people, though. They're about three miles that way," he continued, pointing to the scene of the wreck.

It was as if no one could hear him. He spoke louder, pleading his case.

"You don't understand," he bellowed. "I'm not infected. I'm running *from* the infected. I got into a car accident and people started swarming the scene. I think they killed the woman. They took my girl from me, too."

The weapons didn't budge. He started sobbing, and the loud howls coming from deep inside his chest didn't help his case in proving that he was a sane man.

Such cruel irony it was for Bretton. He had spent so much time doing arguably what was the wrong thing in hopes of saving his own ass. He'd endangered the entire human species for fame, abandoned his daughter in exchange for a quick getaway, and left a poor woman trapped in her car to avoid encountering an infected person. Now, he was going to be gunned down by the only people who could possibly help him. He would die a healthy man. His misdeeds had been completely unjustified.

"Please don't shoot," Bretton cried again, dropping to his knees. "I'm sorry. I'm just so scared." He wept quietly, head bowed.

As he closed his eyes and prepared for death, he heard the rusty screech of the vehicle door opening.

Bretton scrambled to his feet, placing his hands on his head.

"My name is Bretton Vincent," he said quickly. "I work at the University of Washington Virology Lab."

A bald man exited the car and stood in front of Bretton on the dirt road.

"We know, Doctor Vincent. We've been looking for you all day. We need your help."

"You've been looking for me?" he asked, dropping his hands.

"Well, this virus isn't going to stop spreading on its

own, is it?" The man smiled. "Get in the car. We'll brief you on the way to the lab."

Bretton let out a sigh of relief. Maybe he'd get his chance to right some wrongs after all. With the military on his side, he had another shot at working on the cure that would propel him into the spotlight once and for all.

Chapter Six

"Alec Lawrence," the sheriff announced to the group, "you will be paired with Michael Day."

Alec looked across the room toward Michael and gave him a nod. Michael returned the nod and looked back down to the desk he was sitting at. He didn't seem pleased at all to be there, but few officers did.

In fact, morale at the station was at an all-time low. Everyone tried to keep their heads up because it was part of the job, but in quiet moments, you could hear the grumbling of employees who weren't being paid enough to be fighting off virus-stricken residents.

Plus, a lot of officers had family at home that they couldn't afford to infect. These were the ones who scrubbed themselves thoroughly in the precinct showers after being on duty. They'd leave the locker room with pink skin and grim expressions, as if they knew that their exercise was one of futility.

"Like I said before," the sheriff said after reading off the partnerships for the day, "I'd appreciate it if you all wore face masks. The last thing I want is for someone to get coughed on and get the virus. If you choose to wear one, make sure you speak loudly enough for the citizen to hear you. We don't want another accidental shooting case on our hands."

Alec looked down at the ground, but he suspected that there were other eyes on him. The captain wasn't talking about accidental shootings in a general sense. He was referring to one specific incident . . . Alec's incident.

"Things are different now," the sheriff continued. "Before, we were taking all infected into custody to quarantine them. Unfortunately, we lost every single person in the medical cell. So, if you see an infected person causing harm to others, just go ahead and shoot them. Believe me, you'll be saving them a whole lot of suffering later on."

Alec winced. He and his colleagues were police officers because they wanted to protect people, not eliminate them in mass executions. He understood that there was no help for someone infected with the Morgan Virus, but it felt so wrong just to kill people for something they couldn't help.

If he were dealing with rapists and murderers who were trying to cause serious bodily harm, sure, he would pull the trigger and feel very little remorse. Taking a life was always a worst-case scenario, but it was necessary at times.

This felt different. Sure, the infected were extremely dangerous to the healthy population, but they weren't in their right minds. These were everyday people whose only crime was to get sick. All it took was getting too close to the wrong person to be gunned down by his coworkers. That sentiment was not lost on Alec.

When the briefing was over, the officers filed out of the meeting room and walked outside to their patrol vehicles.

"Do you want to drive, or should I?" Alec asked his new partner, trying to initiate conversation. He was feeling a little more alert after finishing a bottle of water during the briefing. For the first time in days, he was functioning without any substances in his system. He didn't necessarily feel good, but he figured he could make it through the shift, and that was good enough for him. He even wondered if he could wait until the next day to pick up a fresh case of beer. He would have to see how he felt after today.

"I'd like to drive, if that's okay with you," Michael said softly, heading toward the driver's side.

"Sure," Alec said brightly. "Not a problem with me. Besides, I've heard you're skilled behind the wheel, and we'll need someone who can navigate this mess. Do you fancy yourself a racecar driver?" he joked.

"No," Michael said, looking at the door handle. "I just don't want to have to discharge my weapon if I can help it."

Alec gritted his teeth. He knew there were a lot of officers who were upset by his actions and didn't want him to come back to work. Apparently, Michael was one of them.

After they got situated in the patrol car, Alec turned

to Michael. He hated anything that resembled talking about feelings, but not having a good trust between partners led to accidents and mistakes.

"Look, man," he started, avoiding Michael's eyes, "do we need to talk about anything before we get out there? It's going to be a long day, and it's better if we get any conflicts out of the way now."

"What do you mean?" Michael asked innocently.

Alec rubbed an aching spot on his forehead. "Nothing. It's just that you don't seem very pleased to be working with me today, that's all."

Michael squirmed uncomfortably in his seat. "The girl you shot? She was friends with my younger sister. She lived across the street from us growing up. She would have never done anything to hurt anyone. The experience completely rattled her whole family. It's just awful."

Alec pursed his lips. "You saw the tapes, though, right?"

"Yeah," Michael replied.

"So you saw that I played things by the book. Also, you realize that we've just been given orders to shoot all infected and dangerous people. We have to follow orders."

"I know," he conceded. "Sometimes, it's hard to accept the fact that things are different now. This virus is killing hundreds and spreading at a rapid pace. All rules for the way we live our daily lives have gone out the window."

"It's rough," Alec said, looking out the window, "but we have to do the best we can. Are we good?"

Michael looked up at Alec. "Yeah, man, we're good."

The pair awkwardly shook hands and drove off to their assigned area. They looked straight ahead as they drove, waiting for the initial awkwardness to wear off. At the very least, there was no outward resentment between them, so Alec felt a little safer in the event that his partner needed to save his ass.

"Look out," Alec said, pointing to a man crossing the street twenty feet from an intersection. Michael slowed down, keeping a close eye on the man.

"I can't tell if we're just in a bad neighborhood or if that guy's got it," Michael said. "What are the signs to watch out for again?"

"Extreme outbursts of rage in typically docile people. How are we supposed to tell if we don't know the people? Otherwise, grayish skin, bloodshot eyes— that also describes some drug users."

"This shit is messed up," Michael said under his breath. "I guess we should just leave people alone until they're trying to do something, right?"

Alec shrugged. "I guess. But then again, if we let an infected person go, are we just allowing them to be free for when they feel the rage coming on?"

Alec and Michael thought about that for a few quiet moments. There was no code of ethics as far as the virus was concerned.

"Up there," Michael said, breaking the silence. "Do you see that crowd of people?"

"Yeah, I see it. We'd better check it out."

The pair pulled up to a gas station where five or six

people had gathered around a car. They were pounding their fists on the frame, shouting at whoever was inside. Michael flicked on the siren lights in hopes that the crowd would disperse. The odd mismatch of people from every demographic didn't seem disturbed by the police presence in the slightest. That was a bad sign.

"What do we do?" Michael asked, his brown doe eyes looking anxiously at Alec. He wasn't much older than Alec. Alec wondered what the sheriff's plan was by sending two rookie cops out into a bad part of town together. Maybe he didn't think they'd have a good chance of survival and they were the most dispensable. He tried to push these thoughts out of his head so he could focus on the work ahead of him. He had too much potential to be treated like a pawn.

"We do our job and break this thing up," Alec replied.

He got out of the car with authority and Michael followed closely behind.

"Step away from the vehicle," he called to the gathering. "I mean it, or else you'll be in the back of my car in cuffs."

No one listened. Instead, they started pounding on the car with more force. Through a small space between two bodies, Alec could make out the face of a middle aged man, a look of pure panic on his face.

"I'm not going to say it again," Alec yelled. "This is your final warning to back away."

After being ignored for the second time, Alec reached for the bundle of zip ties in his belt. There were too many to take in now. He'd have to leave the lot of them on the curb.

"Alec, look," Michael said in a hushed whisper.

He followed Michael's eyes to one of the men surrounding the car. Through a tear in his shirt, he could see angry red boils erupting on his skin.

Alec's eyes widened. These people were almost certainly infected. But he didn't want to make a fatal mistake. He grabbed his nightstick and poked a man, prompting him to turn around and face him.

The man looked like a skeleton covered in too-loose skin. His sunken eyes darted back and forth with no clear direction. A scarlet rash covered his neck and the back of his hands, and his mouth gaped open in a snarl.

Alec quietly drew his gun and aimed at the man. "Sir," he said steadily, "put your hands on your head."

The man took two steps toward him, his expression unchanging.

"On the ground," Alec pleaded with him.

Alec took a quick glance to his left. Michael was aiming a Taser at a man who had also lost interest in the person in the car.

Suddenly, Alec heard a horrific scream and a zap of electricity. Then next thing he knew, Michael was on the ground and the rest of the group had turned toward him. With careful aim, Alec fired a round into anyone who came within a few feet of the two officers.

When the bodies had settled, Alec nudged each one with his boot just to make sure they were dead. Michael scrambled to his feet, looking both alarmed and a little sheepish that he had nearly been taken out by them.

"I didn't think we'd have to kill them," he said, looking pale.

"I was hoping we wouldn't have to either," Alec replied. "Take a look. Definitely infected."

Michael covered his mouth and nose and squatted down to get a closer look. "You're right. By the looks of them, if you hadn't finished them off, they would have been dead in weeks, days even."

Alec strode over to the man in his car and gently rapped on the window with his knuckle. The man reluctantly rolled the window down.

"Good afternoon, sir," Alec said casually. "Did any of these people come into physical contact with you during the altercation?"

"No, no," the man said, clearly shaken. "I haven't been in physical contact with anyone for days."

"That's good to hear," Alec said. "Are you from here?"

The man nodded so hard, his wire glasses nearly fell down his nose.

"The mayor has advised everyone to stay put for a while. Do you have a safe home to go to?"

"Yes. I just went out to get food for my family. We have enough for a few days, yet, but we're running low."

Alec sighed. He wondered how many healthy people like this were in similar situations.

"Give me your name and address, and I'll see if I can have rations delivered to you," Alec said. He hadn't been ordered to do so, but if necessary, he'd make the delivery on his own time.

"Go straight home, and don't stop for anyone," Alec

said after collecting the man's information. "Let's get back out there," he said to Michael. "I have a bad feeling there's a lot more of this out there."

Michael still looked pale as he quietly drove around the neighborhood, looking for any sign of trouble.

"Was that your—you know . . ." Alec asked, trailing off. He was never great with comforting people.

"My first time in a shootout?" he clarified. "I guess it's hardly a shootout when only one guy has a gun," he said quietly. "I'm fine," he said a little louder. "It's just a little startling to have someone infected with a deadly virus run straight at you."

Alec dropped the subject. If Michael was anything like Alec, he would have a lot of booze and sleepless nights in his future. If Michael wanted to voice his concerns with Alec, he would listen. Otherwise, he would just mind his own business.

On the other hand, he was feeling a little smug now. He imagined that most of the officers could now sympathize with what he did to that infected teenager not long ago. There was a good chance a few of his fellow police officers were making the same decisions.

The rest of the day followed the same pattern. They would approach a riot, ask people to stand down, and when they inevitably chased after them, they would draw their weapons and fire. Out of ten of these riots they encountered, only three people appeared to be healthy. They weren't showing symptoms, anyway.

By the time night fell, they were just shooting anyone displaying symptoms. Before, the officers needed to see violent, life-threatening actions toward themselves or others. But eventually, that became too much work. They shot and killed anyone who had the virus rage in them or any of the physical signs. By nine o'clock, they had shot nearly thirty people, only about twenty of which could be identified.

After shooting down a particularly nasty few, Alec was exhausted. He stopped seeing the infected as people. Now, they were just monsters in need of extermination.

Resting behind a burning car for a moment to catch their breath, Alec looked over at Michael. His shivering seemed odd for the situation, given the fact that they were next to a smoldering ball of metal.

"Are you okay, man?" Alec asked. In his short career, he had yet to see anyone snap in the line of duty, but he assumed this is what a ticking time bomb looked like. "I think we should head back to the station."

"Do you?" Michael snapped. He glared at Alec, his eyes looking dark.

"Take it easy," Alec said. "That last one was pretty messed up. No one would blame us if we called it a day. I'm sure we made it a lot longer than some of the others."

"Fuck off," Michael snarled. "I'm surprised that you want to go home. I thought you loved to shoot down civilians. I bet you're having your best day on the job."

Alec furrowed his brow. He didn't know Michael well, but he knew that he was typically a pretty easygoing guy. Alec wondered if he was having a psychotic break from all of the killing they'd had to do. Alec already felt desensitized to the violence, but he knew that he would have nightmares for months.

"I don't like this either," Alec argued, "but we really have no choice. Get back in the car and drive us back to the station. We need some time to decompress."

Michael didn't move. Instead, he glared at Michael, his lips curling into a sneer.

"Fine," Alec said exasperatedly. "If you don't want to go, I'll just leave your ass here. I've had a long day, and I'm not going to sit around and babysit you because you can't keep it together for ten more minutes."

Alec felt a little guilty for being so hard on the guy who was clearly suffering some mental issues, but he was pretty fed up with the situation himself. As he walked toward the car, he heard the sound of a gun being loaded.

"Take another step and I'll blow your brains out," Michael growled.

Alec slowly pivoted so he was facing Michael. Michael had sweat pouring down his pale face.

"What's going on, Michael?" Alec asked in a gentle voice. "Is there something you want to say?"

Michael rubbed his neck. "No," he said casually. "I just don't want to see your stupid face anymore. You've ruined the precinct with your shoot first, ask questions later attitude, and you don't deserve to work for the city anymore."

Alec looked at the spot where Michael kept touching. On the side of his neck were four red, jagged lines that were tinged green on the edges. He was infected, and the virus was moving though his veins quicker than anyone could have predicted.

There was no reasoning with him. He had dealt with

too many infected today to think that saving him was an option either. Michael was dead, as far as he was concerned. The only problem Alec had was making sure he didn't kill him first.

"Put your hands where I can see them," Michael said, rubbing more vigorously at his wound.

Alec complied, trying to figure out how to unholster and fire his gun while being held at gunpoint himself.

"Turn around," Michael added. "Slowly."

Alec obeyed, slowly shuffling his feet until he was no longer facing Michael. It was completely dark now. The lack of light from the cities made the stars so much brighter. He looked into the glittering abyss, aware that it could be the last sight he ever saw.

"I'll tell the station about everything," Michael slurred. "They'll hear about all of the killings you committed tonight. They'll know how I saved the city from your destruction."

He had worked so hard to become a police officer, and for what? Not only did he have to commit atrocities against sick citizens, but now he was about to be killed by one of his own. Alec looked up into the starry sky, felt the cool breeze of the night surround him, and then heard the gunshot.

Chapter Seven

W alking on the balls of her feet down the tile corridor, Elaina followed the echoing shrieks. Her stomach churned as she neared the commotion, knowing that she wasn't well-equipped to engage in a fight. Physical education had always been the bane of her academic career, and she was fortunate that she was naturally quick on her feet. She could run forever, but the moment she had to lift anything heavy, she was useless.

For Elaina, her flight response was much stronger than her fight response. However, spending most of her upbringing indoors, she rarely used either. For the first time in her life, Elaina Morgan found herself wishing she would have listened to her father and spent a little more time doing physical activity. Or, at the very least, enrolled in a self-defense class.

The hallway was dark, but when Elaina squinted, she could see three shapes in the distance. They continued walking through a doorway into the school library.

Looking in from the window, Elaina saw the three people illuminated by the light from the exit signs and the motion-sensor emergency lights. One of the men looked to be in his thirties or forties with a thick neck and a trucker cap on his head. Chubby rolls poked out from underneath his too-tight t-shirt.

The other man looked even younger than Elaina. Tall and lanky, he had a mop of shaggy brown hair that touched his shoulders. The older man was definitely the leader in this duo, as the younger man always observed the other man before acting.

Between them, a slender bicep cupped by each of the men, was a girl in her late teens. Something about her seemed familiar, but Elaina couldn't put her finger on it. Her straight, long hair hung in curtains around her tearstained face.

Elaina continued to watch from the hall, waiting for the right moment to step in. She was positive that she couldn't overtake the men, even with the girl's help. She looked exhausted already, and Elaina wasn't about to make up for any strength deficit.

"I'm sorry we took you away from that old guy," the ringleader said menacingly. "But I know you'd rather be with someone like me. I'll keep you safe from the virus. I've got a bunker and a couple of shotguns. No zombie freaks can get you there."

The girl squirmed in a futile attempt to get away. "Why are you doing this?" she asked her captors. By the sound of exasperation in her voice, it wasn't her first time with that query.

"You just don't appreciate nothin'," the man said. "You're safer here than you are anywhere else. I've been prepping for this kind of shit to go down for years." He dragged out the last word for emphasis. "Pretty soon, everyone will be dead because the virus wiped them clean out. When that happens, guess who will still be standing?"

"We will," the other man replied.

"Darn tootin'," the fat man said. "And you know what? We'll be left to repopulate the planet once the shit hits the fan."

Elaina crinkled her nose, disgusted by the man's grand plan. While the population would certainly take a hit once it was all said and done, it was obvious that the girl had no intentions of repopulating with her captors.

"If that's your plan," the girl asked, "then why are we in a high school?"

The older man let out a chilling cackle. The younger man chimed in with a high-pitched giggle.

"I'm a gentleman," he replied. "I figured it was best if you got to know the two of us before we got down to business."

The girl shuddered violently. Elaina wanted to help her, but she didn't know what to do. She needed to come up with a precise plan of action. Otherwise, she might also be kidnapped and taken to his bunker, wherever it was.

Then, Elaina saw the man jam his pudgy arm up the

girl's shirt. There was no plan anymore—just white-hot rage.

"Clint," the man said, holding the girl down. "I think we're fine over here. Give us some privacy, won't you?"

The younger man nodded and walked toward the door. This was Elaina's chance. She swiftly grabbed the fire extinguisher from the wall, raised it over her head, and—

"Let me go!" the girl screamed, drowning out the sound of the loud thud of the metal fire extinguisher hitting the side of the skinny man's head. He toppled to the ground, and Elaina dragged him by his feet out of view from the library. The fat man would be too preoccupied to even consider or care that something had happened to his friend.

Clint, the younger man, lay flat on his back in the middle of the hall, a red welt forming on the side of his face. Elaina checked to make sure he was breathing and then left him when she was certain she hadn't killed the guy.

Now there was only one more target to take out. This one appeared to be far more dangerous than the other, and Elaina hoped the girl could help her overtake him. She didn't have time to think too much about it—the man was trying to unbutton the girl's jeans.

Elaina sprinted into the library at full speed, running straight into the man, knocking him off-balance.

"What the hell?" he roared, swinging his arms at whomever he could reach. The girl, in shock from

Elaina's entrance, scrambled up to her feet and crossed her arms over her body, shivering.

"Help me take him down," Elaina pleaded.

It was too late. The man pulled a handgun from his pocket, one of many in his doomsday cache. Without warning, he fired a shot straight into the air.

"Are you infected?" he screamed in Elaina's face.

"No, I'm not infected," she fired back.

"If that's the case," he asked suspiciously, "then why did you charge me? You only see that kind of rage in the infected."

"I saw what you were trying to do to this girl," she replied, scowling. "I'm calling the police."

"Shame," he said, aiming his gun at Elaina. "I thought you would've made a good wife when repopulation time came."

Elaina backpedaled, her palms held at chest level. "Just let us go. You don't need to do this."

"Sorry, little girl. Either you come with me or you don't. What's your choice?"

Before Elaina could speak, the girl came flying toward the man, tackling him to the ground. The gun went off, the bullet just grazing Elaina's arm.

The girl had surprised the shooter enough to knock him to the ground, but she couldn't hold him for long. Elaina stomped her boots on his hand, freeing the gun from his grip. She kicked it as hard as she could, sending the weapon skidding on the floor, where it landed somewhere underneath a bookshelf.

Clearly fed up, the girl delivered a few swift kicks to the man's plush abdomen, knocking the wind out of him. He wheezed, scrambling to his hands and knees, and crawled away from the girls.

Forgetting his gun and his friend, who was starting to stir just outside the library, the man booked it, abandoning the girl he'd fought so hard to call his own. Elaina listened as heavy footsteps landed on the tiles until they grew fainter and fainter. Finally, with a loud slam, the man left the school through the heavy doors.

"Are you okay?" Elaina asked the girl.

"I'm fine. You're the one who's bleeding."

Elaina looked at her arm. The good news was that the bullet wasn't lodged in her flesh. The bad news was that any serious wound left her susceptible to infection if she got too close to anyone with the virus.

"It's not a big wound," Elaina said, pressing the sleeve of her jacket to her arm. "I know this is going to sound a little weird, but do I know you from somewhere?"

The girl revealed a dazzling smile. "You're Elaina Morgan," she replied. "I don't think you've seen me in a while, but you work with my dad. I've heard so much about you over the past few months."

Elaina clapped a hand to her mouth. "Are you . . ." She trailed off.

"Natalia Vincent, at your service."

Chapter Eight

"**C**ome on," Natalia urged, grabbing Elaina by her uninjured arm. "Let's get that cleaned up," she said, pointing to the red blossoming on her shirtsleeve.

Elaina remained frozen on the spot, stunned by the odd chain of events that had led her to rescuing the daughter of her colleague.

Not just any colleague though. In fact, she had a terrible thought that if she saw Bretton being attacked, instead of his teenage daughter, she would look the other way.

Elaina wasn't a malicious person by any means, but she had been suspicious of Bretton Vincent for a while now. It seemed as though whenever anything went wrong for Elaina at work, Bretton was hiding in the shadows.

One time, after one of her interviews was published in a medical journal, Elaina received a warning from an environmental agency for using unsafe biohazard disposal measures. When she called the agency for an explanation, they said that they'd received an anonymous tip.

Embarrassed about potentially receiving a fine for something she didn't do, she went through the proper channels to undergo a fair investigation. Luckily, once the environmental agency realized that the claim they received was, at best, misguided, they dropped any allegations against her. Still, the potential damage to her career made her wonder if there were something more to it than just a petty mistake.

After that incident, she took a closer look at how her colleagues acted around her. Whenever something good happened, whether it be an award or a new breakthrough on her research, she watched the people around her. Her observations showed a curious pattern—Bretton Vincent was never supportive of her success.

It wasn't just that he wasn't excited for her good news. He was much more sullen when things were going right for Elaina. Even more damning was the fact that when she shared failures with her team, he was almost gleeful. The others would at least give her a sympathetic nod. He was silent, but with a huge grin on his face.

It was no secret that Bretton Vincent was kind of an ass. No one in the lab really had any serious conflicts, but that didn't mean that there wasn't any eye rolling when Bretton made pompous comments about his accomplishments. It was never anything big enough to call him out on, but any scientist in the lab would giggle about Bretton's latest antics after a few beers.

Then, the virus hit. Naturally, everyone looked to Elaina first. After all, it was her life's work that was wreaking havoc in the community. Though she wasn't prone to silly mistakes, her coworkers wondered if she had been careless and had accidentally taken the specimen outside the lab.

No one likened her as an evil genius set on releasing her dangerous viruses into the world, but it seemed suspicious that the quiet prodigy's big creation was suddenly spreading through town like wildfire. When interviewed by detectives, her colleagues couldn't defend her by saying that they knew Elaina would never do something so dangerous. The fact was that no one really knew Elaina that well. To say that releasing a virus would be out of character for her would be a lie. No one knew what would be in character for her. The "quiet girl who mostly kept to herself" persona didn't bode well with police, hence, the warrant for her arrest.

So, when Elaina realized that Bretton's daughter was helping her up from the floor, she was hesitant to go along with her. She couldn't help but wonder if Bretton were somewhere nearby, the police using him to get to Elaina. However, since she was rapidly losing blood, she needed all the help she could get.

"Come on," Natalia urged, now yanking her up. Elaina reluctantly followed her down the dark hall. "There should be a nurse's office around here somewhere," she said.

She silently followed the girl down the hall, her mind on high alert. At the first sign of trouble, she would bolt. The science lab was just down the hall, so she could grab her things and exit out the emergency door. It would be tough, especially with a bleeding arm, but she could manage it.

"The nurse's office is usually somewhere within the front office," Natalia mused to no one in particular. "I spent enough time in them as a kid—I should know."

"Were you sick a lot?" Elaina asked, trying to make polite small talk.

"I'm a child of divorce. When things were really bad at home, I used to get terrible stomachaches. Once I got older and realized that divorce is part of the average kid's life, the symptoms disappeared. Funny how that works, isn't it?"

Elaina nodded. She had no experience on the subject, but she didn't want to have to discuss Bretton's failed marriage.

"Yep," Natalia said, "this is it. Sit on the cot and I'll find something for that arm."

"No," Elaina protested. "I'm fine. I just need a bandage to wrap around it. You don't have to do this."

"Just let me." Natalia huffed. "I want to go to nursing school one day. I like this kind of stuff."

Elaina relented and plopped down on the cot, exposing her arm.

"Just to be safe, we should disinfect the wound," Natalia hummed, clearly in her zone. She pulled bottles down from the cabinet, examining the labels. Then, before Elaina could ask her what she was doing, she was dabbing liquids into the stinging wound. Then, she applied gauze to her arm and wrapped it snugly in an elastic bandage.

"Thanks," Elaina said awkwardly as Natalia leaned in close to wrap the bandage.

"I should be thanking you," Natalia replied. "You're the one who saved me from those creeps."

"How did that happen, anyway?" Elaina interjected, her curiosity getting the better of her. "You don't even go to this school."

Natalia sighed as she pinned the bandage into place and sat down on the stool behind her. Her breath quivered in her throat as she pushed a strand of hair behind her ear.

"How well do you know my dad?"

Elaina pursed her lips, afraid of where this conversation was going. She nonchalantly looked toward the door, waiting for it to swing open.

"Honestly," Elaina answered, "not that well. I tend to keep to myself at work. I know about the work he's doing in the lab, for the most part, but that's about it. I only know about you because I've seen pictures of you on his desk."

She nodded. Elaina became uncomfortable with the silence between them. She felt like she needed to say something—anything.

"I didn't know about your parents," she blurted out. "I'm sorry. That must be really hard on you. I'm sure your parents are very proud of you, though."

Without warning, Natalia suddenly started sobbing. Elaina clammed up. She wasn't good with these situations.

"What's wrong?" she gasped, digging her fingernails

into her palms. She was already chastising herself for being so socially inept.

It took a while for Natalia to calm down enough to speak coherently, but when she did, she did not spare any details.

"I know my dad's never been the most nurturing man. I get that," Natalia said, wiping a tear with the sleeve of her shirt. "But I still thought that he cared about me, even if it was only a little."

"I'm sure he cares about you," Elaina said hesitantly. "What happened?"

Natalia shook her head. "We were on our way to my grandma's house. He said it wasn't safe in the city, so we had to leave. I didn't want to go. I was supposed to go to my mom's house in a week when she got home from her vacation. I didn't want to be stuck at my grandma's house with him. So, I was in the car with him when those creeps grabbed me from the seat."

"What?"

"Our car was surrounded. Someone smashed the window and pulled me out. My dad did nothing but watch. Once I was out of the car, I managed to fight my way free, but he was already driving away. If he would have waited a minute, I could have gotten back into the car. If he had helped me, we would have been out of there in seconds. He didn't even try."

Elaina looked at the ground. This story confirmed her judgment of Bretton's character.

"Were the people infected?" Elaina asked.

"I'm not entirely sure," she said. "Some might have been, but then there are the others who are just taking advantage of the situation. I was trying to get back to my house when another group of people approached me. Some looked pretty scary with weird skin lesions. But those two guys who grabbed me and took me here weren't infected at all. Not with your virus, anyway," she said, raising an eyebrow at Elaina.

Your virus. A chill ran down Elaina's spine. Once again, she was being blamed for something that wasn't her fault. Also, she was still in disbelief that it was her virus that did all of this in the first place. Something wasn't right, but she was in no position to figure out what it was when there were so many dangers to watch out for.

"What do you know about the virus?" Elaina asked, preparing to have her worst suspicions about Bretton Vincent confirmed.

Natalia bit her lip. "Can I ask you one thing?" she said softly.

Elaina nodded, knowing exactly what she wanted to know.

"Did you release the virus?"

"No."

Natalia looked into Elaina's eyes as if she were searching for some sort of tell, some indication that Elaina was lying.

"Okay," she said finally.

Elaina was expecting more of a discussion, but if Natalia wasn't looking for any more information, she didn't want to push it. It seemed like she believed her. Even one ally at this stage would be big for Elaina, and she didn't want to screw that up.

Still, accepting an answer didn't necessarily mean that Natalia believed her. All she was confirming was that she heard Elaina's perception of the truth, nothing more and nothing less.

"I need to go back to the lab to work on some stuff," she said vaguely. "That's what I was doing when I heard you scream."

"Oh," Natalia said flatly. "Should I go?"

"I don't think that's a good idea. It's probably best if we stick together. At least until we find a safer place to be," she added. "If you want to come to the lab with me, I don't mind."

"Thanks, that would actually be pretty cool. I really don't want to be alone right now. Is there anything that I can help with?"

"I don't think so," Elaina said hesitantly, still not sure what to make of Natalia Vincent. "Sorry."

"That's fine." She sighed. "I have no problems sitting back and minding my own business if it means that I have a little protection from the crazy assholes of the world."

With that, Elaina headed back to the high school chemistry lab with her new companion in tow. While she wasn't always the best at keeping people entertained, she was relieved to have someone with her. There was something so eerie about being alone while the world around you was crumbling.

They had rounded the last corner when they heard a sound coming from in front of them. Natalia clutched Elaina's forearm tightly.

"What do we do?" Natalia whispered.

"Maybe it's nothing," Elaina whispered back. "I need to get into the lab and grab my samples. Then we can leave if we're in danger."

However, there was no time for that. Standing directly in front of the science room were four women with their teeth bared. Elaina knew at once that they were infected and that they were ready to attack.

Natalia squeezed her arm tighter. "Are they . . .?"

"Yep."

"Let's go," Natalia urged, pulling Elaina back to where they came from. Elaina froze in her tracks.

"My samples," she breathed, feeling her pockets. She only had a little bit of the original virus and one vial of LILY.

"They're going to infect us. We have to go."

Elaina pulled toward the science lab. She wondered if she could outrun the infected women before they caught her.

There was no time to test her hypothesis. The second she took a step forward, the women lunged forward, taking off into a full sprint toward the two girls. Elaina and Natalia ran toward the front exit when two men blocked their path. They couldn't tell if they were infected, but at that point, they didn't trust anyone who was running at them. Elaina pulled Natalia down another empty corridor. Eventually, they made it outside through an emergency door and ran until they could no longer hear the door alarm.

Panting, Elaina turned back to look at the school, worried about the samples she'd left behind. She wondered if she still had a chance to work on the cure without them.

In the back of her mind, she also wondered if anyone would find her samples and understand what they were. At this rate, it hardly mattered if someone became infected from her work. She was more concerned that she was leaving a trail of evidence wherever she went. She would need to be much more careful at her next lab.

If she found a new lab. Part of the pain involved with leaving her work behind was not knowing if she'd be able to pick it up again anytime soon. If she couldn't, more and more people would become infected. The more people who progressed to the rage symptoms, the more people who would potentially stand in her way.

"Where do we go?" Natalia asked, looking toward the slightly older girl for guidance. Even though she had earned her doctorate in Virology, in many respects, Elaina still felt like a child herself. She wasn't ready to be fully responsible for herself or others.

"We keep walking," Elaina said quietly, heading toward the soft glow of the early morning horizon.

Chapter Nine

The girls trekked down side streets and dirt roads, avoiding contact with anyone, infected or not. Elaina knew that it just took one good citizen spotting her for her to be arrested, and Natalia had a complete distrust of everyone save for Elaina. They were the perfect traveling companions.

"Can we stop now?" Natalia whined after an hour of running and walking. "We haven't seen anyone in over an hour. Can we go back to your car?"

"My car is in the school parking lot. There's no way that it's sat untouched all this time. Car thefts have been on the rise in the last few weeks."

"I say it's worth going back for. I hate running."

"I'm surprised you want to get back in a car so soon, especially after what happened the last time you tried to drive away to safety," Elaina said in a matter-of-fact tone. This point silenced Natalia for the next twenty minutes of their journey.

Elaina's arm throbbed, but she didn't want to show any signs of weakness, especially after prodding Natalia to continue moving forward. She had to set a good example for the girl if she wanted to keep her safe.

A few times, Elaina considered talking to Natalia about her father, just to search for some clues as to what he was up to. But she saw how distraught it made her to talk about him, so she kept her mouth shut. They carried on in silence.

As the birds began their morning song, exhaustion struck Elaina. She had pulled numerous all-nighters during her academic career, but never like this. Many times, if she found herself lost in a textbook, she hardly flinched when her wake-up alarm sounded. Now, the signs of morning filled her with dread. With no safe haven in sight, she would continue the routine of running and searching for a lab well into the next day, if need be.

In the hours since their evacuation from the high school, they'd had a couple of close calls, both with the infected and the seemingly normal crowd. As time went on, it became harder and harder to distinguish between the two.

"Do you ever just fantasize about giving up?" Natalia asked as they slid down from an oak tree where they had briefly taken refuge after a close call. "The odds are stacked against us. At some point, we're going to come in contact with the virus. Why not just get it over with now and save ourselves a few days of misery running around as a healthy person?"

Elaina stopped dead in her tracks and turned to face

the girl. She pursed her lips, thinking of something inspiring to say to boost her morale. But nothing came to mind.

In fact, that thought had been swirling around her consciousness ever since it escaped. If the spawn of her creation was ultimately the end of her, then it would somehow be just. Plus, if any virus were to take her out, she only wanted it to be one of her own design.

On the other hand, she still felt partially responsible for what had happened. Besides, if she weren't around to find a cure, then the virus would ultimately wipe out all of human civilization. Of course, if everyone were dead, it wouldn't really matter, but the thought of causing the human race to go extinct was too much for her conscience.

"You can't think that way," Elaina replied plainly.

"Why not?"

Natalia had a good point. It would probably be much easier to accept fate than to deal with the struggle that would most likely not lead to a positive outcome. More than likely, at least one of them would succumb to the virus within months. Regular viruses were bad enough—there were so many humans on earth that it was hard to teach everyone that normal human contact, the very actions that made people human, would spread disease. Shaking hands, cuddling, even making love could all conceivably spread communicable diseases from one person to another.

With the Morgan Strain, the infected spread disease intentionally. They bruised and battered healthy individuals until the breaks in their skin absorbed the virus.

This disease wasn't spread by engaging in normal social situations. An unexplainable hatred of others spread it.

"We can't let it win," Elaina said softly.

"What do you mean?"

"The virus wasn't supposed to be a bad thing. In fact, it was meant to be harmless to healthy people and extremely beneficial to sick people with no other chances."

"But it's not, don't you see? What difference does it make whether it was intentional or not? We're still running from maniacs who want to kill us."

"I can stop it. And if I can stop it, then I'll keep you safe. You'll be first in line for the vaccine once it's ready."

"Really?" Natalia asked, her eyes wide and shiny. "You're not just saying that so I won't leave you, right?"

Elaina shook her head. "I mean it."

"Do you really think you can stop this?"

Elaina raised her chin, standing tall. It was a trick her mother taught her for shaking off the nerves when public speaking. Manufactured confidence was nearly as good as the real thing.

"Yes," she replied with full confidence. "I really think I can."

"Then I want to help," Natalia answered. "I just want this to be over so I can go back home."

"Me too."

"I'm starving," Natalia whined after walking through an abandoned downtown of suburbia. "Can we stop in this convenience store and grab something to eat? We're going to need food eventually."

Elaina nodded. She was right. The reserves she purchased at the grocery store were still in her car. Her stomach grumbled furiously when she thought about the sugary snacks she'd left behind.

"Fine, but let's make it quick. If it hasn't been fully raided, then it probably will be soon. We'll grab a few small things that we can carry with us, and then we have to get out of here."

Natalia beamed. "I've always wanted to take whatever I wanted from a store like this," she said, eyeing the gas station. "Somehow, it's not nearly as exciting as I imagined, you know, running from the infected."

Elaina cracked a small smile. She wanted to seem like an adult, but she secretly held the same desire. As it turned out, there were still small joys that even the downfall of humanity could not take away.

Cautiously, the pair entered the store through a broken glass door, ready to stuff their pockets with all of the saturated fats and sugar they could carry. Natalia made a beeline to the chocolate bars while Elaina mused over the different flavors of chips. They each made a few selections when they heard the sound of a door slamming shut.

They jumped up and turned toward each other, hoping that it was in their imagination. By the other's reaction, they knew it was not. Someone was in the store with them.

Elaina felt a wave of panic wash over her. Whoever was in the back room of the store was coming nearer.

They had two options—run or hide.

If they ran, the person in the back would give chase,

and they would have to run down the commercial area looking for shelter. Businesses with goods worth stealing were already occupied, and those that held no interest to the average infected or criminal were locked. There were no great places to hide once pursued.

If they hid, the person in the store could potentially attack them if they were found. But if they weren't found, then they'd have a little time to make a calculated getaway. They'd be able to find a lab instead of being chased into a grocery store.

"Hide," Elaina whispered, pushing Natalia toward a storage cupboard under the coffee machine. The girl folded her legs like a contortionist and squeezed into the small space.

When Elaina could ensure that her travelling companion was well hidden, she tucked herself behind a display of postcards and magazines. In natural daylight, she would likely be seen, but in the dark store, she was camouflaged. If they could just stay silent long enough for the looter to get what they wanted and leave, then they would be free to go.

With a loud blast, the back door burst open, revealing a beast of a man. His wide shoulders gave way to hulking arms. Elaina estimated that he was about six feet, five inches and weighed around three hundred pounds.

He stomped around the store, grabbing whatever was in reach—cigarettes, emergency flares, and rope. He moved as if he had no clear aim, but the items he grabbed told a story. He wasn't in the store hunting for snack cakes like Elaina and Natalia were.

Elaina clamped a hand over her mouth, knowing that one little whimper could send the man into a violent frenzy. She saw the oozing gash on his face. If he hadn't felt any symptoms yet, he soon would.

She was glad that she'd ordered Natalia to hide in the cupboard. If the girl saw who they were up against, she would have screamed. No, it was better for her to imagine that the danger was smaller.

The man, pleased with his selection, walked back toward the heavy back door. Elaina closed her eyes, feeling relief wash over her. She listened as his footsteps fell fainter and fainter.

When she was almost certain that they were safe, Elaina heard a tiny sneeze from the storage cupboard. Before she could even move, the man came barreling back into the store, massive arms ready to strike.

Elaina covered her mouth again, stifling a scream in the back of her throat. He wildly looked around, searching for the source of the noise.

"I heard you," he growled. "I know you people are trying to kill me, but I'm not going to let that happen. I didn't ask to get sick. If everyone would just leave me alone, then we wouldn't have any problems. But no," he shouted, kicking over shelves, "I'm not just going to roll over and die. I'm going to get my revenge first."

He leaned down and wrenched the cupboard door right off its hinges, exposing Natalia's hiding spot. She let out a shrill scream and pulled her former captor's gun from under her sweatshirt, firing a bullet.

It went wide, nearly hitting Elaina. The man

grabbed Natalia by the wrist and pulled her out into the open.

"I'm not going to let some stupid girl kill me," the man roared, pushing her against the wall.

Elaina abandoned her hiding place by pushing the wire magazine racks over onto the man. He was big enough that the racks left little damage, but they startled him enough for him to relinquish his grip on Natalia.

"Run," Elaina shouted, climbing out of the hole in the front door. She quickly looked back to see Natalia sprinting after her. Following her was the man, quick for his size.

Elaina led the way down the street, looking for somewhere, anywhere to go. The man chasing them was gaining speed and practically frothing at the mouth. Natalia was panting and starting to slow down. Elaina worried that she wouldn't be able to keep up for much longer, so she led the chase into an abandoned carwash.

Weaving through the different stalls, Elaina stopped to grab Natalia and pull her to the side. Then, she took the girl by the hand to hide between two gigantic mechanical scrubbing arms.

Natalia was shaking like a leaf, so Elaina pulled her close to her body to calm her down. A protective instinct kicked in, and she squeezed Natalia tighter while silently promising to keep her safe. She was sisterless herself, but as she embraced the girl, she felt a kinship toward her that she wished she could have experienced in normal circumstances.

After what seemed like an hour, Elaina released Natalia.

"I think the coast is clear," she whispered, slowly walking out of the dark tunnel. "Where the hell did you get that gun to shoot at him?"

"I grabbed it after the guy who kidnapped me dropped it. There was only one bullet left though. I'd never actually shot a gun before."

A cool morning breeze blew past Elaina, sending a chill down her spine. Usually, the silence was a good sign, a sign that they weren't in danger. But at this moment, the quiet was eerie. The soft hairs on her forearms stood up.

"Something's not right," she whispered.

"What?" Natalia asked.

Just then, the man who Elaina was sure had moved on jumped out in front of them.

"Did you think you could run away from me?" he snarled. "You stupid bitches are going to die now."

The girls screamed and bolted toward the other side of the tunnel. Elaina felt a large hand brush the back of her neck, then she heard a gunshot.

She toppled to the ground, stunned. She lay there, feeling nothing, then feeling faint. Strong hands rolled her onto her back, and when she opened her eyes, she was staring at a gun.

"Are you infected?" a voice barked at her.

"What?" she moaned.

"Are you infected?"

He remembered that moment when he thought his life was going to end. That moment after hearing the gunshot, looking down to see where he was hit. He realized he wasn't. He remembered how he turned around and saw his partner had shot himself to save him, knowing he was infected.

She slowly sat up. The man on the other side of the gun was wearing a police uniform. The man who had been chasing them lay dead on the street, a bleeding hole between the eyes.

"No, I'm not infected," she protested. "Can you get that gun out of my face, please?" she asked.

The police officer didn't move. "What are your names? What are you doing here?"

"I'm Natalia Vincent," Natalia said quickly, her hands still shaking. "And this is—"

"Lainey," Elaina interjected quickly. Natalia gave her a quizzical look, and Elaina returned it with a flat stare. The last thing she needed was to be picked up by police for the crimes she never committed.

"What are you girls doing out here?" he asked again.

"Trying to find food," Elaina answered quickly. She flashed Natalia a warning look. She didn't need to give him any more information than absolutely necessary.

"Come with me," he said, gesturing to his cop car. "You can't stay here. It's not safe."

Elaina rolled her eyes. It was very clear to her that they weren't safe in their current location. She wondered if the cop was so dense to think that she'd willingly placed herself in the middle of a deserted town.

"You never told me your name," she fired back.

"My name is Officer Alec Lawrence. You can just call me Alec."

Chapter Ten

"Stop," Alec said suddenly, drawing his gun again. Elaina turned to look behind her, wondering what hidden danger he saw that she didn't.

"Don't move," he barked.

"What?" she asked.

"Your arm," he said flatly.

"My what?" she started. "Oh, it's a long story."

"I bet it is," he grumbled. "How did you get it?"

"There were these two hillbilly assholes who tried to attack us," she explained. "The gun went off and it nicked my arm. It bled a lot and it hurts, but it's no big deal. Natalia wrapped it up pretty well."

Natalia smiled but Alec did not.

"Was the man infected?"

"No—well, I don't think so," she answered. "I think he was just trying to capitalize on the epidemic."

"You realize that you could be infected," Alec said

sternly, still pointing his gun. "The man I just shot was definitely infected."

"Sure," she replied, "but he didn't touch me. I assure you, I cleaned and wrapped this wound immediately after I got shot. It's not infected. I'm not infected. Natalia's not infected. Trust me."

Natalia looked confused. "Why are you pointing a gun at her? I though you were here to help us."

"I'm here to protect healthy citizens from the infected ones. If there's a threat to healthy citizens, I need to know about it."

"I promise you, I'm healthy," Elaina said.

"Of all people, she should know," Natalia added before realizing what she'd said.

"What do you mean?" he questioned.

"Nothing," Elaina tried to cover up. "I'm just a Biology major at the University of Washington. We study viruses sometimes."

"I don't care if you're a Nobel Prize-winning scientist," he retorted. "Let me see your arm."

Exasperated, Elaina unwrapped her bandage and exposed her wounded arm. The abrasion was clean and had nearly stopped bleeding.

Alec held her cold arm in his warm hands and closely examined the wound, checking for any sign of infection. When he couldn't find any, he gently released her arm.

"Happy?" Elaina asked.

"Well, Lainey, it doesn't appear that the wound has been infected, but you need to make sure it stays under wraps and away from others, do you understand?"

"Yes," she said, giving him a sarcastic smile.

"Good. Get in the car, and we'll find a place for the two of you to go."

Natalia hopped in the back seat and Elaina slid in next to her on the opposite side. Elaina wished she'd had just a little more time alone with Natalia to explain what needed to happen, or more importantly, what couldn't happen here.

Alec slammed the door behind him. "You know, you're not under arrest. You can sit in the front seat if you want."

"No, thanks," Elaina said coldly. "This is fine back here."

"Do you need anything?" he asked, scratching his head. His inexperience shone through his tough exterior in these moments. He was clearly out of his element, both in dealing with disasters and dealing with women. "I think we've got a first aid kit and some emergency blankets in here."

"What about food?" Natalia asked, squeezing her empty stomach.

"Oh, right," he said, reaching into the glove compartment. "I've only got a few protein bars and a bottle of water. Will that do for now?"

The girls greedily split up the rations, hardly stopping their chewing to breathe. Alec awkwardly watched them, not knowing what to say.

"Where are you girls from?" he asked, turning on the car to warm the shivering girls up.

"Seattle," Natalia replied with her mouth full. "I was kidnapped from my dad's car. The guys who took me were real creeps. If you come across two guys in a bunker, you should probably arrest them for kidnapping. Actually, they've probably found a new wife already. Maybe you should look into that."

"Okay," Alec said, writing something in a notepad. "Can you tell me everything you know about them?"

"The only thing I know is that they're disgusting," she replied. The young one is tall and skinny and the older one is fat and has terrible body odor. If you've got any dogs on the case, I bet you'd find them in a heartbeat."

Elaina stifled a giggle. Having a talkative person with her would be helpful in distracting the police from her business. All she had to do was keep Natalia talking about the right things to keep the heat off her.

"Are you two sisters or something?" Alec asked, wagging a finger between the two.

"No," Elaina answered. "I was trying to hide from the infected people chasing me when I heard her screaming. I ran inside the school and we fought her kidnappers off together. Ever since then, we've run into a lot of people. For the most part, they just chased us away from their territory."

"Are you positive they were infected?" Alec asked grimly. "How many people would you estimate?"

"Maybe fourteen, fifteen?" Elaina guessed. "And they were definitely infected."

Alec groaned and rubbed the side of his face. He hadn't shaved in a few days, and dark stubble was forming across the lower half of his face. It suited him, though. The bloodshot eyes from lack of sleep and poor nutrition didn't as much.

"What's wrong?" Natalia asked. "Have you seen a lot of infected people too?"

Alec nodded. "I'm afraid so. I was hoping I'd be able to go home now, but at this rate, I'm not sure if I'll ever get to end this shift."

Elaina felt a little bad for Alec. As much as she disliked the police and everyone on a witch hunt for her, seeing him be just as eager to go home as she was returned a little humanity to him. He was caught up in a bad situation with limited options. She could relate to that.

"Oh," Natalia said sympathetically. "I bet you want to get back to your family too."

"I live alone," he said. "I'd just like to get back home and go to sleep."

Natalia nodded. "Have any of your friends gotten the virus? A girlfriend, perhaps?" she pried.

"Natalia," Elaina scolded.

"It's okay, Lainey," he answered. "Just a coworker, so far. But even then, it's hard to know if they've been infected and it's still dormant in their body."

Natalia looked down at her lap, hiding a smug smile. Elaina wasn't sure why she was asking a stranger such personal questions. Maybe she was just so traumatized by everything that had occurred in the past twenty-four hours that she turned to inappropriate questions.

"Well, girls," Alec said, looking in his rearview window at the two, "should we go to the station downtown? We've got plenty of supplies there, so you can stay until someone can come pick you up."

"No," Elaina said quickly, a cold sweat forming under her arms. "We can't go to the police station."

"Why not?" Alec asked, genuinely confused. "No one can kidnap you there—it's filled with uniformed officers. There's no safer place in the city."

"I disagree," she replied. "I don't really have anyone to pick me up. Neither does Natalia. If we stay at the station for a few days, where will we sleep?"

Alec thought for a moment. "We have cots in our holding cells. You can crash there until you figure something out."

"We're going to be sleeping in a jail cell?" Natalia asked.

"No," Alec said. "It's not like that. You know you're not under arrest. We wouldn't put you in the same cell as the real criminals. Maybe I can talk to the captain and we can make the drunk tank into a safe place for displaced citizens."

"Let me out of the car," Elaina said firmly.

"What?" Alec asked.

"Here's the thing—we're going to be mixed in with infected people. There's no doubt about that. If I'm stuck in a cage and someone goes into a rage, I'm going to get infected. Then I'm dead. I'm not going to a police station. If that's where you're going, you can let me go here."

"Lainey," he protested.

"It's just not safe. Thank you for all of your help. I

really appreciate it. I just can't be locked into a death cell."

He thought for a moment, considering what Elaina had to say. He, too, had felt concerned about working in an environment where many of the people in holding cells were likely infected. It would be wrong to force them into a place that was supposed to be safe, only to see them fall victim to the virus.

"I just don't know where else I can take you that would be any safer," he said.

Elaina clenched her fists. Her heart was racing. She slid her hand to the door handle just in case he started to drive and she needed to make a quick escape.

"If we're going to get infected at the police station, I don't want to go there," Natalia said.

"Please, let's think of a better solution," Elaina pleaded.

"You're right," Alec said, to which Elaina breathed a small sigh of relief. If Alec didn't recognize her, someone else at his place of employment certainly would. "Do you have any ideas?"

The car was silent as the three tried to think of one place in the city that would be even remotely safe. Elaina needed a place with a lab and few interruptions. Natalia just wanted protection from creeps.

"How about a school?" Alec suggested.

"No," the girls said in unison.

"We came from a school, remember?" Natalia said. "I'm in no hurry to go back. They're filled with infected.

They thought quietly again, Natalia's head bobbing as she started to doze off.

"How about a hospital?" Elaina offered. "There should be enough rooms that Natalia and I can stay safe."

"I wouldn't do that unless you were well rested and on top of your game," Alec replied. "When people get sick, where's the first place they go?"

Elaina frowned. Save for a professional laboratory, any medical setting would be the next best bet. Even a veterinary clinic would suffice. But she couldn't let on to Alec why she wanted lab equipment without drawing suspicion.

After a few more minutes of silence, Elaina broke.

"I can hardly think anymore," she cried, throwing her hands in the air. Natalia woke up at the noise, startled into sitting up straight.

"Let's not worry about a permanent safe space then," Alec said firmly. "Let's find somewhere safe to rest for a little bit, and then we'll figure out where to go. I could use a little rest myself. It's not safe to be out there when we're tired like this. Is that fine with the two of you?"

Natalia nodded enthusiastically. Elaina bit her lip.

"Fine," she said, crossing her arms across her chest. "But once we feel rested, I'm out of here. I realize that it's probably best if we stick together so we can sleep in shifts. Besides, you've got a gun and you know how to use it. That's more than we have right now."

Alec cracked a small smile. He was finally getting somewhere.

"I have an idea," he said. "The shipping district is full of warehouses. I'm sure it wouldn't be too hard to find an empty one. Plus, they're filled with supplies. We just have to find the right one and set up a little shelter there."

"Don't homeless people sleep in those?" Natalia protested.

"Do you have a home to go to?" Alec retorted.

She fell silent. "As long as you promise to protect me, I don't care where we go."

"Lainey?" he asked.

She nodded. "Once our basic needs are met, we can look for a better place. After some rest, we'll be able to think much more clearly. Let's go before Natalia falls asleep again."

Natalia reached across the backseat and squeezed Elaina's hand. She gave her a squeeze back. She felt as though they had wordlessly created an alliance. Now, sticking with Natalia was almost equally important to working on a cure. As much as she liked to be independent, Elaina knew she couldn't do it alone. She needed all the help she could get.

When she got the chance, she would explain more of her situation to Natalia. Bretton's daughter wouldn't be her first choice for confidant under normal circumstances, but the world that they lived in was pure chaos. Elaina couldn't afford to let a single resource go to waste.

"Thank goodness." Alec smiled. "I know it's strange for me to say this since I just met you, but you have no idea how glad I am that I'm actually able to help."

"I'm glad that we could be your damsels in distress," Elaina said sarcastically, flashing him a smile.

Chapter Eleven

Dr. Bretton Vincent took a deep breath and walked past the commanding officer's office, hoping he wouldn't be seen. It wasn't that he was scared of the man, it was just hard to look him in the eyes and tell him that he wasn't making any progress. Coleridge, as he knew him by, was a tall, muscular man, like an older version of GI Joe. Coleridge was the first man he was formally introduced to at the military base. No one else really spoke to him, except for a few lower-ranked individuals. His job was to take orders from Coleridge and report any findings to him first.

"Here are the samples our team collected, Doctor Vincent," an eager lab assistant named Smith said to Bretton, handing a bunch of test tubes to him. "We've collected five different samples from five different corpses. The deceased were all shot by police officers and military personnel due to displaying violent tendencies, so we can assume they reached the rage period fairly recently."

Bretton nodded and placed the tubes in the rack, clearly labeling them with the date. So far, he had managed to collect a wide variety of virus samples in hopes that one would lead him toward some type of solution. Instead, it confirmed what he already knew to be true—people were dying from his mutation of Elaina Morgan's virus.

No one could know this, though. In fact, when the military brought him in for questioning and briefing, he made sure to emphasize that he'd had little to no involvement in Elaina's work. He figured he probably knew about it better than most virologists, but he was not at fault for its release.

Because Elaina Morgan was still missing, he was the next best scientist to work on the cure. Besides, if she was wanted for possible bioterrorism, she was hardly trusted to create a vaccine or cure.

Because he was tasked with a top-secret operation, he only had lab assistants that the military provided for him. They were well-trained and qualified to be assistants on complicated work, but they only followed orders. This meant that their leader needed to know exactly what he was doing in order for them to be useful. Unfortunately, Bretton was stuck.

He stared under microscopes and studied the little squiggling virus, but no inspiration came to him. It made him furious that Elaina could see these viruses and come up with ideas that would never even occur to him. He was a gifted and knowledgeable scientist, but she was doing things in the lab that no one else could do. It was unfair that he was tasked with working on something that would be a struggle for even her.

He didn't really have a choice, though. The military had offered him something that no one else could—complete protection. Left out on the streets to fend for himself, Bretton probably wouldn't last more than a few weeks. He couldn't even protect an eighteen-year-old girl—how was he supposed to protect himself?

When the armored car turned up on the road that day, it was like a gift from heaven. He was so scared and lost, and the military scooped him off the road and gave him a job. A job which, if he completed successfully, would provide him with the wealth and power he desired. In fact, if he pulled this one off, he could even contract with the government to work on other big projects. The thought of working on top-secret projects was much sexier than co-authoring a paper that no one would even read.

Bretton was getting ahead of himself. If he didn't deliver, then there would be no future as a military contractor. In fact, if he didn't come up with the results they needed, there might not be a future for him at all.

When he was briefed, it was made clear that the military wasn't doing him a favor by giving him a safe place to work. If Bretton couldn't come up with results in a reasonable amount of time, then he would be released and he would have to go out on his own. Since the number of infected grew at an exponential rate, he knew the odds of staying healthy weren't spectacular.

What was reasonable for creating a vaccine or cure,

he didn't know. From the way Coleridge spoke, it seemed like a shorter amount of time than Bretton would have liked. It had been just a couple of days, but he didn't even know where to start. He'd tried working on a vaccine, but every time he checked back on the virus, it had changed enough that his vaccine was useless. He couldn't stop or predict how it was going to mutate next. It just all happened too quickly. He felt the pressure from the officers who oversaw the progress. They didn't work in virology. They didn't know how slow progress could be.

The military had bigger problems on their hands than sheltering a mediocre virologist. They needed to stop the spread of the disease. This went beyond quarantines and education methods—they had to physically stop the infected from willingly infecting others. No one liked to speak of it, but the government was killing their own sick citizens by the hundreds every day.

The government was having a hard time keeping the virus contained. What began in Seattle had spread to the suburbs and now had roots in other states. Before long, there was an international travel ban put in place. No one was entering or exiting the country. Traveling in and out of the state was first left to the discretion of the individual, but once it started spreading out of control, the National Guard was deployed to guard each state border. This helped some, but it wasn't enough.

It was a tricky situation for the country's different government departments who all had plans for this sort of thing but never dreamed of having to put them in action. The idea of a massive epidemic wiping out the population was so absurd to some that putting the plans into practice was much harder in real life than in the yearly drills that elicited eye rolling and half-hearted participation.

Plans that had been created years ago were left to sit and become outdated. Administrations changed hands, and no one thought to brief incoming staff on how to handle these things. Some of the literature on epidemics was so outdated that it was laughable. Many didn't account for new forms of transportation and new technologies. A lot of it just wasn't around during the days of the Polio or Ebola outbreaks. Those outbreaks happened so long ago that history books had to be pulled from libraries to see how they were dealt with.

No one was prepared, but they were doing everything they could to stop the spread of disease. Unfortunately, these measures became dramatic once the panic set in. No one was immune to the virus, just as no one was immune to the panic that came along with it. Even the most cool and collected officials had fears that kept them up at night—*Will I be next?*

The only known creator of the virus, Elaina Morgan, was missing. This didn't make her look innocent in the eyes of the law. The longer she hid, the more she was suspected of being a malevolent scientist, hellbent on watching the world burn.

Bretton Vincent, on the other hand, was becoming a shining light in a dark world. Out of all the other virologists in their research lab, he was the only one who'd agreed to help. The ones who could be found were sure that they knew nothing about Elaina's virus and weren't remotely capable of understanding it. But Bretton, with false confidence and the desire to succeed, had agreed to do the impossible.

Setting his wire glasses on the lab table, he rubbed the sweat from his forehead. He needed to focus if he wanted to beat the clock.

A chicken's egg in hand, he carefully injected a tiny sample of his virus inside, then placed it back in its incubator. He repeated the process over and over again until the incubator was full. Next, he formulated a standard catalyst and added it to his vaccine. He didn't want to rush things, but he hoped it would speed the process up enough that he could begin trials.

Bretton knew that he could create a vaccine for just about any run-of-the-mill virus out there. What he was struggling with was one that frequently changed. If he could get his vaccine released quickly enough, it might work. But it wouldn't work forever. It was like making a key that opened one door when what he really needed was to make a master key that could open hundreds of locks. He might get lucky in a few isolated cases, but by and large, it wouldn't suffice.

"I've never seen that technology being used in that way before," Smith said. "I thought people stopped using eggs for vaccines years ago. I've also never seen a catalyst that works that quickly."

"You're young," Bretton said. "Besides, in emergencies, you have to be resourceful. Do you have any subjects for testing?"

Smith looked uncomfortable. He was an excellent

scientist and soldier, but he had yet to be hardened by the horrors of the world.

"What?" Bretton asked. "Don't tell me that you haven't found any subjects yet. I should have cages full of rats ready to go. What's the holdup?"

Smith looked at the floor. "I have orders, sir."

"What kind of orders?" Bretton groaned.

"Have you ever worked with primates before?"

Bretton put his glasses back on. "It's usually not considered ethical to test on animals larger than a rat. Even with rodents, there are still rules. I'm going to need a large sample size. At this stage, ten rats are more valuable to me than one orangutan."

"Sir, this is the military. You can get whatever you need in any quantity you want. This is a desperate situation. Our commanding officer wants to move things as quickly as possible."

This made Bretton nervous—not because he had any problems testing on animals of various sizes and intellects, but because he knew that these guys were not messing around. If they could wipe out infected people without batting an eye, bring in all sorts of animals for testing, and do so without the public knowing, then what could they do to him if things didn't go well?

"It's fine," he said, "but I feel more comfortable working with rats. Besides, their DNA is similar enough to humans' that it doesn't sacrifice quality. Please ask your supervising officer if we can start with rats first."

"Yes, sir," Smith responded, turning on his heel. He strode out of the room, just as he was conditioned to do in basic training.

Bretton sat back on his lab stool, a sick feeling in his stomach. He was working with a very powerful, very dangerous employer. He needed to do whatever he could to get on their good side.

Later that night when he walked back to his barracks, he wondered if his daughter were still alive. Natalia was a sheltered child. If she were still out there somewhere, he hoped that someone was taking good care of her. She was stubborn and tried to be as independent as possible, but she had never experienced a hard day in her life, as far as he could recall.

But he knew that if he were being honest with himself, she was gone. If not from the attackers themselves, then the virus would have taken its toll on her delicate frame. She was just a wisp of a girl. Her body would have been ravished in days. Bretton tried to convince himself that she was still alive, but at the very least, she'd passed peacefully instead of being overcome with the rage.

A tear slid down his face that he quickly brushed away. Bretton stood still for a moment and closed his eyes, breathing in the fresh air. He imagined himself standing on a stage, accepting an award for his advances in virology. *The Natalia Vaccine*, he'd call it, and then his daughter's name would be on the lips of everyone around the world. He may have let her go, but he would make sure that her memory would last forever.

Bretton brushed his teeth in front of the tiny mirror and swallowed a tiny blue pill that the medic told him would help him sleep. Then, he lifted the tightly tucked sheets and slid onto the mattress, finally free from the watchful eyes of his superiors.

Tomorrow would be a fresh start for the scientist. Sleep would renew his focus and he'd suddenly become inspired once he stopped stressing out about it so much.

At least that was what he had been telling himself every night since the virus was released from the lab. He couldn't lose hope yet. There was too much on the line —fame, money, and protection from the very thing he adapted and released into the world.

Chapter Twelve

"How well do you know this area?" Elaina asked Alec as he drove back into the city they'd abandoned not long ago. The air smelled of burned plastic, and a thick smog hung over them.

"I've been living here my whole life," Alec answered. "Don't you worry."

"I wasn't worried," Elaina lied. "I was just making polite conversation."

Elaina wasn't yet convinced of the police officer's competency. He looked to be about her age. She wondered if she would have been in a class appropriate to her age if they had met in school. She doubted it though. She went to a private science and technology high school. He seemed like a public school kid.

Elaina tried to relax, but her type-A tendencies tried to take over. Many called her a know-it-all, but she just had a very good idea of what was rational and what was not. Going to an abandoned warehouse didn't seem like a good idea when much of the population was looking for shelter and supplies. They certainly weren't the only ones with those same needs and the intelligence to know where to get it.

"There are so many of them." Natalia yawned as they drove through the rows of metal buildings. "How do we choose which one to stay in?"

Elaina looked to Alec for an answer. She didn't think that he had one.

"Well," he said, slowing down, "we want something that's empty. And it would help if there were some good supplies inside. The problem is, we have no way of knowing what's inside without checking ourselves."

"That's going to take forever." Elaina sighed. "Shall we split up?"

"No," Natalia said quickly, clutching her seatbelt.

"I don't think it's a great idea either," Alec agreed. "Don't worry, we'll find something in no time."

Elaina rolled her eyes. There was no reason she should trust him. If he were a little more aware of the news, he would have arrested her without asking questions. Still, she figured she was lucky to meet up with a dumb cop. He could provide protection for a brief length of time until he realized who she was.

"It's now or never," Alec said after coming to a halt in the middle of four different storage buildings. "Let's see what we're working with."

Elaina thought he seemed a little too cheery to stop, but she reasoned that one might be at more ease in this kind of situation if they had weapons and the means to use them effectively.

"Stay here," he ordered, getting out of the car and opening his trunk. Elaina watched him through the rearview window, wondering what kind of firearms he had stored back there.

Instead, he pulled out a backpack and started unbuttoning his uniform shirt to reveal a snug white t-shirt underneath. Natalia snickered softly, and it took Elaina all the composure she had not to join in. She hated to admit it to herself, but Alec was not a bad looking man.

Reaching into the bag, he pulled out a hooded sweatshirt and jeans. His lower half was hidden from view, much to Natalia's disappointment, but when he returned to the driver's seat, he didn't look like a cop at all. Instead, he could have fit in at any college campus.

"Are those your undercover clothes?" Natalia asked, a wicked smile spreading out across her face.

"Something like that," Alec replied. He reached into the storage console and tossed an extra handgun into his backpack, along with the empty water bottle and various other items he could find.

Elaina and Natalia followed him from the cop car to the first warehouse. The sliding metal door was cracked open, so they squeezed in to see what was inside.

Much to their surprise, there were people inside, quite a few of them. Fires were burning in metal barrels around the expanse, and people from all walks of life were gathered around to absorb some of the warmth.

Natalia opened her mouth to speak, but Alec placed his finger to his lips, signaling silence. He was being cautious for good reason—there was no way of knowing if these strangers posed a threat from this distance.

After creeping around for a short while, Alec led them back outside.

"I think it's probably too crowded in there," Alec said softly. "I think we should keep looking."

Elaina nodded in agreement. The fewer people to identify her, the better.

The sight of the people seeking refuge in the warehouses was haunting for Elaina. These weren't just homeless people in tattered clothing looking for a warm place to sleep. Instead, average people occupied the buildings. Teachers, retail workers, and accountants were huddled together. The only difference they shared from the usual vagrants was that they once had homes. But once society's only concern is staying alive, it's easy to be pushed out of a home with nowhere to turn.

Even Alec knew that his position as a police officer was much different than the job he signed up for. He felt useless in doing the usual work that filled his days. He couldn't stop every carjacking and kidnapping in the city. He couldn't fight off the squatters that displaced people from their homes with violence. He definitely couldn't prevent the virus from spreading at an alarming rate. It gave him some small comfort that he had two citizens who trusted him enough to follow him through the shipping district.

The trio explored different warehouses, all of them a little too full for comfort. A few times, they were unsure if the inhabitants were healthy or infected. Finally, after three or four attempts, they found one that was good enough.

For the three of them, good enough meant that they could expect to keep to themselves and avoid being attacked or bothered for supplies for a couple of hours.

"Look," Elaina whispered when they entered. "Shipping containers."

This particular warehouse hadn't even been unloaded before the virus struck. A few metal containers had been opened and emptied, but most remained latched shut.

Alec led the girls over to a quiet corner. They weren't completely alone, but their other housemates appeared generally uninterested in knowing who was setting up residency on the other side.

Elaina wrenched the latch of a container open. She struggled and strained, but she eventually managed to reveal crates full of pet supplies. She laughed as she pulled dog beds of varying sizes out of a protective plastic bag. Rawhide bones and tiny stuffed mice lay at her feet.

She wondered if all of the cubes would be full of mostly worthless items. It had been foolish of her to imagine crates filled with bottled water and canned food.

She exited the container to watch Alec open his latch with ease. She rubbed her tired muscles, wishing he had used her free pass to the university's recreation center once or twice.

"What's in there?" she called to him. Alec returned, holding two large plastic flower pots in his hands.

Before she could stop herself, she burst out giggling again. How incredibly bad their luck must be if a warehouse full of merchandise for the taking turned out to be completely useless.

Alec looked surprised to see Elaina in either surprisingly high spirits or on the verge of a mental breakdown. He studied her face with concern, wondering if inappropriate giggling was a symptom of the virus.

"I'm sorry," she said. "This is just so incredibly ridiculous. We could take whatever we want, but we're stuck in a warehouse full of pet supplies and gardening items. What do we do? We have no food and water and nowhere to go. Is this the end for us?"

"Hey, you guys," Natalia called. "I think I've got something."

Elaina jumped down from her perch and followed Alec to the other container. Alec shone his flashlight into the dark space.

"What did you find?" he asked.

"Baby stuff," Natalia answered, flinging a mobile with stuffed animals out of the way. "It's not much, but it's better than nothing," she said, pulling out a box of tiny glass jars.

"Baby food." Alec chuckled. "You're right, it's better than nothing. And you know what? I think it's going to rain today. If we put a few of those flowerpots outside, we could collect enough rain water to last us a few days."

"I guess we can spread out those dog beds and blankets and try to get some sleep," Elaina said, starting to feel rational again.

"Good thinking," Alec said, resting his hand on Elaina's shoulder and giving it a little shake. "Everything is going to be just fine."

"Let's sort through our containers and collect the best stuff. We can put it all in one central area for easier access," Alec suggested. "I'll put the pots out, and you two can grab your stuff."

They got to work straight away, Alec hauling as many containers as his arms would carry, Elaina sorting through the squishy cushions, and Natalia searching for anything edible. When they finished, they met in the spot between their respective searching places.

"This place kind of reminds me of a capsule hotel I stayed at for a conference in Japan," Elaina thought out loud. "But this is on a much larger scale, of course. I guess we can all choose our own containers and get a little rest."

"No way in hell," Natalia interjected. "These containers are pretty massive. If someone comes after me, it would take about a minute for someone to hear my screams and come find me. By that time, I'd already be dead or infected. We stick together."

Elaina started to protest. She spent much of her time alone, so being paired with two other people really threw off her routine. She just wanted a little time to chill out and decompress before the next day. She was hardly even tired anymore. It was the middle of the afternoon, after all.

As much as she had been through with Natalia, and now Alec, they still weren't close. Even though she was starting to think of Natalia as a younger sister, she was still an acquaintance. In fact, being Bretton's daughter almost made her an enemy.

Alec was also somewhere between a stranger and an enemy. Whether he realized it or not, he should have arrested Elaina. He may have saved their life, but that didn't make him a friend. They were all just in the right place at the right time.

Elaina thought about it and decided that if she were in a situation where she could save herself by leaving the other two, she would. As much as she hated to admit it, it made sense to travel in a group, but she was not going to let herself grow too attached to either of them.

"I don't mind staying in the same container," Alec said, looking between the two girls. "Lainey?" he appealed to the older girl, using her family's childhood nickname.

"Yeah, Lainey." Natalia smirked. "We don't have to cuddle together. I just don't want to be alone."

"Fine." Elaina exhaled, grabbing a handful of blankets and tossing them into a container. "Let's set up camp."

Natalia looked pleased with herself and carried the boxes of supplies she found into the container. Alec followed behind, securing the area before he closed one half of the door.

"Should we sleep in shifts?" Natalia asked.

"You two go ahead," Alec offered. "I think I can handle things for the time being,"

"Awesome," Natalia said, spreading out on her personal cushion pile. She draped fluffy pink blankets over herself and fell asleep almost instantly.

"Poor thing," Alec said quietly once Natalia fell asleep. "She looks completely exhausted."

"She is," Elaina answered, glad that her young companion was finally getting some rest.

"You can sleep too, you know," he said. "You're safe with me."

Elaina closed her eyes for a second and tried to imagine a scenario in which that sentiment was true. His words meant little in what felt like the end of the world, but somehow, it was still a little comforting.

"Thanks," she said, leaning back on her own stack of pillows. "I'll try to rest. I'm just not feeling very tired all of a sudden."

"I understand," he said. "It's hard to relax when you feel the burden of responsibility. I don't think I slept for more than a few hours a night when I started working. It just always feels like you should be doing something, you know?"

Elaina understood. In every spare moment of time, she was thinking about what she would do when she got to a lab. She had imagined the procedure so many times that she knew the motions would be automatic and efficient when she got to where she needed to be.

"Did you two really just meet?" Alec asked skeptically. "It seems like you two know each other from something," he said. "If I had to guess, I'd say you two are sisters."

"Nope. I don't have a sister. I just have to look out for her, you know? She's too young to be on her own."

"That's really good of you," he said, to her annoyance. She didn't want him to portray her as the hero. Not yet, anyway.

"She's been through a lot," Elaina said, watching Natalia snore. "A lot of people have."

"Did she really get snatched out of her dad's car?" Alec asked. "That just sounds crazy. How did that even happen?"

"Well, from what I know, her dad's a real piece of shit," Elaina said, feeling some of the anger flow out of her body. She wanted to help keep his daughter alive, if only to use it to mock him for the rest of his life.

"He sounds like it," he answered, chuckling.

"You know what?" Elaina said, "I think I'll try to get some sleep after all."

"Great," Alec said, his voice tinged with disappointment. "Rest up. I'll let you know if anything happens."

Elaina retreated to her cushion pile and turned her back toward Alec. As she pulled the blanket up over her head, completely awake and alert, she tried to pretend that she was alone in her bed instead of sleeping in a metal box with a cop and her rival's daughter.

As she pretended to sleep, she tried to replace the feelings of fear and anxiety with laboratory procedures. She pictured herself filling test tubes and looking under the microscope. Somewhere along the way, she finally fell asleep, watching the centrifuge spin in her head.

Chapter Thirteen

E laina woke with a dry mouth and cold feet, but otherwise feeling good. Her arms and legs were a little sore, but once she stretched out, she felt fine.

She looked at her watch. It was nearly eight o'clock in the morning, meaning that she'd slept for about sixteen hours, something that she had never done in her life.

Stomach rumbling, she searched around in the dark for something to eat. Natalia had made it seem like she hit the jackpot of edible treats in her container, when in reality, they had a small box of mushy baby food and toddler snacks. Even if they managed to choke down the green sludge, it wouldn't be enough to sustain them for more than a handful of hours.

She chose a jar of fruit cocktail and wrenched it open, scooping the purple slime onto her finger and into her mouth. It didn't taste terrible, but it certainly wasn't good. She finished the rest and tucked the jar into the pocket of her jacket.

It took her a few minutes of adjusting to the low light to realize that Alec was gone. Natalia was still snoozing in her corner, but her loud breathing and occasional mumbled phrases made her well known to the others. Alec's absence was odd because he'd promised to keep Elaina updated on any new findings.

Curious, she squeezed out of the crack in the doors and left the warehouse. Others were milling about on the other end, no doubt searching for supplies. She wanted to make it known that there was nothing worth rifling though on their end, but then she would have to communicate with others. She kept her head down and let her hair fall like curtains on her face.

Perhaps it was the much needed sleep she got or the sound of the birds chirping their morning tune, but Elaina felt much better about the position she was in. With everyone rested and ready to go, Alec could drive her to a hospital or school on his way back to work. Then, she could get back to business and do the tasks she could only do in her head from the warehouse.

That was, if she could only find Alec.

Elaina figured that it wouldn't be in her best interest to walk around asking people if they knew where her police officer friend was. Government officials were under fire at the moment for their perceived poor response to the disaster, and none would be very happy to see a police officer walking around collecting supplies of his own. Plus, the fewer people who saw her face, the better.

She started walking back toward his patrol car when she heard a hissing sound from the edge of the building.

"Hey, Lainey," he hissed, waving his hand at her. "Come here."

She jogged over to him, looking behind her shoulder to see if anyone noticed her. The coast was clear.

"What are you doing?" she asked.

Alec pointed to the flowerpots with a grin on his face. "Look," he said, sloshing around a few inches of water in each plastic receptacle. "Drink up. It's important to stay hydrated, especially when we don't know how much longer it'll be until we get more. With any hope, it will rain again soon, but it's hard to know."

She took a planter from him and held it to her lips. It smelled like newly manufactured plastic, but her mouth and throat were parched. She gulped it down without tasting, letting the cool liquid quench her thirst.

"Thanks," she said, swallowing again. "That's much better."

"I refilled the plastic water bottle I had," he said. "I just wish I had more."

She pulled the empty jar from her pocket. "We can use these."

He laughed. "I can't believe you ate that. Was it gross?"

She blushed. "I thought we were all going to," she said quickly.

"I'm just teasing you," he smiled, lightly shoving her shoulder. "Do you want to help me with these?" he asked, pouring the water into larger pots.

Elaina grabbed one, her face still pink, and quietly

carried it into their temporary shelter. Unsurprisingly, Natalia was still sleeping.

"She's a heavy sleeper," Alec whispered. "I had to nudge her at one point in the night to make sure she was still alive. So, what's for breakfast?"

Alec grabbed a few jars and squinted to see the labels. "Butternut squash or banana?" he asked Elaina. She didn't respond.

"We'll give the squash a go," he said, popping off the top and pouring the mixture into his mouth. He grimaced.

"I can't believe you ate that," Elaina mocked.

"We're in the middle of a crisis, Lainey. We don't have time to be picky. How do you think Natalia's going to react to our new cuisine?"

Elaina cracked a smile. The often dramatic teen would probably have a lot to say over the slim pickings.

"I know this sounds weird," Alec said after a long silence, "but you look really familiar. Do I know you from somewhere?"

Elaina froze. This was the moment she had been dreading. Maybe he was awake during the briefing about her after all. With her face plastered all over the news, it was only a matter of time before it clicked and he realized who she was.

"I don't think so. I have a pretty good memory, and I know I haven't met you before."

"Okay, maybe we didn't meet, but I think I've seen you around somewhere. Do you frequent the bars downtown? Or did you go to the University of Washington a few years ago?"

"No," she answered, hoping he would get tired of questioning her and just wake up. For a moment, she thought about nudging Natalia awake, but she was too far away to wake without Alec noticing something was up.

"Okay," he said skeptically, still trying to figure out how he knew her. She scrambled to change the subject, to fluster him somehow.

"I'm flattered, really," she said, batting her eyelashes like she'd seen women do in the movies, "but if you're looking for someone to spend the end of the world with, I don't think I'm your girl. Besides, getting too close to someone is a great way to catch a virus."

His eyes widened, then narrowed. "Wait, what?" he asked.

"I wouldn't claim to be a hot item, but I've had men flirt with me before," she said. "It's actually rather sweet that you would want to spend more time with me, but you have work to do. You can't get caught up in a relationship right now. It's just terrible timing."

That did it. He was officially rattled. His ears turned pink and a thin line of sweat formed on his brow.

"You think I'm flirting with you? I honestly thought I knew you from somewhere," he said, a curious smile forming on his face.

"Yes, it really seems that way. Are you not?"

She hoped that this would be enough to throw him off of her scent. Elaina had clearly embarrassed him, and with any luck, they would go back to silence.

What happened next was something Elaina hadn't accounted for. Instead of taking his embarrassment and chalking it up to a misunderstanding, he ran with her taunting and threw it right back at her.

"Well, then, if you're so sure I'm not your type, then why are you flirting with me?" he asked.

Elaina was speechless. Even though she told Alec that she had experienced men flirting with her before, she really hadn't. She'd shut herself so far away from others that she hadn't had enough social encounters for anyone to flirt with her. That, and she had always been so disinterested in dating that it didn't seem worth it to let men talk to her that way.

Now, in a situation that she was in no way prepared for, the wheels in her head spun without gaining traction. She knew a lot about a few things, and interacting in certain social situations was not one of them. Not only did her face turn red, but she imagined that her entire body glowed fuchsia.

"I'm sorry," she said quietly. "I didn't mean to go into this. I was just kidding. Let's just drop the whole conversation."

"No," he said, raising his eyebrows.

"No?"

"We're stuck in this stupid little shipping container like rats. We have nowhere to go and nothing to do. If we're going to be dead in a week, I'd like to go out having had a few interesting conversations. I'm not asking you to marry me. I just want to know why you think I'm not your type. It's more of a scholarly inquiry, really."

"There's nothing scholarly about this," Elaina said, confused. Unless he was monitoring her vitals to glean the effect of humiliation on the human body, or this was a sociology experiment about how sheltered women react to men, this was nothing more than an uncomfortable conversation that she had unwittingly crawled into.

"Just humor me."

"Fine," she said, feeling the pureed fruits swimming around her stomach. "What was your question?"

"Why am I not your type?"

She wasn't sure how to answer that question in any coy or even off-putting way, so she told him the only thing she could. She told him the truth.

"I guess I don't really have an answer for that. The truth is, I'm not really good at this."

"At flirting?"

"At talking to people in general. I've always been really socially awkward. It counts double when I'm talking to men."

"You don't say." Alec grinned.

"Don't do this to me. I really hate this sort of thing. I'm not good at it and it makes me uncomfortable."

Alec frowned, seeing her big doe eyes full of discomfort.

"I'm surprised. I would have never guessed that this sort of thing made you so uncomfortable."

"Why is that?"

He shrugged his shoulders. "Usually, it's the pretty girls who make guys like me feel nervous."

She blushed again. She had never really been told that she was attractive, save for friends and family members trying to make her feel good. When they said it, it didn't really mean much to her. She would much rather receive compliments on her smarts or talents than her looks. But there was something about hearing it from Alec that felt different. She wasn't sure how, exactly, but it just did.

"Can I ask you something kind of personal?" he asked.

"I feel like you already have, but sure, go ahead," she said.

"How many people have you dated?"

She bit her lip. "Actually, I've never dated anyone."

"Oh," he said, the tone of surprise evident. She knew that once you got into your twenties and had never had a boyfriend, people wondered things.

"How many people have you dated?" she fired back, trying to relieve a little embarrassment.

"Only a couple," he answered honestly. "Neither lasted very long. I guess I'm not great at this thing either."

She smiled awkwardly, hoping he would be out of invasive questions. Still, she didn't completely hate talking to him. He was nice enough, from what she knew about him.

"I guess I just don't really go out much," she said. "I'm committed to my job and I don't have much of a social life. When I'm home, I just like to relax. I've always felt like complicating my life with a relationship would be more than I could handle."

"I often feel the same way too. Like, I don't know if I can give a girl the attention she needs. I always hear about my friends whose girls are mad at them because they don't want to go out on romantic dates and stuff like that."

"It sounds like your friends are dating the wrong girls."

"I don't know. I can see where they're coming from. Some people just have different needs."

"If that's the case, I think I'd be the lowest-maintenance girlfriend," Elaina scoffed before going quiet.

"You know what?" he asked, breaking the silence.

"What?"

"I think that makes you exactly my type."

Elaina looked up at Alec. In the last twenty-four hours, she had never gotten a good look at him. His eyes were so kind and his face was rugged, yet youthful. He swept a hand through his thick hair, pushing it to one side and then the other.

It took her a few seconds to realize that he was looking right back at her.

She quickly looked away and coughed as a way to break the tension. Luckily, this sound was enough to wake Natalia from her deep sleep.

"What time is it?" she croaked, rising from her makeshift bed like a vampire from a coffin.

"A little after ten in the morning," Elaina said, checking her watch. "You slept for almost an entire day."

Natalia flopped back down on her pile, exhausted from sleeping for so long.

"How did I sleep so long? What did I miss?"

"Nothing," Elaina and Alec said in unison.

"Drink some water," Alec said. "It's all we have right now, but it should rain again soon."

"Have some food," Elaina said. "We saved the banana for you," she joked, tossing a little jar at Natalia.

"Great," she said flatly. "I'm so glad I woke up for this. I've been asleep for a whole day. You can't tell me that I haven't missed anything."

"I promise," Elaina said. "We haven't done anything but drink acrid water and eat mushy fruits and vegetables since you fell asleep."

"Good," she said, sitting up again. "I really hate missing out on things."

"Then maybe we should just stay here forever," Alec said. "We could hibernate through this whole virus."

Elaina smiled, but she was eager to get out of there. She entertained the idea of hiding away with Alec and Natalia for longer. The shipping container wasn't an ideal home, but it was comfortable. Alec and Natalia weren't exactly friends, but they were okay. Maybe they could wait it out.

She shook that idea out of her head as quickly as it entered. She had too much work to do to sleep through the days. She needed to go.

Chapter Fourteen

"I've been thinking about it," Alec said after a morning of rummaging around abandoned shipping containers, finding nothing of use, "and I think it's time to move on from here. We came here for the resources, and there's not much here. If we don't find a better source of food and water, we're not going to make it much longer."

Elaina nodded enthusiastically. She had been waiting for someone to plant the idea. If she brought it up herself, she thought she might seem suspicious. She thought back to other conversations where she might have made her motives known. She still wasn't sure how sharp Alec was, and she didn't want to risk getting busted just because she'd underestimated him.

"Where are we going?" Alec asked, filling an empty jar with the little water they had left.

"We?" Elaina asked. "I thought you could drop us off on your way back to work."

Alec scoffed. "Work? If the station even remembers that I'm still technically out on patrol, then they don't care what I'm doing. I realized after the fifth person I killed that I need to look after myself first. I'll try to help wherever I can, but this is chaos. Who knows if the station is even still standing?"

"So what now?" Elaina asked. "You're just doing your own thing? You've gone rogue?"

He suppressed a smile. Apparently, he enjoyed that idea. "I'd probably do more good if I didn't have to answer to my superiors. Besides, I don't think I could sleep at night if I didn't know if you two were okay. I don't like to just abandon people like that."

"Why do you care about us? You helped us out of a tough situation and we can handle it from here."

Alec frowned. He didn't know how to articulate the way he felt about the girls. Perhaps it had something to do with taking that teen girl's life. He didn't want to see any more young people get to that point. Besides, he knew that they'd probably run into other infected people the second he left them alone. That was just how things worked. Nothing good could ever last.

"Lainey," Natalie scolded, "why don't you want him to stay with us? He's generously offered us his professional protection. Can't we just stay with him for as long as we can?"

Natalia was scowling at Elaina now. Elaina could see the fear in her eyes. Alec offered a service that they needed. The only problem was, the longer they stayed with Alec, the longer she would be away from a place to do her work. She didn't know how to choose which was more important—safety or progress.

"If we stay with you to find supplies," Elaina said cautiously, "where do you think we should go?"

"I've been thinking about it a lot. We don't have to stay for long, but we can stop at my house. I have some food and drinks there. My house is pretty small, so I don't think it would be a target for looters."

"Why is that?" Elaina asked, not pleased with his idea.

"If you could rob any house you wanted to, without the risk of being caught, where would you go? Would you rob a mansion with champagne and caviar in the fridge, or a little house that might not have any food at all?"

"Fine," Elaina said. "We can go to your house, only because you seem so confident that there will be the supplies we need there."

Elaina pouted, but Natalia was clearly relieved. "This is the best option for us, Lainey," she said, grabbing onto her arm. "It will be fine."

"Okay," Elaina said calmly, though she wanted to scream out in objection. "Let's go."

They gathered the little drinking water they had left and walked to the spot where they'd left the patrol car. If she couldn't get her way, Elaina was glad that they could continue forward, knowing that eventually, they would stumble upon a useful place.

"Where's the car?" Elaina asked, panic rising through her voice.

Alec froze on the spot and looked around wildly. "It was here, right?"

Natalia walked forward. "Are we sure this is where we left it?"

Elaina nodded. "I'm absolutely positive. We were right in the intersection of these two roads. Someone stole the cop car."

Elaina closed her eyes and tilted her head toward the sky. Tiny water particles speckled her face. She was so frustrated that she couldn't speak. Once again, she was being held back from the place where she needed to be.

"What do we do?" Natalia asked.

"We walk," Alec answered simply. "My house isn't far from here."

Without looking back, Alec began walking toward his home. Natalia followed a few paces behind, her feet already dragging. However, this time, it wasn't out of exhaustion—she just needed to add some dramatic effect so no one could mistake the fact that she was unhappy with their situation.

Elaina paused for a moment and noticed a small puddle of blood at the site of the missing car and had a sudden moment of inspiration. While she couldn't be sure that the fluid belonged to an infected person or just a careless car thief, she decided that she needed fluids from the infected for further testing.

Squatting down, she quickly collected the sample in hopes that it would provide answers once she got to a laboratory. Then, once it was safely tucked in her pocket, she followed the others, hardly focusing on where she was going because she was so inspired to work.

The three walked in silence. Alec was determined to provide food and shelter, Natalia was focused on staying safe, and Elaina was lost in her own discovery. No one felt like talking, so they carried on, placing one foot in front of the other.

Elaina held a hand to her pocket so the growing collection of glass and plastic vials wouldn't give away her secret by jingling a telling tale. Now that she had gotten back on track with her work, her spirits had been lifted and she hardly even noticed the chill in the air.

Seeing the puddle of blood made her realize that she had been looking at the wrong fluid samples. Her virus had yet to show signs of mutation in the limited trials she'd managed to start. But, the news reported that symptoms changed quickly, leading her to think that mutations did as well. It boggled her mind that she was unable to replicate something that was clearly happening around her, right in front of her eyes.

In her frenzy to figure out what was wrong with her original sample, she neglected to look at any other samples. The city was full of human incubators, packed full of the virus she needed to study. All she had to do was collect body fluids from a few infected people, and she was sure that she would be able to figure out what was going on with her virus.

There was also the issue of testing her potential cure weighing heavily on her mind. The logistics of testing cures in her normal fashion just weren't practical, given the circumstances.

When it came to animal testing, rodents were safe choices. They were small and easy to work with and showed symptoms not unlike humans. Plus, the general public didn't feel a lot of outrage when a rat was injected with all sorts of things. Plus, they were cheap and easy to get.

Elaina's issue was that she didn't foresee herself getting to a place with test subjects and lab equipment. Even if she managed to find a pet store that still had live rodents, she would have to wait for the virus to progress in them before testing her serum. That would take days. What Elaina needed was something that would take hours, or even minutes.

She knew that what she needed was crazy and probably impossible to manage. But if she happened to inject a virus victim with her serum and hold them for long enough to see results, then she would be so much closer to having her cure ready.

How she would do that was beyond her current level of scientific inspiration. In any normal circumstance, she would immediately dismiss the crazy idea and try to think of a better solution. But, accelerating trials by jumping directly to already infected humans in different stages of the virus would make up for all of the lost time she'd spent being chased and hiding out in abandoned warehouses.

As she walked, she constantly scanned her surroundings, but for other reasons than her companions did. Instead of watching out for potential threats, she saw it more as looking out for incredible opportunities. She hoped that she would stumble across someone in the early stages of the virus and she could quietly get them to consent to being injected without anyone noticing.

She would have to ditch Alec before that happened, though. The second she revealed her identity, she would be handcuffed immediately. If the police didn't already think she was crazy, they definitely would if they saw her injecting strangers with strange liquids.

Elaina would have to wait a little longer. She would do whatever she could to continue progress on her project in secret, but she would also reap the benefits of having travel companions. Not only were they highly motivated to search for necessary supplies, but when Elaina was deep into research, it often helped to have people around her to remind her that she still needed to eat and drink.

Elaina was broken from her trance by the sight of Natalia lagging even further behind than she already was. She even turned her head a few times to look at Elaina, which concerned her.

"What's going on?" Elaina whispered once Natalia was in earshot.

"Not much. I'm bored. How much further do you think we have to walk?"

"I don't know. Why don't you ask Alec?"

"You should ask Alec," Natalia said, wiggling her eyebrows.

"Why?" Elaina asked.

"I think he likes you, Lainey," she said in a singsong voice.

Elaina rolled her eyes. She was glad she was never

really boy crazy in her teenage years. She found the whispering and giggling so intolerable.

"Whatever," Natalia groaned, annoyed that Elaina wasn't playing her game correctly. "You do have to admit, he's pretty cute."

Elaina felt her face heat up again. She looked forward and watched him walk for a while. He stood up straight and walked with authority. Wide shoulders tapered down into narrow hips. He had the physique of an athlete. Elaina wondered if he had the jock persona to go along with it. But, he was nice to her, and it seemed unusual for a meathead to be so friendly to a nerd.

"I don't have to admit anything," Elaina replied simply, turning up her nose as if she had nothing to say on the subject.

"Look at his butt," Natalia continued. "He has a really nice butt."

Elaina let her eyes wander for a fraction of a second to confirm Natalia's observation before turning to her.

"I have more important things on my mind than his butt."

"Like?"

Elaina bit her lip. If the time was ever right, she would tell Natalia about what she needed to do. However, standing fifteen feet behind a police officer was not the right place to do that.

"Like staying alive," she replied, covering the basis of her concerns.

"The world's basically over," Natalia said, throwing up her hands for dramatic effect. "Shouldn't you just enjoy yourself? Alec is cute, and I think he likes you. If you wanted to hit that, you totally could."

"The world is not 'basically over'," Elaina said. "If I truly thought that, then why would we be doing what we're doing? Wouldn't we just lie down in the street and wait for the infected to come ravage our bodies?"

"I don't know," Natalia said, rubbing her empty stomach.

"I'll figure something out," she said, more for her own benefit than for Natalia's. "I just need a little more time. If we ever get to the point where I think it's a hopeless cause, I'll let you know."

"You can let me know by hooking up with Alec," she said with a wink. "But don't let the destruction of the human race stop you."

Elaina reached over to playfully shove Natalia, but Alec turned around first. She didn't want to give him the idea that they were talking in secret.

"It's not much further from here," he called, waving them closer with his hand. "Maybe ten more minutes."

"Oh, thank God," Natalia said, picking up her pace. "Do you think he knows he lives in a sketchy area?"

"He's a cop." Elaina laughed. "I think he knows. Besides, do you know any safe areas in this town at the moment? Because if you do, I'd like to go there now."

"Stay close," Alec said, slowing down so they could catch up. "If you see anything unusual, I want you to let me know."

"How about how unusually handsome he is?" Natalia whispered to Elaina.

Elaina gave her a death glare in return. She didn't

want to give Alec any reason to try to get closer to her. First, she didn't want the police to know of her whereabouts. Second, she didn't want to get close to someone who might not make it out alive.

Finally, and perhaps the most frightening for her, was the fact that if something did happen between them, she would have to figure out what to do. She felt less prepared to take on a relationship than she did to take on a deadly epidemic. She had been studying her whole life to tackle the most complicated viruses. She had missed out on everything related to dealing with guys while doing so.

Chapter Fifteen

As they neared Alec's small house, it was apparent to him how much the city had changed in just a few days since he left to go to work. When he left, his already shady neighborhood had been awash with break-ins and robberies. Just a few blocks from his house, an entire bar had been set on fire, not to mention all of the smaller car fires scattered throughout the streets. Everywhere Alec went on that first day of patrol had been consumed by absolute chaos.

Now, as Alec walked down the street, he saw nothing. It wasn't just nothing out of the ordinary—but nothing at all. There were no gangs of street youths talking and laughing loudly as they walked to the park, there were no drug dealers driving slowly in their tinted cars, and there were no cop cars doing the rounds, just looking for someone to bust. In fact, if he overlooked the fact that most of the houses were in various states of disrepair, he would have guessed that he was walking down the middle of a suburb on a school day. There was not a single person to be seen.

This made his even more uneasy than the regular riffraff did. Something had gone terribly wrong in the last two days for things to change so much. He was afraid that the moment he walked in his front door, he would find out.

"Come here," he said to the girls, waving them closer once again. They picked up the pace and he held a finger to his lips.

"Why do we need to be quiet?" Natalia whispered, her eyes wide.

"It's just a precaution," he replied, trying to ease her nerves. "That's my house right there. That brown one with the silver truck in front, you see? A lot of these houses have considerable damage done to them. I want to make sure everything is fine with mine before I take you in there. There's no need to be afraid, but it's best if we stay alert."

As they got closer, they noticed that one of the front windows had been broken. By the look on Alec's face, the girls knew that it wasn't a preexisting defect. Even the police officer had fallen victim to the mass hysteria.

"I don't think you should go inside," he said to Elaina and Natalia. "I don't like the look of this place. How about we ditch our original plan and take my truck somewhere else?"

"That's fine with me," Elaina said.

"But what about the supplies you said you had?" Natalia asked.

Alec tried to swallow, but his throat was too dry. He wasn't sure how much longer he could go on without having something to drink first. The girl was right—he couldn't leave his house without at least checking to see if there was food and water in there first.

"You're right," he responded, "but I think I should go in there alone."

Natalia tensed up. Even Elaina looked nervous.

He drew his weapon from his belt. "Can you two just wait for me right here, behind that car?" he asked, pointing to the edge of the street. "If anyone runs out, I don't want them to see you before I have a chance to take care of them, okay? When I've checked the whole place and it's clear, you can come in and take whatever you want. Then we'll go find another spot. How does that sound?"

"Just hurry," Elaina said, looking around. "There's something about this that's giving me the creeps."

"I will," he said. "Give me five to ten minutes to do a thorough sweep, then you can come in."

"What if something happens out here?" Natalia asked.

"Get my attention. Scream, yell, and make a lot of noise. But nothing should happen. I'll be right here."

With a reassuring nod, he unlocked his house with the key in his pocket and opened the door, gun drawn. He walked with heavy footsteps, as to not catch any intruder off-guard. Then, he stood in the entrance for a moment, waiting.

Alec had searched a fair number of homes in his short stint as a police officer. He had burst into houses as drugs were being manufactured and had even been bitten on the leg by a guard dog. He had chased criminals through a series of never ending hallways and alleys without batting an eye.

Yet, the task of searching his own home for a danger he didn't know was scarier than any of those other things.

It was personal, now. Someone had destroyed his property by smashing a window. This wasn't the type of crime he could leave at work.

"Seattle Police Department," he called, announcing his presence. This was usually enough to get whoever was inside the busted house to fight or flee. He stood up straight with his gun drawn, ready to take on an attacker.

But no attacker came. That meant that it was time to start the search. Fortunately for Alec, his home was small, and it wouldn't take long to check the handful of rooms he could afford to buy.

He worked cautiously, entering each room without exposing himself to any angle. He turned frequently, like well-rehearsed choreography, checking each corner for criminals. Closet doors were flung open with a flourish and hanging clothes were swept from side to side.

When one room was safe, he moved to the next, repeating the same procedure. He stayed focused, not letting his mind wander to the crackers in the cupboard or the beer he forgot about in the vegetable crisper. It was like meditating for him, his mind completely consumed with everything his senses could tell him about the particular place.

Much to his surprise, he found nothing. Not even one infected person.

Once his sweep was over, he started walking toward the door to invite the girls in. Then he remembered something that made him pause and turn back to his living room.

He was suddenly embarrassed by the state that his home was in and didn't want Elaina to see that he had been living in squalor. Before he was called in to work, he had hardly left his couch because he was in such a funk. Fast food and takeout boxes littered the floor, and empty beer cans sat on all surfaces. He hadn't washed clothes in weeks, and his trash can was definitely molding. The few actual dishes he'd used since the shooting incident had sat untouched in the sink, covered in slime. It was disgusting.

The smell alone embarrassed him. It smelled like a fraternity house after a big party—body odor, stale beer, and other mysterious smells permeated the air. There was no way he would feel comfortable letting anyone see that, let alone the cute girl he was trying to keep safe.

With haste, he piled trash into plastic bags, and when that failed, he just kicked things into the corner and into closets. He tried to run the water before realizing that the water had been turned off. He even found an old can of spray deodorant and fruitlessly tried to freshen the air in the living room, but it was worthless. When he stepped back and looked at his home, he knew that it looked like the house of a crazy person who was not to be trusted. That was the opposite of what he was going for.

The girls could wait a little bit longer. He had yet to hear any screams, which meant that they hadn't been attacked. A few more minutes wouldn't hurt. He knew that if he let them inside, he would have to explain why his place was in such disrepair. That was a conversation he didn't want to have—not when he was trying to display his worth to the girls.

Alec grabbed a duffel bag, emptied it of its dirty gym clothes, and tossed in a fresh change of clothes. He wasn't sure how long he'd be away, and he didn't want to repel the healthy people with his smell. Then, he went to the cupboard and took everything he had. It wasn't much, but he packed his bag with protein bars, crackers, chips, and a few cans of soup. Finally, he filled a jug with water from the pitcher and threw in a few cans of soda. Then, he dug to his hidden spot in the fridge, past the wilted lettuce, and popped six beers in. He hoped he'd soon find a safe enough spot to enjoy them.

Wildly searching around, he tossed in anything that he thought could be of use to him—spare batteries, a pocketknife, and a couple of surgical masks, among other things. When he was finished, he tossed the bag toward the door.

Before leaving his home for an undetermined amount of time, he did one last sweep of the place. Not only did he check for things he might have missed, but for things that had gone missing. While most of the destruction had resulted from his own messiness, someone had definitely been in his house at one time or another. His bedroom television was gone and his expensive stereo system had been ripped from the cabinet. Besides that, everything else was mostly intact.

Finally, he went into his bedroom and lifted the mattress. Reaching underneath, he felt around until his fingers made contact with the tattered spiral notebook. Knowing that his innermost thoughts were safe, he lowered the mattress and sat down for a moment.

After the incident, he had been urged to see a therapist, but talking wasn't his thing. Instead, he bought a twenty-cent notebook and started pouring his heart into the blue-lined pages every night. He couldn't reveal how he felt about killing a young girl to his closest friends and family, but he could get it out on ink.

Once he started writing in there, he couldn't stop. It was a cathartic practice, and it made him feel like he could deal with life, at least well enough to sit on the couch and drink without wanting to kill himself. He wrote down his hopes for the future, his goals, and his deepest fears. Every secret he had was in that notebook, and he didn't want to lose it for anything. Even if a thief took it and immediately disposed of it, the thought of it being read and taken from its spot sent a shiver down his spine.

With everything in its place—for the most part—he could leave. He'd tell the girls that he decided it would be quicker if he gathered the supplies himself since he knew where everything was. He wouldn't mention the fact that he was too embarrassed to let anyone see how he was living. If they really wanted to come inside for whatever reason, he figured he'd just tell them that he was robbed and someone was staying in his place in the time he was gone. After all, it did look like something criminal had happened there.

He went back outside and locked the door out of habit, knowing too well that anyone could come and go as they pleased. Then, he tossed the bag and the big jug of water into the back of his old pickup truck.

Those girls are good at hiding, he thought to himself as he squinted to see them behind the broken-down car. He waved his hand in their direction, hoping to catch their attention without having to call for them out loud.

"Come on, girls," he grumbled, walking toward the car to fetch them himself. Something strange was going on, and he didn't want to wait around long enough to find out what it was.

"Lainey, Natalia," he hissed, trying to get their attention, but no heads popped up over the car.

Then, he saw a couple of figures out of the corner of his eye. He squinted to see what was going on. He told the girls to stay behind the car. What were they doing so far down that end of the street?

Alec called out to them, this time waving more frantically. He wanted to get the hell out of there. He'd had pretty good luck, and he didn't want to challenge that by lingering around too long and getting into an altercation with anyone.

As the two people came closer, he realized that they looked absolutely nothing like Elaina and Natalia. The two were fighting in the middle of the street, absolutely tearing into each other. They beat each other with such ferocity, but neither showed any signs of slowing down.

Alec felt a terrible chill come over him and his

stomach rose to his throat. He ran to the girls' hiding place, hoping they were just frozen in fear, but no one was there. He ran back toward his house, spinning in circles, hoping they'd appear and they could hop in the truck and get out of there. That didn't happen either.

He remembered that he was a police officer and that his job required him to see why the two people were beating the crap out of each other, but he suspected he knew why. He touched his holster, ready to aim and fire at a moment's notice.

Anger and worry filled his veins. If the girls had listened to him, they would have been on their way out of there. If he had lived like a normal person and not a disgusting slob, they could have just come inside after his search was done. So many things could have gone differently.

Alec was just about to yell the girls' names again when figures came from the fog. More infected had descended upon his home, and he was alone.

"Where are you two?" Alec whimpered, feeling completely dejected. He had given himself two priorities —to stay alive and to keep the two girls alive. He wasn't entirely sure if he'd manage to do either of those things.

Chapter Sixteen

Elaina had some reservations about waiting behind the old Cadillac down the street for Alec to return from checking the house, but she was too mentally exhausted to voice them. He seemed to know what he was doing, and Elaina knew that arguing would only delay progress.

Perhaps she would have been more at ease if she were ordered to wait alone. Ever since their brief discussion on the walk toward Alec's house, Natalia had been giving her sneaky glances and grins that were nothing but trouble. It appeared that Natalia found one of Elaina's greatest insecurities and latched onto it like a leech to its host. She knew that Elaina had secrets, and she wanted in on the excitement.

"When are you going to tell me what's really going on?" Natalia asked the second Alec was out of earshot.

"I don't have a clue what you're referring to," Elaina deflected.

"You told him to call you Lainey. It's a cute name. If I met a guy I liked, I'd maybe introduce myself with a cutesy nickname."

"Drop it," Elaina warned. "If you haven't noticed, I'm not into him."

"Okay," she hummed, clearly not convinced. "Still, why the nickname?"

Elaina let out a long sigh. She had told herself that she would explain her situation to the girl the second they were alone. Yet, the second she unbottled her secrets, she knew she couldn't stuff them back inside. Teenage girls were notoriously bad at keeping secrets.

"You know who I am," Elaina explained. "You know that I work with your father. How much do you know about our work?"

"A little," she said. "I know that you work with dangerous viruses and your lab is busy during flu season or whenever a big epidemic strikes somewhere in the world. But if you haven't noticed, I'm not really that close with my dad. I play the role of daddy's little girl when it benefits me, but we don't talk a lot. I don't know a lot of the specifics of what you guys do. I'm also just not that interested."

"Okay, so you can assume that our lab had something to do with our current situation?"

Natalia nodded.

"By the way," Elaina added. "Everything that's happened is not a direct result of the virus," she defended herself. "In fact, I bet most of the crimes are in response to the hysteria surrounding the media coverage. Why would you show images of an infected person suffering violent mania and act like it was happening everywhere? There were stories of kids going crazy and killing their parents. Did you know that there were very, very few reported cases of children and adolescents with violent reactions? It was rare, yet the news made it sound like it was the norm."

"Yeah, I guess," Natalia said, interrupting the rant. "Most kids and adolescents just dropped dead before they could reach that stage, huh?"

Elaina went quiet.

"You said yourself that you're in a bit of trouble," Natalia said. "You're wanted by police for the virus getting out. Your virus?"

Elaina shrugged.

"So you use a fake name so our police officer friend doesn't realize who you are? Out of all of the names you could have picked, you chose one that sounds almost exactly like your real name." She sniggered.

"I panicked," Elaina exclaimed. "Everything happened so quickly. I was worried you were going to give something away."

"I'm not a snitch."

"I didn't say you were. I just didn't want anything to accidentally slip out. I wasn't sure if you knew how serious this was for me. If I'm in jail, I can't get any work done. You know this."

"I know. And if you think you can put a stop to this, I'm not going to get in your way."

Elaina smiled. She had not given the girl enough credit. She wasn't some ditzy teenager with a one-track mind. She truly cared about the state of the world and wanted to help if she could.

"Does this mean you'll help me out?" Elaina asked hopefully, finally making an official deal with her travel companion.

"I just need to know one thing for certain," she said, looking at the ground. "Did you do it? I mean, release the virus, either purposefully or accidentally?"

Elaina took in a deep breath. There was so much to explain, and she didn't know how much time she would have to do it. She needed to start at the beginning of her story and tell her that the work she was doing wouldn't cause harm to normal, healthy people. She needed to tell her that she had made a lot of progress on an antidote of sorts.

Finally, she needed to explain how she would have never infected anyone, intentionally or unintentionally, and how she suspected that there was foul play involved.

But how do you tell your travelling companion that you suspect that her father was behind all of the destruction happening right in front of your eyes?

Maybe she would leave that part of the story out for now. Until she could see some current samples from infected victims, she had no way of knowing if her hypothesis was remotely accurate. Once she had some evidence to back up her claims, she would tell her. For now, there were just some secrets too terrible to share.

Elaina didn't have time to profess her innocence to Natalia. As she opened her mouth to speak, a gasp came out instead.

They were so deep in their own secret conversation,

carefully watching Alec's house, that they didn't notice the people approaching them from behind. Quietly, as if they had been stalked like animals, they were ambushed by a group of the infected.

One reached for Natalia and put their hand over her mouth before she had a chance to let out a scream. She pursed her lips tightly and held her breath in case the virus was capable of entering her nose and mouth.

The infected girl holding onto Natalia looked to be about her age, but taller and bigger than the slender girl. She struggled to free herself from the infected girl's tight grip until Elaina delivered a blow to her stomach that slackened her fingers.

Natalia broke free and ran down the street, not caring about where she was going as long as she could get away without being chased. In her fear, she could hardly breathe, let alone scream for Alec's help.

A couple broke off from the pack and stumbled after her, their legs appearing to have undergone some sort of muscular breakdown. Atrophied legs like stilts limped after the girl, their ultimate aim unknown.

It was in this moment that Elaina saw the infected in a new light. They were no longer bloodthirsty maniacs, but test subjects. As she jogged down the street, she carefully watched their motions, trying to figure out what was going on with them.

As far as she knew, no medical professional had examined a patient in this stage of the illness, probably because it was extremely dangerous. Not only was there a huge risk of passing along an infection, but the doctor could be attacked just from asking banal questions about symptoms. No physician in their right mind wanted to work with these patients, not that anything they could do would be of much help.

But when she thought about it, these were helpless people who had fallen victim to their virus-ravaged brains. Were they seeking healthy people out in an attempt to get help, only to turn violent? Or, as many believed, were they seeking revenge on those who had managed to dodge the disease? So little was known about them because their would-be victims had no choice but to run from them.

Elaina knew a good opportunity when she saw one. Being attacked by disease-ridden people wasn't an ideal testing facility, but it was the closest she had been to them since she'd decided she needed to test on humans. If she could find a way to collect samples from them without getting injured herself, she would be in good shape.

Fumbling in her pocket, she grabbed LILY and clutched it in her fist. If she could load it into a syringe and inject it into someone, or even just drop a little serum into an open sore, she might have the chance to see if there were any immediate effects.

She looked around for her perfect candidate. A rail-thin woman sat on the ground, muttering to herself. Elaina figured that the drug would work the best on her since she had the least amount of body mass. She seemed like she was pretty sick, but not currently violent.

Elaina felt a surge of adrenaline course through her veins. She was so close to running a test, the test that she had been waiting ages to conduct. Even if it didn't heal the woman of her ailment, at least she would finally get to find out if it worked.

She carefully crept closer to the woman, who had yet to take notice of her. She had her eyes on a particularly deep, oozing sore on her chest. With all of the blood flow in that area, Elaina hoped that it would be spread throughout her body quickly. She had to work quickly before Alec came out and before they were attacked.

Like sneaking up on a sleeping animal, Elaina tiptoed through the rubble in the street, trying not to disturb her subject who was muttering about some son-of-a-bitch named Robert who had taken her baby. Elaina grasped the rubber stopper in the bottle with trembling hands and pulled.

A scream tore through the air. Elaina knew that it was Natalia. She had heard it before when they met in the school.

Reflexively, Elaina shoved the bottle into her pocket and ran in the direction of the scream. She wasn't about to let her partner be attacked.

She found her about two blocks away, cowering behind a gardening shed. The girl that had grabbed her before was searching for her, blood seeping from her eyes. The look of pure determination on the infected girl's face told Elaina that Natalia didn't have much time.

Elaina crept toward them, just as she did before with her potential test subject. She knew she couldn't over-power her, so she picked up a short length of pipe buried in the tall grass.

With a squeal that sounded like it came from a

monster and not a human, the infected girl lunged at Natalia. Before she could make contact, Elaina swung the pipe with all her might and brought it down directly on top of the crouching girl's skull. With a crack, Elaina felt the pipe contact the hard bone, then break through the tough exterior. She had left a dent in the infected girl's head, leaving Natalia free to scurry out from under her heavy corpse.

"Where the hell is Alec?" Natalia cried, shuddering after removing herself from the person's clutches. "We have to get out of here, now!"

Elaina ran back down the street without looking back at the body that lay crumpled near the shed. She would have time to process the atrocities of the virus later. For now, she needed to get the hell out of there.

"What good is it having a police officer with us if he can't even keep us safe?" Natalia raged, booking it back to Alec's house.

"I don't know, but I hope he shows up here soon."

They were nearly there when a man dropped down from a large oak tree hanging over the street. His arm was bent at a strange angle, and for a second, the girls thought that he had been hiding from the infected when he saw them.

"Holy shit," Natalia gasped. "Are you okay?"

The man didn't respond. Instead, he swiped at them with his good arm. Natalia let out another blood curdling scream, this time, full of frustration at Alec.

Elaina pulled her down an alley. They were running further and further away from Alec's house, but there were fewer infected people back that way.

"It might just be the two of us from here on out if Alec doesn't hurry up and find us," Elaina panted as they ran.

"If we ever see that asshole again," Natalia gasped, "I'm going to give him a piece of my mind."

As if Alec had heard them, the girls heard a gunshot in the direction of his house. They slowed to a stop, looking at each other for answers.

"Do we go back?" Natalia asked.

Elaina looked in the direction of his house. More and more infected were flocking to the area as they spoke. Going back would be a major risk.

"I don't think that's a good idea. If Alec survives, he can find us. We have bigger things to worry about."

Chapter Seventeen

The moment he realized the infected were closing in on him, he heard a scream a few blocks down from his house. The sound, if anything, drew the people closer to him, as if they couldn't discern where it came from, but they knew they had a prime subject standing in front of them who would do.

"Lainey," he yelled, surprised to hear that his words came out in a squeak. He thought about getting in his car and driving away, but there were too many of them now. If he didn't fight, then the girls would certainly die. He stood with his gun drawn, just waiting for someone to make one wrong move. He was ready.

As far as he was concerned, every infected person who died by his hand would be one less infected person who could harm the girls. He despised killing, but he needed to protect those girls.

The first attacker, a short, fat man, came waddling

up to him. With so much flesh preventing him from being agile, Alec took him out with a swift blow to the temple with the butt of his gun. With a loud groan, the man hit the ground hard.

But, as he was fighting off that man, a woman came hurling toward him with her hand extended. In the overcast light, Alec caught a glimpse of something metallic in her hand. As she wildly reached forward to stab him, he fired off a shot, squarely in her forehead.

The loud noise must have momentarily startled the infected, because they quickly retreated a few feet. They didn't disappear completely, just regrouped and waited for a better opportunity to strike.

Alec knew he needed to leave immediately, but he couldn't help himself. He bent down to get a quick look at the life he ended. He knew it would give him nightmares for years, but curiosity got the better of him.

Bleeding from the head was the woman he had waved to every morning on his way to work for years. His neighbor lady, Mrs. Daniels, was currently on his driveway, staining the concrete with her blood.

Alec clasped a hand to his mouth. She was a kind, middle aged woman with a deadbeat ex-husband who could never make his child support payments on time. Her two boys often played in his yard in the evenings when she was making supper before leaving for her night shift at the supermarket. She, unlike a lot of the other neighbors, liked the fact that he was a cop. She said she always felt safer when he was home.

He wondered where her boys were now. Her house looked like it had been vacant for days. She loved her boys—she would have never let anything bad happen to them. If she knew she were ill, she would have found somewhere safe for the kids to go. That, or they had fallen ill before she had.

Alec's throat felt thick. Breaths came out ragged through his choked up throat. He had just killed the kind of citizen that came to mind when he talked about keeping his community safe. Mrs. Daniels could do no wrong in his eyes.

Yet, here she was, a shell of her former self. Alec staggered back and sat on the concrete before his wobbly legs gave out.

He closed his eyes for a second and was transported back to the shopping mall on the day that he fired his weapon in the line of duty for the first time. After the deafening shots, he heard nothing. Time seemed to move by in slow motion. The girl, pretty as could be, fell to the ground and ceased to move. Motionless, she looked completely harmless. In fact, Alec wondered if he had imagined seeing her attempt to kill him.

At first, Alec really believed that he could help her. As she reacted to the tormenters in the crowd, he spoke over them, reassuring her. He promised that whatever was going on, he could save her from it. He truly believed his words, too. If she just listened to him, he knew he could get through to her. For all he knew, she was just a troubled kid in need of someone to listen to her.

Those words seemed to have had an effect on her. She turned toward him and sort of cocked her head, as if she was interested in what he had to say. He gave her clear instructions to drop her weapon, but she didn't. It was as if it were an extension of her hand. She didn't even look down at the weapon as if to consider her options.

Then, she started coughing up blood. A few sputters, and then crimson splattered the sidewalk like paint. First, it was a little bit that dotted her top, then more. Alec had never seen someone become so ill so quickly. He called for an ambulance into his walkie talkie, perhaps one equipped with hazmat gear. There was something seriously wrong with her.

"We're going to get you some help, okay?" he said gently, holding out his arms to her. For a moment, he saw the light return to her eyes. She slowly walked toward him—he had gotten through to her.

As quickly as the light appeared, it had vanished again. Then, all hell broke loose. She ran toward him at full speed, ready to strike, and he stopped her.

Then, as if someone had turned the sound back on, he heard the screams. Much of the crowd had stayed to watch, even though he'd ordered them to vacate the premises. Somehow, the thin glass of their camera phones would protect them as they greedily fantasized about the fame their crazy footage would capture. Now, they were collecting evidence.

The worst screams of all came from the girl's mother. After seeing the commotion, she worried that her daughter, a regular at the mall, might be present. She searched through the crowd in hopes that she could spot her daughter and bring her to safety from whatever madman was wielding a knife in a crowd.

Instead, she arrived to find her varsity cheerleader, honor student dead, bleeding from a perfect round hole shot by Alec as if she were nothing but a paper target at a shooting range.

The wails from the mother of the girl instantly made his heart ache. He had no children of his own, yet he felt like he'd just watched one of his own die. Through her tears, he felt the pain of someone who had suffered a tremendous loss.

It was all such a waste of a life, too. If it had been a treatable illness, she would have gone to a doctor or a therapist, talked about what was going on, taken a few pills, and would be right as rain. She could go back to school, graduate, go to college, and begin her life. Instead, her face was plastered all over the news, sharing the gory details of her last act, something that was out of character for the teen.

Everything about it was so unfair. There was nothing but chance that separated Alec from the people he was gunning down in the name of safety and security. He could have easily been infected when he killed the girl. If it weren't for his leave from work, he probably would have been infected some other way. Yet, here he was, ending the life of his good neighbor, who only wanted her young children to have a good life. He felt like a monster.

He had known Mrs. Daniels fairly well, too. At least, he knew of her problems. He had visited her home in uniform more times than not for different issues with her ex. One time, he had slapped her around so hard that he left her bloodied and battered. He nearly lost it and would have put his fist through the guy's face if his partner hadn't talked him down. She was a good woman who didn't deserve that.

In fact, her kids were great, too, and if by the off chance they were still in the house, he needed to make sure they were okay. Alec fired off a few warning shots into the lurking infected before jogging to her house.

"Michael," he called into the house. "John, are you in there?"

He started searching frantically, not as calm and precise as when he searched in his own home.

"Please be in here," he whispered to himself, opening and closing closets. "Please be okay."

He paused when he reached the refrigerator. Attached to the front with a pizza restaurant magnet, next to a Chinese takeout menu, was a picture he vaguely remembered taking.

He had volunteered to go to a community outreach event and cook burgers for families in his neighborhood. It was something the department liked to do to create good rapport with the citizens. The Daniels family attended, likely due to the fact that money was scarce in their household and a free meal was a free meal. He normally hated taking pictures, but the boys looked up to him, so he crouched down and smiled, the kids matching his wide grin.

That was years ago, though. Now those boys were around ten or twelve. Wherever they were.

He sifted through the mail on the kitchen table. The most recent was postmarked about a week ago. He swept a finger along a counter and inspected it for dust. No one had been in there for a few days.

In order to believe that nothing bad had happened to the kids, he needed a little more evidence. He searched for something, anything that would tell him that their mother had sent them away to a relative out of state. Or, at the very least, they were in protective custody.

He found nothing, so he kept searching. He looked in their bedrooms for any written account of what they were going through, or maybe even a packed bag. Then, he searched to make sure there was no hint that something had gone terribly wrong. There were no bodies and there was no blood. It was like they had vanished without a trace, but their mother had returned to the home she once shared with them.

Then, he saw something that made his breath catch in his throat. Michael had approached him one day to show him a baseball card that he had acquired. Alec couldn't remember who was on the card, but he realized that it was a big deal to the kid. Alec had endured a rough day at work, but seeing Mrs. Daniels's kids made him feel a little better.

As the years went on, he learned that Michael never went anywhere without it. When a kid at his school stole it from his book bag, he enlisted Alec's help to get it back. He laughed at how startled that kid was when he showed up at his house to get it back. Alec was professional and kind to the little thief, and he hoped that he had learned a lesson. Mrs. Daniels was horrified that her son had bothered a real police officer with his playground problems, but it was no problem for Alec. It was as if he were getting justice from his own playground bullies. From then on, he always saw that baseball card on Michael, either in his hand or tucked into his pocket. It was his lucky charm.

So, the fact that it was on the ground with no child to be found was striking to Alec. He wanted to drop everything and piece together the mystery of the missing boys. Then he heard the screaming again.

The weight of his responsibility was crushing to Alec. There were just too many innocent people to save and not enough people to help. Alec was just one man—he couldn't take on more than one case. He couldn't protect them all.

He tucked his mouth into his hoodie and took a few quick breaths. The heat from his accelerated breathing made his face feel moist and clammy. He closed his eyes and tried to focus on something that would calm him down, at least enough to make him stop hyperventilating. Elaina came to mind, and instead of forcing her out, he focused on her piercing eyes and pink lips. He imagined sitting with her, just talking, nothing more. Finally, he calmed down enough to catch his breath.

There was nothing left for him in that house, but outside, there were two girls who needed his help. He was going to get into his truck, find them, and take them to safety. That he could do.

He marched out of the child's bedroom, a renewed feeling of confidence in him. He turned the corner and opened the door when he heard quiet rustling behind him. He paused for a moment and expected to turn around and see one of the boys laughing. Maybe it had all been a game of hide and seek, and they had become too eager to properly hide.

The next sound he heard was a loud crack, and then his ears started ringing.

Alec felt a weird, sudden pressure on the crown of his head. His scalp and neck felt warm and wet. He touched a hand to the back of his head and brought it back to examine. Hot, sticky blood covered his fingertips. He slowly wiggled his fingers in front of his eyes, unable to comprehend what was on them. Then, dread struck him.

Before he could understand what had happened to cause the blood and pain, everything went black. He fell, and in his mind, it was like drifting off to sleep. He leaned backward and hit the carpet of his neighbor's house, floating off into the darkness.

Natalia and Elaina continued to scream and plead for help, but it was no use. Before everything went dark and silent, Alec could have sworn he heard Elaina call his name, and that he called hers, too. *Once I wake up*, he thought as he lost consciousness, *I'll be with her.*

Chapter Eighteen

E laina's legs were starting to burn. She wanted to stop running, but every time they stopped, they spotted someone who could be infected. After a while, she wasn't sure if the people she saw were real or imaginary. The girls just kept running until they found something better.

They had been on the move for about an hour and a half when they finally stopped to rest at a campground. It had started to rain again, so the girls found shelter underneath a weathered picnic shelter. Elaina swished the contents from her last jar of water around her mouth before setting the container outside. It was a futile practice, seeing as they couldn't stay long enough to collect enough fluids, but every drop counted.

"I don't know about you," Natalia said, "but I'm starting to feel really guilty about leaving Alec behind."

Elaina nervously cracked her knuckles. "I'm sure he's fine."

"I'm not. Did you see how many infected were in the area by the time we got out of there? I know he's a police officer and all, but that's a lot of people to fight off without backup."

"You heard the gunshot. I'm sure he's in his truck right now, driving around town. Maybe he's even looking for us."

"Maybe," the younger girl said, swinging her legs from the bench of the table, just sweeping the ground with the tips of her toes. "Do you think that was his gun that went off?"

"Whose gun would it be if not Alec's?" Elaina asked, shivering.

"The police aren't the only ones with guns," she said darkly. "Those rednecks who took me had them. I'm certain a lot of the infected do too. Everyone does."

"Except for us," Elaina added.

"Except for us."

"Call me crazy," Natalia said after a few moments of quiet, "but I was starting to like Alec. He's not a bad guy."

"No, he's not," Elaina mused. "But that's only because he didn't know who I was. If he'd paid a little more attention to the wanted posters, it would have been a different story."

"I'd like to think that even if he did know, he would help you out."

Elaina scoffed. "Yeah, right. Why do you think that?"

"I don't know," she said dreamily. "I think he has a strong sense of justice. Not like he always has to follow

172

the rules. You don't give him enough credit. I think that if you would have told him what you were up to, he would have helped us."

Elaina bit her lip. She wasn't as sure of their companion as Natalia was, but she wondered if there were more to him than just the clean-cut cop she saw. Would he help them?

It didn't matter now. She didn't want to spoil Natalia's hopes that he would rejoin them, but it didn't look good for him. But if she could boost her spirits by telling her everything would be fine, then it was worth lying to herself.

All of Natalia's doubts were warranted. He had been outnumbered. It would be one thing to go up against a group of healthy people. However, there was something about the virus that made adults a lot more violent than any one person could be. It was like taking on a bunch of bodybuilders who had taken too many steroids, if those bodybuilders also contained a lethal dose of poison in their bodies.

And while she would have never admitted it to Natalia, she was sad that she would probably never see him again. Even if he did survive, which would be miraculous, he wouldn't be able to find them again. They lived in a large city, and there were too many places to hide. It just wasn't practical for them to search for him, nor was it for him to search for the girls.

If circumstances were different, Elaina wondered if she would have pursued a friendship with Alec. She wasn't great at meeting or keeping friends, but he seemed different from other friends she'd let drift away.

Her problem with maintaining relationships was that no one seemed to understand that her work would always come first in her life. When she had to decline coffee dates or girls' night outs because she had a big project to work on or was writing a journal article, it always sounded like an excuse. Eventually, after declining too many invitations, the invitations would cease altogether. One by one, friends turned into acquaintances, who turned into strangers.

Alec seemed like he was a bit of a loner, too. That was one type that could fit into her busy work schedule. It would be nice to have a friend who understood that she had important work to do, and that she'd hang out when she could. That could possibly work with the right kind of friend, but that setup would never be successful for anything more than casual friendship.

Dating was out of the question for Elaina. First, she refused to sacrifice her work or study time for anything else. Secondly, she had yet to meet anyone who changed her mind about the first point. Men could come and go, but her studies could last a lifetime, even beyond that. A really good discovery could change the shape of the future of the planet. A few months of casual dating would change nothing.

Yet, whenever Natalia tried to tease her about Alec taking a liking to her, she couldn't help but wonder if that were the truth. It shouldn't have mattered to her whether it was factual or not, but for some strange reason, it did.

Perhaps it was because Elaina knew that the human species was in decline. From a biological standpoint, the fact that the population was plummeting would be a good enough cause to begin having feelings for a member of the opposite sex. At some point, repopulation would have to happen, and it made sense to reproduce with someone whose qualities you admired.

But Elaina wasn't a bonobo chimp. She was a human being who was very confused by the thoughts and feelings running through her head. She needed to get back to work. That always helped her keep her mind at peace.

"Should we go back and check on him at least?" Natalia asked.

She entertained the idea in her head for a moment. While it would be a nice gesture, by the time they got back to his house, he would certainly be gone. Then, they would have wasted an entire day on a walk that would most likely be dangerous. But if they spent the day looking for a lab, then she'd be one step closer to finding a cure.

"Let's keep going," Elaina said, standing up from her damp seat. "We can't afford to waste any more time. He'll find us eventually," she added in response to Natalia's glum expression.

The girls continued walking through the barren streets with nothing but a faint feeling of hope to guide them.

Chapter Nineteen

Alec could see nothing but blinding light when he opened his eyelids. He couldn't move his limbs, and his pulse throbbed in his head. He felt nauseated and sweaty. He tried to open his mouth, not sure if he could speak, and tasted the metallic flavor of blood. He tried to form words, but it all came out as one loud groan.

"Oh, sorry," a male voice said, clicking off his flashlight.

Alec's eyes adjusted to the change in light and surveyed his surroundings. He was lying on a couch in a home he didn't recognize. His arms and legs were bound around his body with what looked like neckties. He felt like death, so the fact that he was alive in the mortal world and not experiencing some strange form of purgatory was a wonder to him.

"I thought that when someone has a concussion, you're supposed to shine a light into their eyes and see if their pupils dilate," the young man said. "That's what the trainers did in high school football when someone got hit really hard."

"Who the hell are you?" Alec hollered at the boy, who looked to be around the same age as Natalia.

The kid jumped, as if he were surprised that the police officer would be upset about being tied up in a strange house. Alec struggled against the bindings, finding the strength returning to his arms and legs.

"My name is Will Domenica," he answered. He was short, slender, and had big brown eyes with long lashes. He held his hand to Alec's as if he were trying to formally introduce himself, then he awkwardly dropped it back to his side when he realized that Alec was incapable of that kind of movement in his current condition.

"I guess I should untie those. You can never be too careful nowadays, you know?" he said cheerfully, working at the knots. "You're not going to hurt me, right?" he added, leaning down close to Alec's face.

"That's to be determined," Alec muttered. The boy was too cheery for the headache he was currently experiencing. It was like a hangover times a million. "But if you're asking if I'm infected or a criminal, I'm neither," he said.

"That's great to hear. I've seen too many of both types lately. It's a crazy world we're living in."

"I know. I'm a police officer," Alec said, rubbing the marks where the restraints touched his flesh. "I've seen some crazy shit in the past few weeks."

"So have I," Will said. "I try not to think about those things, though. It distracts me from moving forward."

Alec could see sadness in his eyes, even though he masked it with a toothy smile. Something traumatic had happened to Will, but he knew better than to pry in other people's private business. Alec hated when people made him talk about things he didn't want to talk about.

"So," Alec said, changing the subject, "how were my pupils?"

"What?" Will said, snapping out of a trance. "Oh, I think they're fine. I'm not exactly sure what they're supposed to look like, I guess. But you're awake now —that's good."

"About that," Alec said, "can you tell me anything about how I got here? What happened to me?"

"It's a long story," Will muttered, playing with his dark brown hair.

"I've got time. I'd really like to know what happened to me."

Alec reached his hand toward the site of the searing pain, and Will's eyes opened wide.

"I wouldn't—" he said quickly, trying to stop Alec from touching his head wound.

But it was too late. Alec felt the crusted blood of his swollen head around the haphazardly placed bandages.

"How did this happen?" Alec asked, feeling panicky. "The last thing I remember, I was walking around Mrs. Daniels' house, looking for her boys. Then, I woke up here. You were with me for at least some of the time in between. What happened?"

"I—" he stuttered. "I may have hit you in the head with a baseball bat."

179

"May have?" Alec growled, lightly touching the tender spot on his skull.

"I'm really sorry about that. I guess you could say that I was a little on edge with everything that was happening."

"Just start from the beginning," Alec said, getting irritated.

"Okay, so, I had been hopping from house to house, looking for supplies. I wasn't breaking into homes where anyone lived or anything. I was very careful to make sure that people were gone and not coming back before collecting the things I needed. Things like food, water, clothes, that sort of stuff."

"I'm not going to arrest you for theft, if that's what you're worried about."

Will seemed to relax a little.

"Thanks. I appreciate it," he said softly. "This has all been a bit of a moral dilemma."

"I know," Alec said wearily. He had also been thinking about how the line between right and wrong was blurred in times of chaos. Rules that society adhered to for hundreds and thousands of years were suddenly put on the backburner. "Go on."

"I was in that house you were searching through. But I didn't know what you were doing. I'd seen sick people in the area, and I was looking for a place to hide out for a while before moving on. So, I tucked myself underneath the table and waited until they left."

"But then I came in," Alec said, filling in the blanks.

"Exactly. You were searching around, but I couldn't get a good look at you. I didn't know who you were and what you were doing in there. You weren't taking anything, so I knew you weren't a thief."

"So you thought I was infected?"

Will gave him an apologetic look. "It can be hard to tell as it is. It's harder to tell when you don't have a good look at someone. I knew that you were seconds from finding me, and I didn't know what you would do if you did. You started to turn around toward me, so I cracked you over the head with my bat," he said, pointing to the wooden bat propped up in the corner.

"You could have killed me with that thing," Alec protested.

"That was my intention," he replied grimly. "It's a good thing my swing sucks."

Alec sighed. He could hardly be mad at the kid. He probably would have done the same thing in that situation. Will was just a scared kid trying to survive the city. His head hurt like hell, but he couldn't blame him.

"Okay," Alec said. "So you hit me in the head and I went out like a light. What next?"

"Once you were down, I took a closer look at you and realized that you were still alive and that you weren't showing signs of infection. I felt so guilty that I dragged you across a few yards to my parents' house and propped you up on the couch. I tried to stop the bleeding and get you cleaned up, but I'm not really good with blood."

"Why the ties?" Alec asked, holding up the strips of silk in an array of colors and patterns.

Will grinned. "You can never be too careful, right?

You didn't appear to be infected, but in case you suddenly hulked out on me, I wanted a little protection."

Alec cracked a smile for the first time that afternoon. "That's pretty smart of you. How long was I out?"

"About an hour, hour and a half. I was pretty worried that you weren't going to make it. I'm glad you did."

"Me too. Where's your bathroom? I think I have some more blood to wash off."

"Down the hall and to the right," Will answered, turning pale. "We don't have running water, so I have a few jugs by the sink for washing up and flushing."

Alec padded down the hall in his socks. Somewhere along the line, Will had taken off his boots. He was a sweet kid, but something was just a little bit off about him.

He tried to get a glimpse of his injury, but he couldn't crane his neck far enough to get a good look. The back of his hair felt sharp and spiky, like he'd put too much gel in it. Yet, when he dabbed at it with a damp washcloth, he turned the beige linens red. He worked at the spot until it was rinsed clean. It was the most he had washed in days.

Alec opened the medicine cabinet and rummaged through different bottles of shampoo and soap until he found some rubbing alcohol. He drained the contents on a fresh washcloth, and with a deep breath, he pressed the stinging liquid to his wound. He clenched his jaw to keep from screaming out in pain.

Once he felt like he had cleaned it enough, he pressed a fresh piece of gauze to his head, which immediately turned red with blood. Tired of dabbing at his head, he took the rest of the roll and wrapped it around his head from crown to chin, and around again. He examined his reflection and knew he looked ridiculous, but the added pressure would stop the bleeding.

Next, he looked for something to help with the pain. Behind the over-the-counter pain pills was a little orange bottle with a couple of prescription painkillers—the good stuff. He carefully took two from the bottle and placed them in his pocket, just in case he needed them later. He felt terrible stealing from this kid and his family, but he did crack him over the head with a Louisville Slugger. It was the least they could give him.

Then, he dropped three little red ibuprofen tablets into his mouth and swallowed with a swig from the plastic jug. It would hardly take the edge off the pain, but it would keep him sharp until he was allowed to let his guard down.

Finally, Alec decided it was best to freshen up while he had the chance. He wiped himself down with a damp towel, rubbed a stick of deodorant under his arms, and squeezed a ribbon of toothpaste on his finger and worked it around for a few seconds. He still looked like he hadn't showered in a few days, but at least he kept his natural odors at bay.

Feeling the strong urge to snoop around, Alec crept into the adjacent room, the master bedroom once he finished up in the bathroom. The bed was neatly made, and pictures of two smiling parents and their teenaged son, Will, sat on the dresser. For a home that someone was still living in, it looked just as vacant as the others in the area.

"Looking for something?" Will asked, popping around the corner out of nowhere. Alec jumped.

"Shit, you scared me," he said sheepishly. "Sorry, I was just having a look around. It's an old habit as a cop."

"Always watching your back." He nodded. "Is there anything else I can get for you? I still feel really bad about what happened."

"Don't worry about it," Alec said, waving him off. "It was an honest mistake."

"I have a few beers in the fridge if you want one," he offered.

Alec squinted his eyes at Will. "Are you sure you're old enough?"

Will laughed. "I'm nineteen. Let me guess, you've spent a lot of time busting underage drinkers?"

"A fair amount," Alec admitted. "But what the hell, it's the end of the world. One won't hurt."

Will grinned and pulled two beers from a cooler and cracked them open. They tasted a little skunked, but Alec was not one to complain. He had gone a few days without drinking—it was a cause for celebration.

"Where are your folks?" Alec asked, taking a sip of the lukewarm drink.

"Gone," Will said flatly.

"They left you here?" Alec sputtered. "I'm sorry, man. That's rough. I wouldn't take it personally. People do strange things in an emergency."

"No, I mean they're gone. They're dead."

Will's head fell. His eyes stared fixed on a spot in the floor.

Alec felt uncomfortable, but he needed to say something to break the tension.

"I'm really sorry. That's terrible."

"It really is."

"Did they get sick?" Alec asked, throwing him an easy question. He could basically guarantee that anyone who died in the last few weeks was a virus victim. It claimed lives so quickly.

"My mom did," he said after clearing his throat. "But that seems like a lifetime ago. In reality, it was less than a month ago."

Will's voice sounded thick, as if he were on the verge of tears.

"You don't have to talk about it if you don't want to," Alec said.

"No, no, it's all good. In fact, I haven't said the words out loud. I think it would help me process some of it if I told someone what happened."

"Okay," Alec said gently. "I'll listen."

"I think my mom was one of the early cases," he said, his voice steadying. "She was a nurse, so when she started feeling under the weather, she assumed it was something she picked up from a patient. That kind of thing happened all the time. She had a high fever and was really achy, so she called into work and said she needed a few days off. No big deal."

"But then she got worse?"

Will nodded. "She started having terrible headaches and stomach pain. We tried to convince her to go to the

185

doctor, but she refused. She just chalked it up to a virus. She said she just needed rest. My dad was really worried, but he couldn't stay home with her. I was taking pre-requisite classes at the community college, so I took a week off and came home to take care of her."

"How did you stay healthy?" Alec asked, trying to make his voice sound like the question was out of curiosity and not suspicion.

"I'm kind of a germaphobe," he answered. "So as you can imagine, being in a home with someone with some strange illness made me very nervous. But my dad was really worried, so I told her I was on a school break, and I watched her from a distance. I disinfected every surface of the house while she slept, and I wore gloves and a mask whenever I was around her. It used to make her laugh that I was so serious about protecting myself. It's probably the thing that's kept me alive this long."

"Did your dad get sick soon after?" Alec asked.

Will shook his head. "Surprisingly, he didn't get sick at all."

"What do you mean?"

He took a deep breath and clenched his fists. "Come to find out, my dad was having an affair at that time. He said that he had to go on a business trip, but then when we saw him again, he said he had to put in a long night of work and that he'd catch a few hours of sleep at the office. Even when he was home, he was distant. He didn't get too close to my mom because he didn't want to catch whatever she had. In reality, he probably didn't want her to smell another woman's perfume on him. It was almost the perfect cover."

Alec's jaw gaped open. "Holy shit."

Will nodded in agreement. "It gets worse. During this time, my mom was getting sicker and sicker by the minute. I wanted to take her to the emergency room, but the virus was really going around then, and hospitals were packed. No medical staff went into work because it was too dangerous. There was nothing to do but wait. I was trying to keep my mom comfortable because she looked like death."

Will took a long drink before setting his empty can on the table.

"Then suddenly, something changed. She still looked ill, but her energy was back. She could sit at the table and eat supper with us again. So to celebrate, my dad made steaks. We figured that the red meat would give her a boost of energy. She had hardly eaten anything but soup broth for the past few weeks. Then, something clicked inside her mind."

"She figured out about the affair," Alec breathed.

"Bingo. There was makeup on my dad's collar, much too dark to be my mom's. Besides, she hadn't worn makeup in weeks. She asked him about it. At first, he tried to deny it, played stupid. Then she pressed him. She was getting angrier and angrier by the second. My mom was the sweetest woman in the world. I had never even heard her yell before."

"Really?"

"Nope. And I wasn't the best kid, either. If the cops caught me doing something stupid and dropped me off on her porch, she'd just shake her head and give me a disapproving look, and that would be it. I'd never seen her angry until that night."

"Do you think it was the rage?" Alec asked. He had seen that symptom in too many people.

"I know it was. My dad's not a good liar. She broke him down. Then, she jumped up on the table and stuck her steak knife straight through his chest."

"That's horrible."

"It was so strange," Will said, his voice sounding disconnected. "She was a tiny thing, but somehow, the knife went all the way through. Then she kept stabbing and stabbing."

"I'm so sorry," Alec gasped. His head was starting to feel woozy. He leaned back on the couch and stared at the ceiling.

"Yeah," Will said quietly. "The scariest part was that she came after me when I tried to stop her. She was completely gone by that point. It was as if she were a completely different person, a monster even. I ran into my room and barricaded myself in there until she stopped screaming and clawing at the door. I called the police, but they were so swamped that it was hardly worth it for them to come at all. After an hour or so, she just stopped."

The two were silent for a moment, Alec focusing on muddy shoeprints on the floor. He thought Will had finished his story, but he continued.

"I think she had tired herself out," he said weakly. "She didn't have a lot of strength left. I think her rage just burned through the rest of the life she had in her. I found her on her bed. Blood was coming out of her mouth. She was just gone. There was no one to tell and nowhere to go. I cleaned the place up, completely sterilized everything, and put everything back in its place. I've been trying to keep this place stocked, but it's been tough. I know I'm not the only one who's gone through something like this."

"Another drink?" Alec offered, walking to the cooler. If he couldn't keep this young man from witnessing terrible tragedy, then at the very least, he could try to be of some comfort to him.

"Why not?" Will said, wiping a tear from his cheek. "You know what? It feels good to get that off my chest. Thanks—" he started, realizing that he knew nothing about the man he'd told his story to.

"Alec," he said, offering his hand to shake.

"It's really nice to meet you, Alec. It's been lonely here. It's nice to be around someone who hasn't completely lost his mind."

"Cheers to that," Alec said, tapping can against Will's.

"Have you been out on your own?" Will asked, jogging Alec's broken memory.

In everything that had happened, he had forgotten about Elaina and Natalia.

"Holy shit," Alec gasped, bolting up from his seat. He stood up too quickly, and little black orbs danced in his vision. "The girls!"

He fell back to his seat and focused on his remaining vision.

"Take it easy," Will warned. "What are you talking about?"

"I was with two girls. One was in her mid-twenties, and the other was in high school. Did you see them?"

"No, I didn't," Will said, looking alarmed. "Are you sure? You were alone."

"I'm positive. Lainey and Natalia," he said, saying their names in almost a whisper.

"Where do you think they are now?" Will asked.

"No idea. I hope they're okay," Alec said, suddenly feeling ill.

"I'm sure they're fine. If you want, I can help you look for them."

"Don't worry about it. I just need you to take me back to where you found me. I need to get to my truck."

"I don't think you should be driving in your current condition," Will said. "Let me drive. It'll be easier to find them with two sets of eyes. Besides, I don't want to be alone. You're the first healthy person I've seen in a long time."

"Fine," Alec said, "but we have to leave now. Is there anything you need to bring with you?"

Will shook his head. "There's not much left for me here. If it's okay with you, I'd like to get the hell out of here," he said with a smile, his bright teeth on display.

"That makes two of us," Alec said, slowly climbing up from the couch. Will handed him his gun from the coffee table, and they left his home and the horrors it contained behind.

Chapter Twenty

"Okay, how about Na?" Elaina asked Natalia as they walked.

"Easy, that's sodium," she answered.

"K?"

"Potassium,"

"How about Sn?"

"Silver?" Natalia guessed.

"Nope, it's tin," Elaina corrected.

"Ugh, I always forget that one," Natalia groaned. "When does that ever come up in nursing, though?"

"Probably won't, but you have to pass the chemistry classes to get into nursing school. Let's try Ag."

"I'm tired of this game. We've been playing for hours."

"It's silver, by the way. Besides, it's not possible for us to be playing for hours. It's only been—"

Elaina looked at her watch.

"Oh," she said softly. "It's been four hours since we stopped at Alec's house."

Elaina turned to Natalia. She could tell that the girl was trying really hard not to complain, but she was exhausted. Elaina was drained too. The running with intermittent walking was physically taxing, but having to look death in the eye every time they made a wrong turn took its toll.

If the danger were short-lived, it might have produced a euphoric effect. Amusement park rides and haunted houses capitalized on this effect. In the moment, fear is not welcomed. The body sends chemical warnings throughout, preparing the body for whatever it's facing. But once the brain realizes that the danger has passed, the body feels good.

With Elaina and Natalia's situation, there was never that release of stress. Sure, they may be able to run away from one pack of infected, but soon, there would be another. Their world was like being stuck in a horror film, with no hour and a half runtime to contain them. There was no end in sight, no relief on the way.

"We should turn left here," Elaina said, stopping dead in her tracks at an intersection.

"I thought you said you wanted to go east," Natalia protested. "If we turn left, we're going to end up further from where we wanted to go."

"No, I think there's a grocery store over here," she replied. "Let's see if we can find anything good."

Elaina had visited this particular store before, and she had a feeling that it would contain everything they needed. She felt a sense of nostalgia from the past, going to the grocery store on a Sunday afternoon with her parents to stock up for the week ahead. She felt peace in her weekly routine. Each item had its place, and that never changed. Week after week, she could grab the same loaf of wheat bread from its home next to the hamburger buns. As a child, she could convince her parents to let her have a candy bar from the enticing racks near the checkout, and when she was older, it was her parents who tried to sneak a treat past Elaina, who had been on a health kick after a bout of illness in the family. These places offered her fond memories of how she could find pleasure in the mundane.

The store, with its welcoming green façade, appeared to have undergone little damage. A front door had been pried open, but no windows had been smashed. The parking lot was peppered with stray carts and a few vehicles neatly parked out front as if the owners had just stopped in to pick up some milk on their way home. Elaina assumed the vehicle owners had long been gone, if their bodies weren't decaying in the front seats already.

"I'm scared," Natalia said plainly. High-traffic areas like grocery stores were always a risk in the aftermath of the virus outbreak. It was the perfect place for an attacker to hide, as the healthy citizens would eventually come looking for sustenance.

"We'll be quick," Elaina reassured her. "We should make a plan, though. We need water and quite a bit of food since we don't know when we'll be able to stop. But we can't carry too much with us in case we have to get away quickly."

"Got it. We'll either tire ourselves out with lugging around a bunch of stuff but be well-fed, or be light on our feet and starve."

"I know," Elaina said. "Look for high-calorie, nutrient-dense foods."

"Like those milkshakes they give picky little kids who don't eat their vegetables."

"Exactly," Elaina said. "And plenty of water. Try to get some food and fluid in you while we're in here."

"Why are you talking like you're not coming with me? Are you not coming inside?" Natalia asked, panic rising in her voice.

"No, I am. I just wanted to make sure we're on the same page about what we need in case we're momentarily separated. It's a pretty big store."

"Please don't leave me alone in here," Natalia said wearily as they cautiously made their way inside.

"Don't worry," Elaina responded. "It doesn't look like anyone is in here."

The girls stood at the front of the store and waited. If anyone were in there, keen to attack, the sounds of their footsteps would have triggered an ambush.

"I think the coast is clear," Elaina whispered, picking up a pink backpack from a display near the door. "But let's be quiet, just in case. Ten minutes, and then let's get out of here."

Natalia nodded and grabbed a bag of her own, stuffing water bottles into the drink holders on either side. Elaina did the same before they split up, heading into different aisles. Natalia cruised through the health food section while Elaina booked it to the back of the store.

She had hit the jackpot. The in-house pharmacy was one of the best in the city. Elaina's dad's friend used to be a pharmacist at that location, and Elaina, interested in everything, got to visit once in her youth. She marveled at shelf after shelf of clear bottles with pills of every shape and size.

Most importantly, she remembered him taking her to the section where they kept the antiviral medication. That was obviously the highlight for her. In those giant plastic bottles were tablets and nasal sprays specifically designed to stop the viruses that wreaked havoc in the human body. They were the antidote to some of the most powerful destructive forces in the world.

"With these," the pharmacist had told her, "you have to take them at the right time. If you catch it early and take them at the first sign of symptoms, then you're in good shape. You might still have some symptoms, but they'll be a lot more manageable."

"What if you don't take them immediately?" she'd asked, already knowing the answer.

"Then it probably won't do much," he'd said, frowning. "You'll be stuck suffering through whatever nasty bug you've got. That's why they're tricky drugs. No one's really found an easy way to kill a virus off in its late stages. That's why vaccinations are so important. It's easier to prevent a virus than it is to treat it."

Elaina agreed with that concept. It wasn't too hard to make a vaccine for already well-established and frequently studied viruses. Her parents told her all about how big of a deal it was when the HIV vaccine came out. That virus had been officially eradicated when she was still a little girl. A good vaccine could protect billions from completely avoidable illnesses. It was that kind of work that she longed to do.

But there seemed to be bigger issues in the world. With military conflicts popping up all over the world, issues like border security and bioterrorism took center stage. No one thought much about illnesses that people passed through daily human interaction. It just wasn't seen as a big enough threat.

Only people like Elaina knew it was. Travel was faster and easier than it had ever been. You could fly from San Francisco to Shanghai in less time than it took to watch a baseball game. Just one infected person on that flight could spread disease to a multitude of countries. While the government was busy making sure that people crossed the borders with proper visas and identification, no one was stopping to make sure that no one was unintentionally smuggling in deadly diseases. The funding just wasn't there for people in Elaina's line of work. They had to make do with whatever they could get.

It wasn't all bad, though. For that very reason, Elaina could walk into a high school chemistry lab and conduct professional experiments, even though she didn't have all of the state-of-the-art technology that she had grown to love. She could make do with less. She could walk into a partially-raided pharmacy and see opportunity instead of measly leftovers. Part of her brain was one of an inventor's—she had enough vision to make something out of nothing—and that was exactly what she planned to do.

Like a kid in a candy shop, Elaina excitedly glanced around the storeroom of drugs before deciding what she wanted. First, she filled the bottom of her bag with pills that she believed could prove useful. Antivirals of every kind went into the bag. Next, she needed instruments. Lancets, syringes, and specimen containers were grabbed by the handful. Finally, she grabbed a few items for her own protection. Rubber gloves, masks, and disinfecting agents filled the rest of her bag. She slung it over her shoulders and clipped the strap across her chest. It was fairly heavy, but to Elaina, it was arguably more important than food and water.

When she was finished, Lainey returned to the main store and collected a few items to hold her over until their next raid. Energy bars, dried fruits, and trail mix were jammed into the empty spaces in her bag. When that was full, she tucked snacks into her pockets next to her most valuable possessions—her virus and cure samples.

"Where the hell have you been?" Natalia hissed when Elaina rejoined her at the front of the store. "You said ten minutes. I think it's been at least fifteen."

"I'm sorry. I guess I just got lost in all of the choices," Elaina lied. "Did you get everything you needed?"

"Yep," Natalia said, holding up a melting pint of ice cream. She ripped open a package of plastic spoons and dug into the soft dessert. She sat on the cold concrete floor and ate so quickly that Elaina doubted she could even taste it.

"Slow down," Elaina laughed. "You're going to give yourself a brain freeze."

"It's hardly frozen," Natalia mumbled with her mouth full. "I thought it would be nice to get some meat. We could make a fire at one of those parks and cook it. But, the power is out, and I don't know if it would be safe."

"Probably not," she replied.

"I found some dry shampoo and tried to clean myself up a bit, but my hair is so dirty that it just looks like I dumped a bag of cornstarch on top of the grease. I've never gone this long without showering. I feel horrific," Natalia said, scooping another spoonful into her mouth.

"Why don't you go to the bathroom and wash up? This place uses gravity-fed rainwater for its water supply. There isn't much happening in this area, so I can keep watch for a while."

"Are you sure?" she asked, looking around.

"Go ahead," Elaina said, helping herself to the ice cream. "I'll give you a shout if something comes up."

"Thank goodness," Natalia groaned. "I'll hurry, I promise."

"Take your time."

Elaina sat and drank from a sports drink while Natalia rushed off to select some soaps and shampoos. Biting into a rubbery energy bar, she wondered what the best way to use her alone time would be.

Knowing that Natalia took great pride in her appearance, she figured that she could shake off her little shadow by promising something she could not get anywhere else—a nice shower. Albeit, it would have to be contained within a grocery store sink, but it was better than nothing. Elaina just needed some time alone, something that Natalia would not willingly give her.

As she refueled, she decided that it might be worth it to start working on a vaccine just in case she found a lab at their next destination. She wandered through the empty aisles until she found a dozen chicken eggs. Sitting cross-legged on the floor, she carefully took miniscule portions of her original virus and injected them into the eggs, sealing the hole with a little bit of tape. Then, she wrapped each egg in a short length of bubble wrap and tucked them into her jacket pockets. Once her pockets were full, she carefully tucked the last one into the top of her snug camisole. She hoped the body heat would be enough to incubate the virus.

Once she was finished, she picked through a melting bag of frozen berries, sucking on the sweet fruit until it completely thawed in her mouth. After a few handfuls, her stomach started to hurt. It had shrunk over the past few days of their unintentional fast, and all of the food and drink that she craved just couldn't fit.

Natalia hadn't returned yet, but she heard the water running and assumed she was fine. With no other work to be done in the store, Elaina wandered the aisles aimlessly, browsing through the strange hodgepodge of products that hadn't been picked over yet.

The items in the store told a story. The store was low on stock, just as it would be upon the eve of a big storm. Only the molding loaves of bread at the back of the displays were left sitting to decompose, and foods that required work to prepare like meats were left in the freezers to thaw. Bags of flour and sugar sat untouched, while ready-to-eat foods like chips and cookies were scarce. Even in the middle of an emergency, people needed their vices. Elaina opened a sad looking bag of generic chocolate chip cookies, nibbled on one, and tossed the bag back onto the shelf.

"There you are," Natalia said, patting at her damp hair with a handful of paper towels.

"Feeling better?" she asked the girl.

"So much better," Natalia gushed. "Sorry I took so long."

"No problem," Elaina said. She was just happy to see Natalia in a better mood. "Are you ready to go?"

"Aren't you going to wash up?" Natalia asked.

"Do I smell?"

"No."

"Then I think I can make it a little while longer," Elaina replied. "I'm ready to leave. I couldn't possibly eat anything else right now."

"Me neither," Natalia replied.

The girls picked up their bags and headed back out into the world. Neither could guarantee that there would be adequate food or shelter where they were going, but in that current moment, they felt satisfied.

Chapter Twenty-One

"Doctor Vincent," one of the assistants said, jolting Bretton out of a daydream, "I was just informed that you are to meet with the Colonel at the end of the day. Can I tell him that you'll be in his office at six?"

"Oh, yeah, sure," Bretton answered hastily. "Did he say what the meeting was about?"

"Nothing specific, but I'm sure it's not going to be a big deal," the assistant said kindly. "I think he just wants to be briefed on your progress. If you can explain what you've been working on in terms that the average soldier could understand, then there shouldn't be any breakdowns of communication."

"But—" Bretton stuttered, starting to sweat.

"I understand," he said softly. "It can sometimes be, uh, intimidating to talk to your superiors, especially when they're the no-nonsense type. I'd suggest writing down a list of what you've been doing, just in case you forget."

Before Bretton could respond, the assistant was gone, probably off to tell the Colonel that the scientist would report with his findings at the end of the day.

The only problem was that Bretton had no findings.

It had been over a week, and he was no closer to figuring something out than he was when he was picked up by the military. This would be his first official meeting with senior officers, and if he didn't have something with just a hint of potential, he would be in deep shit.

His lack of progress had nothing to do with his surroundings. He had all of the lab equipment, and maybe even better than he had at his lab. He had assistants who could get him anything that he could ever need, and they worked tirelessly around the clock. They followed every order they got without question.

It wasn't enough for him, though. No one could bring him other experts in the field because there were few to be found. If the virus didn't scare them into hiding, then it took their life. Plus, the military didn't want a lot of scientists in on the project. Secrecy was important, and adding too many people to the mix would make it hard to keep under wraps.

A few times, he thought he had come pretty close to figuring something out. Soldiers on the streets were very helpful in bringing in samples of the virus from bodies on the streets. Bretton couldn't keep up with them though—each new sample that came in looked completely different from the last. It was like there were a hundred different viruses out there that all caused the same symptoms.

One time, they even brought in a corpse in a misguided attempt to get some more insight into what was going on. This act nearly sent Bretton into a panic attack. He reminded them, in certain words, that he dealt with viruses, not the bodies that contained them. He made it clear that he was not qualified, nor willing, to perform autopsies.

He was reaching the end of his rope. He worked long hours with no results and was becoming increasingly paranoid that others were starting to figure out that he had nothing to show for his work. It wasn't as if he weren't a gifted scientist—he had many published papers that had forwarded the field. It was just this very specific virus strain that he was having issues with. He felt like his entire reputation and body of work were going down the tubes just because of Elaina Morgan's stupid new strain.

Elaina Morgan was still a touchy subject. Sometimes, he even found himself wishing she would get picked up so she could come into work and figure out how to stop it. Bretton would be completely humiliated and would have to drop off the face of the earth, but at the very least, the crisis would be over.

He still hung onto a shred of hope that he would still somehow manage to pull something together that would work. Maybe the government would send him someone useful to help him, like someone in pharmacology.

There were virologists on different continents who would probably be of some assistance too. Where were they when he needed them?

After another long day of making absolutely no progress, Bretton sheepishly marched into the colonel's office. He waited for the colonel to be seated before sitting in the smaller leather chair.

"Doctor Vincent, I hope you have some good news for us," the large man said gruffly.

"Umm . . . there are a few challenges with this particular virus—"

"You don't need to go into detail," the colonel interrupted. "Just tell me what you've accomplished this far. Is this project worth continuing, or should we find someone else to take over?"

"No!" he exclaimed. "I have a vaccine."

The colonel paused, rubbing his chin. "You do?"

"Yes. It's not quite ready yet, but I believe it should be fairly effective in a few different mutations."

"But it's not a cure?"

"No."

"And it won't protect against all forms of the virus."

"I don't believe so, no."

The colonel sighed. "If you had to guess, in what percentage of cases will it work? We have very important people who need to be protected. The Commander in Chief is going to need something to keep her safe. How effective is your vaccine?"

Bretton gulped. If he had to guess, he figured that it would work in about a tenth of a percent of cases. And that was only if it were administered immediately and there was no incubation period involved. That wasn't good enough. Not for the president, not for the military, not even for himself.

"Maybe twenty, thirty percent," he lied, wincing.

The colonel sat back in his chair, slightly rocking back and forth. He thought for a moment. Bretton held his breath. He was overestimating by a lot, but it still wouldn't be the right answer.

"I'm just not sure if that's good enough. What seems to be the problem?"

Bretton could have rattled off a long list of problems, but it would have made him appear incompetent. He wanted to whine that he was basically set up to fail, but he couldn't do so in front of a senior member of the military. They wouldn't accept any excuses, so he would give none.

"It's just that this is the most complex virus I have ever seen in my life," he admitted. "In most cases, this kind of thing would be studied by a whole team, maybe multiple teams around the world. Remember when the Ebola vaccine became available? Scientists all over the world had been working on that, trying to be the first to complete it. It took decades. This is even trickier than that, I'm afraid."

"Do you know anyone who is better equipped to take on this kind of project?"

Bretton froze. Was he about to get fired? All of his protections would be revoked. He'd be out on his ass in a minute.

"In full honesty," he said, bracing himself, "there might be."

"May I have that individual's name, please?"

He pursed his lips, trying to make his smug smile look more thoughtful.

"Have you located Elaina Morgan yet?"

The colonel gritted his teeth. Bretton shrank back in his chair, ready for the colonel's full wrath. He knew that he would be poking the angry bear with that kind of comment, but it would only solidify his place in the military base.

"Morgan's whereabouts are still unknown. Do you have any information on her that you'd like to share with us?"

That wasn't a request. It was a warning.

"Believe me, if I knew anything about where she was, I'd give her a piece of my mind. I'd be the first person leading the witch hunt against her. Did you know that I lost my daughter because of her? No, I have no motivation to keep Elaina in the shadows. I can promise you that."

"Okay," the colonel said, backing off. He seemed surprised that Bretton had spoken so strongly about her. "Can I ask you a hypothetical question?"

"Sure."

"If we managed to find Elaina Morgan, do you think she would be capable of making a vaccine or a cure?"

Bretton figured she probably could with ease. The virus was her life's work, her little pet project. She knew the ins and outs of it much better than Bretton did. All he'd managed to do was tinker around with it enough that it made the symptoms deadly. If anyone could do it, she could fix the problem.

"It's quite possible, yes," Bretton responded.

"Do you know much about her personal life? Does she have any close family members, friends . . . a significant other, perhaps?"

"I don't know about that. I would say that our relationship is strictly professional. There's nothing really cordial about it."

"Do you know of any other motivations she might have?"

"Motivations?"

The colonel clenched his square jaw again. "Is there anything we can hold over her head in order for her to be compliant?"

Suddenly, what the colonel was really asking clicked.

"You mean torture?"

"Hypothetically, if we find her, she probably won't be willing to help us. It's just nice to have a little information on our subjects so we know what will motivate them to do what we need them to do."

Bretton's stomach hurt. He wanted to get out of the office as quickly as possible.

"Is there anything else you need to know?" Bretton asked. "I was planning on staying late at the lab today."

"No, that's it," the colonel said, looking disappointed. "Let's meet in four days' time. I need to know if any progress is being made."

"Yes, sir," he replied, standing up from his chair.

With shaky legs, he made his way back to the lab.

Before he could return to his workbench, a voice whispered to him from the other side of the hall.

"Doctor Vincent," a man whispered.

Bretton hadn't seen this man before. There were people entering and exiting the base all the time. If Bretton wasn't working directly with them, he didn't take the time to get to know them.

This man didn't look like the other soldiers. He was dressed in a navy blue suit and had slicked back blonde hair.

"If it's okay, I'd like to have a word with you," the man said in a low voice.

It was suspicious to Bretton that the man seemed so secretive, but they were working on a secret operation. There was a lot that Bretton didn't understand about military work.

"Sure," he said, stepping into the small office.

"My name is Agent Stephens," he said, offering his slender hand to Bretton. He shook it and sat down in his chair.

"I understand that you're working on a vaccine for the Morgan Strain, correct."

"Yes," Bretton answered shakily. He wasn't sure who was given clearance to know about it, but the man seemed like he knew a lot. He felt like he could probably trust him.

"You're not having much luck, are you?" the man said sympathetically.

"I wouldn't say that," Bretton fired back, trying to defend himself. "It's a difficult subject to work with."

"Oh, no doubt. I was wondering about something concerning the virus. Just a few quick questions."

"Shoot," Bretton said.

"In your very professional opinion, would you say that the virus could be altered to become easier to control?"

"I'm sure that's possible," Bretton said. After all, he had messed with it and made it harder to control. He figured he could mess with it again and have different results.

"What I had in mind was something practical— something that didn't spread like usual illnesses. Something that could maybe even change the body on a DNA level?"

"Oh, I'm sure of it," Bretton said haughtily. "I bet you I could made a strain of this virus that wouldn't do anything but give you the monster strength without the rage. I could probably make it so it only gave the fatigue without the rage. There's no telling what this thing could be."

"That sounds very promising," Agent Stephens said. "You're a brilliant scientist, Doctor Vincent. I'd like it if you did a little job for me."

Bretton beamed. Finally, someone was giving him the attention he deserved.

"What is it?"

"We'd like to see you make this nasty virus into something the military can use. It will be extremely secret though, so I'm afraid you won't be able to ever write about it in a journal."

Bretton frowned. "Then what's in it for me?"

"We can offer you protection that's unparalleled. Maybe even better than top officials get. Plus, there's money. You might never have to work again."

Bretton hid his smile. He was ready to sign any contract that he needed to. He could do without the fame for now as long as he could ensure that he would be safe.

Chapter Twenty-Two

Will eagerly peered over the steering wheel, adjusting the seat for his short stature. Alec was quite a bit taller than him, so he fiddled with the levers until he was ready.

"Go ahead and adjust the mirrors, too," Alec reminded him, having seen a few accidents caused by reckless teenagers. His truck wasn't particularly nice, but it was the only one he had. He didn't want it to be totaled while riding along helplessly in the passenger seat.

"I used to have a truck like this," Will mentioned as he strapped his seatbelt on.

"Yeah?" Alec asked, pouring a few of the pain pills from Will's house into his hand.

"It was stolen," he said. "It was the day after my parents died. It just disappeared from the driveway. I guess I have to take some of the blame for it—I left the keys in the ignition.

"In our neighborhood?" Alec scoffed.

"You should have seen my truck. Trust me, I'm sure whoever stole it is sorry. It probably broke down halfway out of town."

Alec didn't know if he should feel offended that the kid was comparing his truck to a run-down piece of crap. Alec didn't have a lot of money as he was just starting in his career. He didn't really care about status symbols like cars and clothes. He just needed the basics to get by. That's how he was raised, and that's how he planned to live his life.

"Alrighty, then," Will said, turning the keys in the ignition. "We have a full tank of gas—that's a promising sign. Where are we going to go?"

"What?" Alec asked, unwrapping his bandages. The bleeding had nearly stopped, but the pain had yet to subside and he still felt a little woozy.

"Where should we look first? For the girls, I mean. What were their names, again?"

"Lainey and Natalia. Natalia's short and scrawny, about your age. Lainey is—"

His mind was momentarily lost in thought about the older girl. How could he describe her smooth, porcelain skin, gentle eyes, and long, silky hair to Will? How could he do her description justice without sounding like a kid with a crush on someone way out of his league?"

"Hey," Will said, snapping his fingers. "Are you okay?"

"Yeah," Alec said, snapping to attention. "Why do you ask?"

"You've been silently staring into space for about a minute now. I asked you what Lainey looks like."

"Oh, right. Uh, she's pale, kinda freckly, and has long, brown hair. She was wearing a Seahawks hat the last time I saw her."

"Got it. So basically, if we see two girls walking together and they don't look infected, then it's probably them."

"Sure," Alec said.

Will put the car into reverse, pulling out of the driveway. "Where to?"

"I—I don't know," Alec said.

"Oh, God, did I knock your memory loose? Oh, shit, this is bad. Do you remember my name? What's your last name?"

"Shut up, smart ass," Alec responded. "I'm trying to think."

"Well, where were you guys planning on going next?"

"We didn't have any plans. We were just going to get in my truck and look for a good opportunity."

Alec was furious with himself for not doing any more planning when they still had the chance. All he would have had to do was listen to where they wanted to go, and then he'd have a good starting place. But now, they could be anywhere. It had been hours since he had last seen them.

"That's not a problem," Will said, sensing Alec's rising frustration. "What do you know about them? Is there somewhere they would want to go? Maybe a favorite part of town? Maybe like a school or a library or something? Or were they trying to get out of town and make a run for it?"

Alec shook his head. He didn't know anything about the girls and was a little embarrassed that he didn't know much more about them than Will did.

"That's okay, man," he said, giving Alec a reassuring pat on the shoulder. "Why don't we just start looking in the area? If they're on foot, they couldn't have gotten too far. We'll cruise around the area and keep an eye out for them."

"Yeah, let's go," Alec said. "I'd like to get a good start before it gets dark."

Will took off, driving a little too fast for Alec's comfort. He didn't blame the kid—there was something exhilarating about flying down empty streets, not having to worry about traffic. Most people had the good sense to leave the city days ago once the virus showed no signs of being under control.

They drove through deserted residential areas, circling through culs-de-sac and cruising down windy streets. Will scanned the road ahead of him as Alec stared deeply between homes, hoping he'd catch a glimpse of Elaina's grey jacket disappearing between two houses.

Alec continued to pop a variety of pills into his mouth to keep the pain from his head at a manageable roar, but also to keep him awake and alert. He so badly wanted to close his eyes, but he knew the second he did, he'd miss the girls. The warm, cozy air from the cab of the truck, the quiet hum of the engine, and the gentle motion of the vehicle was trying to lull him to sleep. He fought heavy lids until he couldn't fight them anymore.

"Unless they're posting up inside one of these houses, I don't think they're around here. They move quickly," Will said, jolting Alec back to consciousness.

"Crap, was I asleep?" Alec asked, wiping the drool from the side of his face.

"Yeah," Will said softly. "I was going to wake you up, but you looked so peaceful. I thought you could use a little rest."

"What if we missed them?"

"Relax, you were only out for about twenty minutes. I doubt they're in this area anyway. It's too residential. I'm willing to bet that they ventured out into something more commercial. More supplies, you know?"

Alec frowned. He felt guilty with his bag of food and drinks in the truck when the girls were so hungry and dehydrated. Wherever they were, they must have been absolutely famished, he worried.

"You don't think it would be crazy if we stopped at a McDonald's along the way?" Will asked, testing the waters. "I could go for a Big Mac and some fries right now."

"Do you really think that there's any of them that are open?" Alec asked incredulously. He was starting to wonder if there was something wrong with the kid, apart from a little PTSD.

"I know there probably aren't any functioning ones, but we could always pop in and cook something up from the fridge. You know that stuff's preserved to last through the apocalypse."

"I highly doubt it," Alec said, his stomach reminding him that he hadn't had much to eat. "You'd be the only moron to die of food poisoning in the middle of an epidemic."

"I doubt I'd be the only one," he said darkly. "What do you think is going to happen when there's no electricity to keep the food safe? I guarantee there will be a lot of people desperate to eat the last of their food and take a risk. Besides, food poisoning is probably a lot safer than leaving your house to get food."

Alec went quiet. This kid was not doing his conscience any favors.

"Oh, I know what we could do," Will offered. "Turn on the radio."

"Why?"

"Oh, you'll get a kick out of this."

He pushed the volume button and fiddled around with the tuner.

"Okay, here's the Top 40 station."

Alec listened, wondering if Will was having a psychotic break.

"It's just static. There's nothing playing."

"I know! This is such a popular station, too. They didn't even bother to leave a running playlist. You know that's all they do there—the songs are always the same. But no, they shut that whole thing down."

Will flipped through a few more stations to illustrate his point. All of the stations, classic rock, metal, jazz, even local news were nothing but static. In the middle of Will's channel-changing, Alec swore he heard a few words.

"Wait, what was that one? Go back."

Will slowly pushed the scan button until he found what Alec was talking about. The voice was intermixed with the buzz of static, but it was still audible.

"Dude," Will said, "I think this is National Radio."

He twisted the knob until they could clearly hear what the monotone voice was saying.

We're continuing to get updates from Seattle, Washington, the epicenter of the Morgan Strain outbreak. Understanding the size and scope of this disaster has been difficult, as many city officials have evacuated the city, despite telling their own citizens to stay where they are. We'll be spending this hour talking about what happened in Seattle and what's to come for the bayside city. Milton James has more.

A classical piano interlude played, and Alec and Will exchanged surprised glances. For them, it felt like everything had happened so quickly, yet National Radio was dedicating an entire show to their precarious situation.

I'm standing near the Space Needle in Seattle, wearing a full plastic suit, as if I were visiting an alien planet. If it weren't for the towering landmark, I might forget that I'm in the state's largest city and not in the middle of a warzone. Destruction is everywhere —smoke rises from fires in the distance, crushed cars sit parked in the middle of the street, and rubble crunches under my feet. It's hard to believe that this was the result of a virus released from a university laboratory.

In order to gain access to the city, I had to gain permission from the United States Military. They insisted that I wear the proper protective suit of their design, much like the one that would be worn in the event of chemical warfare.

Along with my safety suit, I am required to be accompanied by armed soldiers. When they first told me this, I laughed at them. Then I realized that it wasn't a joke.

You see, there are many strange symptoms of this new-age virus. First, symptoms start off fairly mild. In fact, many sufferers believed they came down with the flu, packing doctor's offices with sick people. Then, symptoms intensified. The victims felt extreme fatigue, horrible nausea, diarrhea, and coughing fits.

These symptoms led to death in children and young adoles-cents, as their frail bodies would not respond to fluids. However, adults faced a fate that no one could see coming.

Because the virus is so new, no one has had the chance to really study and understand its effects on the human body. Thus, no one can explain why it causes madness in adults.

It's widely reported that the infected in later stages of the virus will undergo a complete personality change. They do not respond to reason and become highly agitated. Once they're upset, there's no telling what they can do. In fact, much of the destruction I see is caused by the moments of rage, a source tells me. These infected individuals are liable to attack healthy people, spreading the illness, if not killing them. Hence, my armed guards.

"This can't be great for tourism," Will joked. Alec shushed him.

The report went on, telling them everything they already knew about the virus and its alleged release from the lab. Then, the report mentioned something they hadn't thought much about.

We talked to a member of the National Guard assigned to securing the perimeter. For reasons you'll soon understand, we cannot disclose any information about them, as they are bound to

218

secrecy. So, this interview will be read by Derek, an actor. Can you tell us some of the things you've heard about the state of the city at the current moment?

Sure, an eager voice replied, no doubt a young actor doing his first gig. *The city had strongly recommended its citizens to stay where they are and not evacuate, yet all citizens of special importance, like the mayor, left weeks ago. But since the spread of the virus, we have now been ordered to make sure that no one enters or exits a twenty-mile radius of the city limits. In fact, if you drive down the road, you'll see armed military keeping anyone from going through in either direction.*

"So we're trapped?" Will breathed.

"No, that's not possible," Alec responded, though with little confidence.

Though our source says that the perimeter is being guarded, that doesn't mean that rule is being enforced.

Money, the actor read. *If you have enough money to pay one of the members of the Guard, you can get through. Unfortunately for the working class, unless you rob a bank, you're not getting through.*

Alec put his head in his hands. That explained a lot of the theft in the area and a motive for people to commit crimes even though they were perfectly healthy. This one was the government's fault. As a public servant, he felt so ashamed of his superiors whom he'd adamantly defended in times of controversy.

But don't think that will continue, the reporter said. *Word is, the soldiers assigned to protect the rest of the country from the city have been told that there are no uninfected survivors left. At best, if you venture to the border, you'll be turned away. At worst, you'll be shot on sight, no questions asked. It appears that the world has given up on Seattle in hopes that diverging more resources to minor breakouts will keep it from spreading beyond control.*

"We're screwed," Will said, slumping over in his seat. "You heard that report. What options do we have if we can't leave the city and go somewhere safer?"

Alec shrugged. "The infected will die off eventually. We just have to wait it out."

"It mutates, though. What if the symptoms change and the rage period lasts months, not days?"

"We'll just keep moving until it clears up. We have to try."

The boy nodded, sitting up a little straighter. "You're right. It's just you and me against the world, Alec. We're not quitters."

"No, we're not," Alec answered. "And I'm not going to give up on those girls either."

"Do you remember anything about where they wanted to go?"

Alec thought for a minute, remembering one debate that went nowhere.

"Lainey wanted to go to a hospital. I think she wanted to be somewhere with a backup generator."

Will winced. "That doesn't sound like a good idea. A hospital is a good place to find a virus."

"That's what I was trying to tell her. I don't know if she believed me."

"If that's the case, they might be dead. I wouldn't be surprised. They had a good run, though. There should be a memorial or a record board for anyone who stayed here and survived for more than a few days."

"What did you say?" Alec snarled.

"A record board for survival times?"

"Why would you say that they're probably dead?" he barked. "You don't even know them."

Alec tried to take a few deep breaths, something they were taught to do while working if they thought they were about to make a stupid decision out of anger. He breathed until he stopped shaking, until he could think clearly again.

"I'm sorry," Will squeaked. "I didn't know that they were this important to you."

"I guess I didn't either," Alec replied, thinking about Elaina. He wanted to rescue her, if anything, to show her that he was a caring person. He wanted her to be in his life, not out on the streets in the middle of an epidemic.

He felt a connection to her that he could not explain. It was probably rooted in stress from the madness that was unfolding around them. Still, it was more than he felt for a lot of people, and he would be damned if he couldn't take a shot at living in a post-virus world with her.

But the kid was right. If it weren't for Alec's experience working in dangerous situations, he would have been a goner ages ago. It wasn't fair for him to snap at Will for logically connecting the dots.

"I'm sorry," Alec said once he regained his composure. "You're probably right."

"No, I'm sorry. They've got as good of a chance as

anybody. Let's keep looking. I've got nowhere to be, now that we know there's nowhere to go."

"Thanks," Alec said wearily, knowing that their energies were being wasted on such a futile mission. But, if there was even a one-in-a-million shot of finding them, he would take that chance.

Chapter Twenty-Three

Reading the billboards as they trekked, Elaina began to pick up the pace. She walked faster and faster until she was nearly jogging.

"Wait up," Natalia called. "I have shorter legs."

"I think this is it," Elaina said, unable to hide the excitement in her voice. "This might be our answer."

Natalia looked up at the signs, then back over to Elaina. "You're not talking about that hospice, are you?"

"That's exactly what I'm talking about. It's not a hospital, but they might have the things I need."

"Sure, if you need a bunch of infected elderly people," she retorted. "Honestly, this worries me."

"Come on. This is a place where people come to live out the few days they have left. They're already going to be in a weakened state, and I wouldn't be the least surprised if the nurses and caregivers have abandoned them. For all we know, everyone in there is already dead."

"For all we know, everyone in there is very much alive and infected. We have no way of protecting ourselves."

Elaina stopped to look at Natalia, who had come to a halt. She could see that the girl's hands were shaking.

"How about this?" Elaina proposed. "You can stand back a little way, and I'll poke my head inside. If people are just roaming around, out for blood, I'll give you a signal and we'll book it out of there. If the coast is clear, we set up shop. Look at this place," Elaina said, gesturing to the empty expanse. "This place is kind of in the middle of nowhere, and I haven't seen signs of life, healthy or otherwise, in over an hour."

"Fine," Natalia said, throwing up her hands. "See if anyone's around."

Elaina nearly skipped up to the front door, opening it with ease. It was mostly dark inside, but faint streaks of sunlight came in through gaps in the blinds. She didn't see or hear anyone, so she walked into the entrance and pulled open the blinds. In the daylight, the building looked like a nursing home, slightly sterile in décor but with a homey twist. The floor was stark white and tiled, but a wreath of autumn foliage hung on the reception desk.

Pleased with what she had found so far, Elaina poked her head out the door and excitedly waved Natalia toward her. She had high hopes for the place.

"You think it's empty?" Natalia asked, cautiously looking around corners.

"As far as I can tell. This place is huge. I wonder if they have a lab for doing in-house exams."

"It smells strongly of alcohol," Natalia said. "I guess that's a good sign. At least it's clean in here."

"Let's check it out," Elaina said, like a child on Christmas morning, waiting to see what surprises could be discovered.

"No, wait," Natalia said, clutching Elaina's arm. "Do you hear that?"

"No," Elaina said. "I think it's in your head."

Natalia took a few steps down the dark hall. "I really think I hear something."

Together, they crept down the hall until Elaina heard the noise too. It sounded as if there were a wounded animal somewhere in the building. It seemed so strange because there was no sign of life in the building. It looked like it had been abandoned, just like everything else.

The sound grew louder and louder and Natalia was digging her nails into Elaina's arm now. They realized that the sound was not coming from one living creature, but several. Natalia peered into one of the thin, rectangular windows in a patient's room and let out a gasp.

Elaina leaned over to see what was so startling and nearly jumped from pure shock. Inside the patient's room were about twelve people, mostly elderly, wandering around. They seemed completely unaware that they were no longer alone.

"I'm getting the hell out of here," Natalia said, doubling back.

"They're locked in," Elaina noted, lightly touching the door handle.

"They're infected," Natalia spat. "What makes you think they won't break down that door this instant?"

"Because they haven't already. How long do you figure they've been in there? I'd be willing to guess around a week. They're in bad enough shape that their rage isn't enough to help them blast down that door. At the very most, they're just going to claw at each other and throw the food the staff so graciously left for them," she said sarcastically. "I'd say we're pretty secure. I'm going to find a lab."

"I hate everything about this," Natalia said. "What do you think happened?"

Elaina looked around. "My guess is that the virus hit, and these guys were infected. The staff didn't know what to do with them besides quarantine them. I don't blame them—it would be too easy to infect everyone in the place. Then, once it got bad, the workers split, but these guys were left behind."

"That's extremely inhumane," Natalia protested. "How could they just lock them up like that? There's not enough room for everyone in there."

"They're infected," Elaina said softly. "There's not much they could do for them. They're already in bad shape anyway. I guess they figured that they would go one way or another."

"I guess," Natalia said sullenly. "It just really gives me the creeps."

"Me too, but I think this is a fairly safe place to be right now. Would you like to come with me, or would you rather stay outside?"

Natalia let go of her arm. "I'll stay with you, but if I

hear that door break down, I will not hesitate to leave you behind."

"Fine with me."

They walked down the long corridor until the terrible howls sounded like faint mewls.

Elaina peeked into every room they passed, hoping to find something useful. Most of the rooms were for patients. Some of them even had bodies, stiff with rigor mortis, in the beds.

"I feel like I'm in a haunted house." Natalia shuddered after finding yet another dead body.

Finally, they entered the heart of the hospice, where the employees spent most of their time. Beside a fully-stocked breakroom, there was an infirmary, complete with a small room used for processing samples and minor medical procedures.

"This is exactly what I needed," Elaina gushed, looking around. She found a lamp and adjusted it so it shone on the work bench. "Yes, this should be enough to make some serious progress."

"How is there electricity?"

"They clearly have the generator going. I guess they just turned off all the lights before they abandoned the infected."

"Want to check out the lounge with me?" Natalia asked.

"No, go ahead," Elaina said, already adjusting the lens of a microscope and wiping the dust off a slide.

"You need food and water," Natalia reasoned, nervous to go into the room for the first time alone. "How do you expect your brain to work at full capacity if you don't have any carbs in your system? We might even be able to find a little caffeine," she persuaded.

"You're right," Elaina said, carefully setting a slide on the bench. "Just a quick look, and then I'm going back to work."

The lounge had couches, vending machines, and even a little cot for sleeping during long night shifts. Without thinking twice, Natalia picked up a paperweight and hurled it at the glass of the vending machine, shattering the front.

"I'm sure there's a key for that around here somewhere," Elaina said, frowning at the mess of broken glass on the carpet.

"No time," she said, pulling snack cakes from the wreckage. "You've got to get to work."

Natalia filled up a plastic cup from the water cooler and handed it to Elaina, along with a variety of snacks.

"Have fun," she said cheerily as she flopped down on the couch, waving at Elaina with her hands full of junk food.

"Believe me, I will."

Elaina spent a few moments rearranging her new sanctuary until everything was just right. She laid out her test tubes to admire the little samples they contained. She pulled the chicken eggs from their hiding spaces until she found a heating pad warmer to tuck them in. She hoped that they were still in good condition and that she could hide out in the hospice and work until they were ready.

Curiosity had been nagging at her for so long. Taking the blood sample she collected from the scene of

Alec's cop car theft, she added a few solvents from the shelf and placed it in the old centrifuge. As it hummed, she prepared a slide of her original virus. Of course, she could probably sketch it from memory, but it was always nice to have for comparison purposes.

When the blood had separated, she decanted the plasma and white blood cells into one tube, leaving the thick, red liquid behind. Then, she added more solvents and separated it down even further. Once that was ready, she prepared another slide of her mystery sample.

She searched around on the slide, increasing the magnification as far as it would go until she found it—her little virus swimming around.

Then, she saw something that nearly took her legs out from underneath her. What she thought was her virus wasn't her virus at all—she even compared her original sample again to make sure her eyes weren't playing tricks on her.

The thing in the mystery sample looked so similar, but it had a few tiny changes. To the untrained eye, it didn't look like much, but to Elaina, it blew the top right off her suspicions.

Elaina's virus, even with the minor side effects, had never created that mutation when it spread. Even if it did, it would have to undergo a lot of change, perhaps years and decades of change to get to that point. Someone had clearly created that virus in a lab and had used her original strain as a template.

There was only one scientist who could have created that abomination, and his daughter was in the adjacent room to Elaina. Dr. Bretton Vincent, for whatever reason, had made changes to her virus and released it into the world.

When Elaina thought hard about it, he had been increasingly moody toward her ever since she'd started trials with it. While others were encouraging her progress, he appeared especially sullen. Then, she started seeing less and less of him. He started spending longer hours in his lab, working on something in secret. Elaina assumed he was working as an independent contractor in his spare time, but would it be so outrageous to believe that he was ripping her off?

She had no idea what would motivate him to do such a thing, but everything was starting to fall into place. He was just the type to steal another scientist's work, the type to leave his daughter behind as she was being kidnapped. Dr. Vincent was just no good.

Elaina tried not to get too hung up on how it happened and just focus on the problem at hand. Even though it wasn't her fault, she was still capable of making things right in the world again. Feeling confident, she relabeled her samples *Evidence #1* and *Evidence #2*. If the time ever came to vindicate herself, the justice would be sweet.

Now, she had a whole new problem. She didn't need vaccines and antidotes for her virus. She needed them for Bretton's take on her virus. Out of eggs, she injected some of the new strain into the tiny holes in the shell, hoping that it would incubate that strain as well.

Then it was time to work on a form of LILY that could stand up to the new imposter virus. She put a drop of each onto a slide and watched them battle it out. LILY put up a good fight, but it didn't make a perfect fit with the virus in order to take it down.

She didn't know much about pharmacology, but Elaina took out the pills she gathered from the pharmacy and lined them up on the desk. If she could separate some of the compounds they contained, she reasoned she could keep the virus at bay long enough for LILY to start working.

Elaina would have to look more closely at what Bretton had done, but he wasn't that inventive—if anything, he had just made an amalgam of viruses, a Frankenstein's Monster of viruses. If the antivirals could affect the altered part of her virus, Elaina could fix the rest.

Excited with what she was finally able to discover, she wanted to share it with someone. Elaina ran over to the lounge to share her findings with Natalia but found her asleep on the couch. She shook her head and chuckled quietly to herself. That girl could sleep through the apocalypse.

Turning off the main light and flicking on a small lamp instead, Elaina went back to the lab and just marveled in what she knew now, as opposed to the things she'd wondered for days.

The makeshift lab in the hospice was a good starting place, but she needed more if she was going to come up with anything substantial. Elaina longed for the university laboratory with her old familiar equipment. She would do her best with the utensils and chemicals these temporary labs contained, but at some point, she wanted to do things right and make medical-grade vaccines and medications.

But the sun was setting, and it would be dark soon. It made no sense for her to venture out and find a proper laboratory. Besides, she figured that there was a live-stream camera in every advanced lab in the state. The cops would be looking for her in the one place she wanted to be. She couldn't give herself up yet—not without the evidence she needed to prove her case.

Until she found a better place to be, she would meddle around with the resources she had. But, when the time was right, she would need a few moments in the right lab to put the finishing touches on her work.

The rest of the evening, Elaina worked tirelessly, testing new combinations of chemicals against the virus. She wished she had a lab assistant, and she almost woke Natalia to help her, but ultimately, she decided to let her rest.

Knowing she needed her sleep too, Elaina pulled a throw pillow and blanket from the lounge into the lab and rested underneath her work bench. She closed her eyes, already excited for her next waking moments. She was so close to figuring out how to end a national cata-strophe. She just needed a little more time.

Chapter Twenty-Four

Elaina heard footsteps trotting down the corridor, the one that was supposed to be empty. She pulled her head up from under the blanket and listened as they multiplied and came nearer. Moonlight altered the appearance of the room as sinister shadows danced on the walls of the lab.

Slowly standing to her feet, Elaina looked for her most valuable test tubes to hide from the intruder, but she realized that the table was bare. Even the syringes and bottles of pills were missing.

The realization sent a jolt of electricity through her body. She felt cold and sweaty, yet her brain was on fire. She let out an involuntary wail and the footsteps stopped in front of the lab door.

Holding her breath, she waited as the doorknob creaked open and the door revealed the source of the footsteps. The inhabitants of the quarantine ward stood staring at her, scowls on their faces.

Elaina couldn't move. Her legs felt impossibly heavy, and every time she tried to walk, her legs shook so badly that she fell down. She tried to call for Natalia, but her throat was so dry and scratchy that the name came out in soft, hoarse stage whispers.

"Help us," the gaunt old man in the front pleaded. The virus had whittled him into a skeleton. His eyelids were drooping, making him look even more pitiful.

"I can't," Elaina cried, holding her hands out, ready to defend herself. "All of my medicines are gone."

She quickly looked back at the workbench just to make sure she hadn't overlooked them. The table was still bare, with no indication where her things may be.

"You can't just lock us in a room and wait for us to die. We didn't ask for this. We didn't mess with nature and release this on the world. Why do we have to get sick?"

"I didn't do this," Elaina argued, tears of frustration in her eyes.

"You're Doctor Elaina Morgan."

"How . . . how did you know?"

"Everybody knows who you are. Your name will be in every history book from here on out. That is, if there's anyone left to tell our history."

"This isn't my fault," she cried as the infected entered the lab. She scrambled backward, but there was nowhere left to go. "I just wanted to help people."

"You didn't help anyone. You can't save us, just like you couldn't save Lily."

"LILY! Do you have it?"

"No, and you don't either. You'll never have her."

As the man's milky white hand reached for her throat, it melted into pink goo and slid down her chest.

Elaina yelped and sat up from her spot on the floor, smacking her forehead on the workbench above her. Her heart was racing and her eyes were wet. She grasped at her throat, expecting the man's melted flesh to still be on her. She was still intact.

The dream felt so real that she climbed up to the table to make sure all of her possessions were as she left them. Everything was where it was supposed to be.

She slumped back down on the ground and let a few tears fall freely to the floor. Elaina was feeling guilty for her role in the outbreak, even though no one with all of the facts would ever fault her for what happened. If the truth never came to the surface, she might forever be known as the one who started the worst epidemic of the century.

She took a deep breath to calm herself and turned on the lamp. There was no chance of getting any more sleep. Looking at the clock, she calculated that she had slept for about four hours, which wasn't bad for her. She cracked the top off a can of acidic energy drink from the fridge and got back to work.

After a few hours, Elaina was at an impasse. Theoretically, a few of the antiviral solutions she made could work in the event of an infection, some more probable than others. But she didn't know if any of them would work without testing.

The logistics of acquiring animals to test on, especially at that hour, were dicey. She didn't know that area particularly well, so venturing out to find a pet store or veterinary clinic would put her at tremendous risk. Plus, she would catch all sorts of hell from Natalia if she tried to uproot her in the middle of the night—or worse, leave her at the hospice.

Instead of staring at her nearly finished work in frustration, Elaina decided to stretch her legs. Besides, there was always the possibility that one of the residents owned a small animal. In her desperation, even a turtle or a parakeet may be of use to her. She just needed some living organism to ensure that her drugs wouldn't cause a worse death than the virus.

Walking down an unexplored corridor, she heard a low moan, not unlike the one from the quarantine ward. This one was softer and monotone, though. She strode toward the sound and peeked in the window.

There, a thin young woman sat rocking back and forth in her chair. Intermittently, she released dreadful groans that sent a shiver down Elaina's spine.

This woman must have been healthy at the time the hospice was abandoned. Otherwise, she would have been placed in the quarantine chamber with the others. She was clearly as sick as the others now—her skin was mottled with oozing sores.

Elaina wondered what a woman her age was doing at a hospice. Her bald head suggested cancer of some sort.

She felt nauseated. The woman looked miserable, but she likely didn't have the mental capacity to understand what was happening to her. She appeared to be in a daze, rocking in her metal chair, then angrily pacing. Eventually, she just slumped over in her bed, resigned.

Elaina had a sudden desire to help the woman in any way that she could, especially after her nightmare had brought those desires to the forefront of her mind.

But seeing the woman in the state that she was, she knew that she couldn't make her well. If the virus didn't kill her, whatever else was ailing her would.

That didn't stop Elaina. Fueled partially by the need to help and partially by academic curiosity, she decided that she would start her human trials that night. She had a subject who looked fairly calm, who was also isolated in her own room. She couldn't pass up on such a good opportunity.

She took off in a jog down the hallway to the administrative office. She pulled open drawer after drawer, looking for a master key that would let her enter a patient's room. She collected a handful of silver keys of different shapes and sizes and started testing them on an empty room. After her fifth attempt, she found one that worked.

Dropping the other keys back into the drawer, she then went looking for something to protect her from the virus. This hospice wasn't equipped to handle serious pathogens, but she rounded up a pair of scrubs, clothing shields, and heavy-duty gloves. She put on protective glasses and placed a mask over her nose and mouth.

Then, she looked for something to arm herself with in case things didn't go well. Her makeshift laboratory contained vials of different sedatives. If her subject began to lash out, she could inject an overdose and hope that it would be enough to keep her from becoming a homicidal maniac.

And if that wasn't enough, Elaina grabbed a knife from the kitchen. She hoped it wouldn't come down to stabbing anyone, but she would defend herself if necessary.

Finally, she went back to the breakroom to see if Natalia had woken from her slumber. Unsurprisingly, she was in the same spot Elaina had left her. Pink sunlight was creeping in through the open windows. The sun was about to rise, their only protection from the mysteries of the night. If her human trial turned out to be a bust and the patients were too hostile to work with, then they could leave.

Elaina debated whether she should wake her traveling companion. If she woke her, she was certain that the girl would protest her plans, being terrified of getting attacked. She would be strong in her protestations too, and it would be hard to keep her out of the way when she carried on with her plan anyway.

Worse yet, she may actually succeed in talking Elaina out of conducting her experiments. Then, she wouldn't be any closer to figuring out how to end this mess. Natalia didn't back down from a fight, especially when her safety was involved.

On the other hand, if she didn't tell Natalia what she was doing, then she would be completely unprepared in case of emergency. Elaina couldn't run from an infected person and protect Natalia. As much as she wanted to save as many infected as possible, Natalia's safety was much more important to her. She might not be able to cure anyone, but she sure as hell would try to prevent anyone else from falling victim.

Plus, it would be nice to have a little help. If she had backup, even just there with a syringe filled with sedatives in hand, it would make her job so much easier.

But, knowing that Natalia would never go for that, Elaina chose to let the girl sleep. The break room door locked from the inside, so if Elaina couldn't make it back, she would at least have everything she needed to survive for a few days in the hospice. Then, when she was ready to leave, the girl could unlock the door and venture back into the world, only having lost a small measure of security.

Yes, there was no other choice in Elaina's mind. She returned to her lab in the adjacent room to gather her supplies. Fully dressed in her protective clothing, she filled her syringes. Standard procedure would have to fall by the wayside—there was no time to sterilize the site of injection or explain to the patient what she was about to do. Instead, she would inject her as quickly as possible and get the hell out of there.

As she began to unlock the door, she tried not to think too much about what she was about to do. Otherwise, she may realize how insane it was to willingly go into a room with an infected person and back out at the last moment.

Taking a deep breath of clean air, she braced herself and opened the door. Then, she closed it behind her. There was nothing separating herself from attack.

Upon closer inspection, Elaina figured that the woman wasn't much older than she was. Her pale skin was covered with powdery makeup, her hollow eyes lined with black. Her lips were painted a rusty red, the color of dried blood.

She sat back in her chair, knees pulled up to her chest, arms wrapped tightly around them. Elaina wondered if she should aim for the blue veins that snaked through her transparent skin or go directly for the chemo port in her chest. If she could inject directly into that area, the serum would travel as quickly as she needed it to go. She would give it a shot.

Though the woman was silent, Elaina shushed her to keep her calm, like a mother would calm a crying baby. She was shocked that the woman didn't try to attack her immediately. She must have been in the end stage of the illness, because she looked exhausted, physically and mentally.

Needle raised, she slowly crept forward, eyes locked on the port in the woman's chest. It would only take a few seconds to inject the cure, then she would depart immediately and watch her progress from the window.

As soon as she was inches from the site of injection, the woman's eyes suddenly locked on Elaina and she bared her teeth. She sprang from her chair and pinned Elaina to the ground.

Elaina pressed her forearm into the woman's neck, trying to avoid her teeth. As thin as she was, she still had a few pounds on Elaina, and she struggled to shake the woman. With her left hand, she jabbed the needle at the woman's chest, just barely hitting the opening in the woman's body. She howled and got up, allowing Elaina to slide out from underneath her.

Elaina had another syringe filled with a sedative and

antiviral that would calm the woman down for long enough to study her reaction to the serum, but there wasn't time for that. Instead, she lunged for the door, just missing the woman's grasp by a few inches.

She locked the door, absolutely exhausted from wrestling with an infected person but ultimately pleased. Finally, after weeks of work, she was able to see if her serum worked in a practical setting. She could spend a few more days at the hospice, monitoring the woman's condition as she rested and used up the supplies in the staff lounge. Perhaps, if the woman responded well to her drug, she could even refine her serum and try it out on the others. There were so many new possibilities now that she had the chance to test her work.

Down the hall, she heard a door open. Thrilled with her breakthrough, she nearly skipped down the corridor to tell Natalia what she had accomplished. Sunlight was now streaming in through the open windows, and Elaina hadn't felt so much hope and optimism in weeks.

"Natalia," she called, unable to hide her excitement. "I have some big news to share with you."

Natalia didn't answer. Elaina couldn't believe how much that girl slept, yet was too drowsy to share in her big news.

"I tested my serum on one of the infected," she cheered. "I knew you wouldn't be happy about it, so I didn't wake you. Now, we can hide out here for a few more days. Isn't that awesome?"

"Hands in the air," a deep voice barked, startling Elaina so badly she felt like her heart was going to explode. "Don't move."

Initially, Elaina thought that Alec had found them and was playing a prank on them. A smile spread back out over her face. Maybe he would be open to hearing about her work now that she was getting somewhere.

Then, she realized that there were dark shadows moving toward her. At least five people, all dressed in black tactical gear, were walking in her direction. When she whipped around, three more were behind her.

"Cops!" Natalia shrieked from behind them as she was being escorted away by a large man.

Elaina broke out in a cold sweat. She could try to run, but she was surrounded. She was outnumbered by a long shot, and they had weapons. She could try to fight them off with the tranquilizers and knife, but she would be shot on site. There was nowhere to go. There was no one to save her.

She glanced to her right. Through the tiny window, she could see that her test subject was soundly sleeping, her chest steadily rising and falling. What if the serum was fighting off her infection? She needed to know what happened to her.

"Elaina Morgan," the man closest to her called, "you are being detained by the United States Army. Put your hands on your head and do not resist arrest."

"You can't do this. Don't I have rights?"

"You've released a biological weapon on the world that has already taken thousands of casualties and shows no signs of stopping."

"I didn't do this," she shouted, placing her arms on her head, tears of frustration threatening. "This isn't my fault."

Two military members handcuffed her hands behind her back, the cold metal cutting into her wrists. Then, taking her by the arms, they walked her outside to an armored car and tossed her inside.

In the hospice, Elaina's serum was coursing through the veins of the sick young woman, putting up a fight against Bretton's virus. However, Elaina never got the chance to see if the solution she'd spent hours laboring over worked.

Chapter Twenty-Five

Since taking the offer from the mysterious agent to find a practical application for his virus, Bretton was feeling much more optimistic about his situation. Suddenly, without the added pressure of getting his military protection yanked away, he felt more inspired. The mental block that clouded his brain was gone. He was going to be a scientific genius. There would be books and documentaries about the work he was doing at that very moment.

Suddenly feeling bolder with his new job, he asked for an even better laboratory than the one he was already in and requested that he have double the number of researchers working under him. He hand-selected the best and brightest that were still willing to come in and work on the virus that was killing thousands. For a young virologist, it was the project of a lifetime—they were raking in a lot of money for a sinister cause.

Bretton had no strong political leanings nor strong opinions on military goings-on. He knew that the atomic bomb was an absolute horror and didn't want to see one being used in his lifetime, but he still envied the scientists who got to work on it. For him, once he sold his virus to the military, he could wash his hands of its eventual effects. But, he could revel in the glory of being the lead scientist working on something that could change the course of history.

So, just like before, Bretton took a virus that had one function and fiddled with it until it was slightly different. He was terrified yet fascinated by the way his strain had caused so much fury in later stages. He knew that it was unlike anything he had ever seen and wanted to capitalize on it.

He found that he could weaken the Vincent Strain to the point where it could not reproduce or mutate. In fact, it was so weak that a healthy person could possibly fight it off in hours. The effects were still horrible, but they didn't cause death—not in the infected, anyway.

To become infected, one would have to consume the virus in a large dose. It wasn't transmitted from person to person very well because it couldn't survive without a human host for very long. Even then, large volumes of the virus would have to be shed from the infected person, and that was rare.

His trials on rats were going extremely well. When injected with a large quantity of his solution, the rats would show symptoms in hours. They couldn't spread the illness to other rats, but when placed together, they would attack. Bretton always had his team report their observations during this test. It was just too much for him to witness himself. He was pleased with the results. The trials were still in their early stages, but this newest virus showed a lot of promise.

He did wonder whatever became of the military's plan to work on a vaccine. He had completely abandoned that project to start on his current one and couldn't be happier about it. It troubled him that as far as he knew, no one was working on a vaccine, but he assumed that they had someone else on the case. As long as his new virus made more money than the vaccine would, he couldn't complain. He'd have to share a little bit of the glory.

Once his rats passed the benchmark tests that he designed, Bretton was ready to present his preliminary findings. He couldn't wait to see the looks on the officers' faces when he showed them how it worked.

After the rats were infected, the rage symptoms only lasted for a few hours. But in that time, they were faster, stronger, and did not react to pain. When the effect wore off, the rats eventually returned to normal, though they were extremely lethargic. Bretton wasn't too concerned with side effects if the main effect was up to snuff.

On Friday afternoon, just as the junior members were heading back to their barracks, Bretton assembled a demonstration in a conference room. As he stood in front of some of the highest-ranking officials in the military, he beamed with pride. All eyes were on him, and he knew that what he had to share was revolutionary.

"Good evening, ladies and gentlemen," he said with a flourish, not sure how to address the mix of military officials. "Over the past week, I have been spearheading a project that will change modern warfare as we know it. Traditionally, biological weapons are used against the enemy to weaken their defenses, making them easier to overtake. But in this case, our armies can use this groundbreaking technology to their aid."

Bretton's hands were shaking from excitement. All he had been told to do was use the Vincent Strain and come up with something more practical. With his creative genius, he'd made something that he assumed the military would want to use immediately.

"Is anyone familiar with the story of the Norse Berserkers?" he asked his audience. A few heads nodded.

"These were warriors who showed a characteristic fury in their fighting unlike anything that had ever been seen. These soldiers would develop so much rage, seemingly out of nowhere, that they could take their opponents by storm. They used their rage as a motivator to come out on top. Afterward, they would calm down and even enter a sort of trance. It was as if the rage had left them altogether."

He looked around to see if anyone knew where he was going with that story. There were definitely some puzzled faces in the crowd.

"No one really knew what caused this fury. Some say that it was a genetic defect—wires in their brain were crossed, which caused them to be fierce warriors. Mental illness was another possibility. Some think that it was pharmacological—perhaps some kind of plant or mushroom was ingested that gave these fighters such strength.

The point is, I have created a virus that works like whatever factor caused the Berserkers to fight in the manner
that they did."

That got people interested. He tried to suppress his
pleasure from their interest. He didn't want to get ahead
of himself, but he knew people were already impressed.

"In preliminary trials in rats, this new virus presents
temporary symptoms. It's like the Morgan Strain that's
going around, but more refined. With my strain, you
don't have any of the other flu-like symptoms. You
might have minor symptoms like muscle aches, but
probably nothing big. Then, you get the fury that we're
looking for."

"Pardon my interruption", the colonel said, standing
up from his seat in the back, "but why do we want to
willingly infect our own army? How will this not end in
the disaster that we're currently in? What makes you
think that these rage symptoms will be useful to our men
and women?"

"I understand that it's risky, but if you're looking for
motivation for your soldiers to fight, this is it. Put it in
their MREs or even call it an energy shot if they don't
want to take it willingly—for exhausted or unmotivated
soldiers who are having a hard time getting into the
fighting spirit."

"And why can't we just recruit soldiers to do the jobs
we need them to do in the matter we need them to
do it?"

"I think I can answer this one, Colonel," Agent
Stephens said. "If you're looking at who you're fighting,
it's not your average soldiers from sovereign nations.

These are smaller fringe groups that really feel like they're fighting for something. They're pissed as hell, and your soldiers just can't match that intensity, especially when you're fighting on behalf of another nation. It's not their battle to fight, and they're doing their job, but not with the intensity you need. This virus could make them so much more efficient."

The colonel sat down, a frown on his face. He didn't look convinced about the proposal, but he didn't look upset about it either.

"As I was saying," Bretton continued, "this virus will give them rage and extra athleticism. In rats, the rage period makes them fifty percent faster and stronger than in their natural state. Think of what this could do to your top soldiers who are in peak physical condition already. This would elevate them to new heights. I know that performance-enhancing drugs are usually frowned upon, but these aren't sports stars. These are our finest military personnel. I predict that one infected soldier could do the work of two uninfected when it comes to combat."

The conference room went silent. Enlistment numbers had been down for years. A mistrust in the government and increased international conflicts had not been good for their numbers. If they could increase efficiency without having to deploy more soldiers, then they were in good shape.

"The good thing about this virus is that it is very temporary. It cannot spread through human contact, and it cannot survive for long in the human body either. Within hours, the effects will go away. We're seeing a lot of lethargy after the rage has worn off, but that's something that can be dealt with. It's perhaps the body's way of recovering from such a high-energy-consuming state. It's probably good for the soldiers to take it easy during this time to be safe. But you can always try traditional drugs like caffeine to counteract the lethargy."

"What's next?" the colonel asked.

Bretton clenched his fists. He felt like he had everybody in the room on board with what he was working on. He took his shot.

"Human trials."

"Do you have reason to believe that your new virus will prove fatal to our soldiers?"

"I don't think so. Rats are easier to kill, and we haven't lost any of those yet. I'd be shocked to see anything more serious than hangover-like symptoms."

"Let's not wait any longer," Agent Stephens said. "Why don't we test this right now? We have no shortage of subjects here. Get one of the privates in here and see what happens."

Bretton looked at the colonel, expecting—and hoping—that he would deny his request. Instead, the colonel gave an unmistakable head nod.

Before he could even think about what was going on, a small group of the senior-most members gathered in the laboratory. A steel-faced young private entered and stood at attention.

"You're going to need to restrain him if you don't want anyone to get hurt," Bretton warned. "Make sure he doesn't injure himself either."

A straightjacket was obtained, and the man's

extremities were bound close to his body. Then, his torso was chained to the wall. When he could no longer move, everyone looked to Bretton.

"Doctor Vincent, go ahead and administer the virus."

Bretton obliged, plunging the syringe into the crook of the soldier's arm. Minutes passed and nothing happened. Bretton was getting nervous. If this didn't work, then all of the excitement around his virus would fly out the window.

Thankfully, after about a half hour, the symptoms started. First, the soldier started to tremor. Then, he snarled and growled like a bear as he fought to break out of the straightjacket. The officers in attendance looked on with interest. Bretton's virus was just what he had advertised.

The next few hours were painful for Bretton to watch. The soldier began to scream like a banshee as his eyes glassed over. The jacket stretched and frayed. Bretton was beginning to get nervous that he was going to break free, though it would only help his case if he did.

By the time the symptoms finally wore off, the jacket was simply pulled off without having to untie him, it was so loose. He lay on the floor, panting and sweating.

"Congratulations, Doctor Vincent," Agent Stephens said, shaking his hand. "You've created something useful from a rogue virus. I'm impressed, and I'll be in contact with you tomorrow about compensation agreements."

"Thank you," he said, relieved that everything had worked out for him. He had completed his task, and he only needed to make a few small adjustments to make the virus perfect and marketable. But he had sealed his fate. He would be protected from whatever horrors were present in the outside world. He would be just fine.

"Keep him in quarantine for the next twenty-four hours, just as a precaution," Bretton said. "If you don't mind, I'd like to go to bed now."

Bretton slept better that night than he had in a long time. The relief he felt was more soothing and relaxing than any sleeping pill he could take.

Chapter Twenty-Six

"How long do you think this virus can keep up?" Will asked as he circled the block for the second time. "Like, there's gotta be more people out there like us who have survived this long."

Alec was tired of the boy's constant questions. Companionship was nice from time to time, but this was a little much for Alec. He was tired, in pain, and worried about Elaina and Natalia. Small talk, or even worse, deep discussions, were not a top priority.

"I don't know," Alec sighed, looking out the window. "If they are really holding everyone in Seattle hostage, then I'm sure the rest of the world is safe."

"Were you not listening to the radio? They said that there are reports of the virus on every continent except for Antarctica now. This doesn't look good for anyone right now. Think about all of the flights that went out of here before the airport was closed—hundreds of people caught the virus in their seats and it spread exponentially. Give it a few days, and I'm sure what's happening here will start happening all over the world."

Alec couldn't even imagine that happening somewhere else. Seattle was a big city, but it had nothing on the populations of other major cities across the globe. In New York City or Beijing, the death toll would be in the millions. Unless everyone in the entire world knew how to prevent the spread of viruses and was committed to staying healthy, there was no way it wouldn't turn into a disaster, especially since there was no surviving it once infected.

"Once we find the girls," Will said, "we should get some of those inflatable plastic bubbles. We could make our own little bunker if we found a building and sealed it up tight. We'd need a ton of food and water, but I'm pretty good at finding resources now. We can all just hang out together and wait it out until the military comes back to clean up the dead. They'll find us, and we'll probably get to go on all of the talk shows as the four who survived the virus from inside the city. That would be a nice way to cash some checks."

Alec rolled his eyes. He couldn't think of anything worse than surviving and becoming a minor celebrity except for not surviving at all. If Will's fantasy came true, then he would let the kid take his airtime. Alec just wanted to start life over again without the baggage of his past hanging over his head.

Will slammed on the brakes. Alec lurched forward, almost hitting his head on the dashboard. A second concussion would have left him down for the count.

"What the hell are you doing?" he chided.

Will's face turned pale, his eyes locked on the rearview mirror. Alec craned his neck around to see what was so startling.

An armored car was stopped behind them. People in army uniforms and black protective masks and gloves exited the vehicle and were walking toward Alec's truck.

"What's going on? What do I do?" Will asked frantically, not knowing if he should keep still or step on the gas.

"I think we'd better see what they want," Alec said with little confidence. He was hardwired to believe that government agencies were to be trusted and respected, but they had also been locked in a city that was crumbling. He really didn't know whom to trust.

He felt for his gun in his pocket. If these were foes and not friends, then he'd do his best to defend himself. Still, he knew that there was little chance of getting out of that fight alive.

Alec rolled down the windows as the masked military men approached. Unsurprisingly, they led with their guns.

"We're not infected," Alec said, holding his hands up. "Don't shoot. I'm a police officer with the Seattle Police Department. I'm trying to help, but there's not much I can do by myself."

"What's your name?" a masked man asked.

"Alec Lawrence."

"And I'm Will Domenica," Will chimed in from the driver's seat.

"Stay where you are. We're going to run your names in the database."

The military personnel left, and Alec quickly rolled up the windows.

"I think this is good," Alec said, looking over his shoulder.

"Do you think they can help us find the girls?"

"Maybe. At the very least, they have some sort of system to keep track of those who have been killed, displaced, or have survived so far. I wonder what their search is going to bring up for us?"

"I don't think we need to worry," Will said. "We haven't done anything wrong."

Alec hoped he was right.

Eventually, the men returned with a small tablet in hand. "Do you know Sharon and Pablo Domenica?" the man asked Will.

"Yes," he sighed. "They're my parents. Both recently deceased."

"I'm sorry to hear that," the man said in a monotone voice. "How long ago was that?"

"Almost two weeks, I believe."

"Have you had any symptoms?"

Will shook his head.

"And you?"

"No, sir," Alec responded.

"Please come with us. Since there has been a travel ban for entering or exiting the city, we have been advised to round up all of the healthy survivors and place them in protective custody."

"Where are we going?" Will asked, his eyes wide.

"We will take you to a camp set up near one of our bases. There, you will have access to clean water and food, along with shelter in a safe environment. However, if you enter, you must stay there until you can be relocated."

"How long do we have to stay there?" Alec asked, suspicious of what they were about to agree to.

"You must remain until our doctors can clear you. I'd say you can expect to wait a week. Then, military personnel will escort you to a different location that has not experienced a breakout."

"Do I have to give consent to this?"

The man shrugged. "Frankly, I don't see why you wouldn't. We're offering protection to the handful of people we can find. Besides, if you don't come with us, we've been ordered to use reasonable force to persuade otherwise. In the end, it's for your own good. It's a chance to get out of here. If I could take that deal, I would."

Alec tried to look through the man's dark sunglasses. He felt some empathy for him. He had also been called into work at a time where he would have rather stayed at home. But, there were some jobs that were non-negotiable.

"One last thing before we go with you," Alec said. "I was traveling with two girls before we got separated. Have you been able to find anyone named Natalia or Lainey?"

The man typed into the tablet. "Do you have any more information about them? A last name, perhaps?"

"No, I only knew them by their first names."

"We've picked up a Natalia Vincent. She's eighteen years old."

"That's her," Alec said with a smile, relieved that they were rescued.

"Yes, my records show that she's been transported to the quarantine unit. I can't find anything about anyone named Lainey, though. If they were together, it's possible that it hasn't registered with the system yet. We've been having trouble with Internet connection. You'll have to talk to her friend about that when you see her."

"Thank you," Alec said, excited to see the girls again. "Am I allowed to bring my personal belongings?"

"Yes, but be advised that they'll be subject to sterilization upon entry to the camp. Now, please come with us and find a seat in the vehicle. We'll arrive at the camp in about an hour as long as we don't have to make any more stops."

Will and Alec eagerly got in the vehicle. Now, they would just have to sit around for a week to prove that they were healthy, but then they would be free to do as they pleased. No longer would they have to worry about hiding out in a bunker as the city fell. They could start over in a new city somewhere safe. Alec hoped for a small rural location. After all of the disease and destruction, he wanted to be somewhere wide open and sparsely populated.

Once they arrived at the camp, they were guided to a blindingly white tent to undergo medical evaluation. Alec was poked and prodded, asked questions about his mental state, and had several glass vials of blood taken from him. His vitals were all within the normal range, and he even had someone examine and take care of his injuries. Finally, he was given an IV with fluids, nutrients, and a painkiller for his head. Once he was cleared, he was sent to the decontamination center.

This tent was a large room with one large shower, like the ones he used to shower in during his high school gym years. Steaming hot water blasted him as he was instructed to cover his entire body with a soap that made his skin sting. When he got out, he was handed a towel and a pair of cotton pants and shirt. His bag was returned to him and he checked the contents. Everything was intact and smelling of disinfectant, but his gun was missing. He'd inquire about it later, but for now, he just wanted to rest.

He found Will in the quarantine tent, talking to some girl wearing a matching outfit and couldn't help but laugh at the absurdity of their situation. Here they were, after being rescued, scrubbed within an inch of their life and placed in a holding tank, and Will was already flirting with some girl who probably wanted nothing to do with him.

Alec went to rescue the poor girl from Will's overeager conversation and realized that he girl he was talking to was Natalia.

"Alec," she gasped when she recognized him. "I never thought we'd find you again."

"Same," he replied, letting the girl wrap her slender arms around his waist in a tight embrace. "I'm glad you got picked up. You'll have to fill me in on everything that happened when we got separated. By the way, where's Lainey?"

Her face fell. In fact, she looked like she wanted to cry.

"Oh, my God," Alec said. "She's okay, right?"

"She was picked up with me, but they've kept her."

"What?"

"Is that your other friend?" Will asked. "Why don't you introduce me to this one right here?"

Alec ignored him. "Why would they keep her?"

Natalia shrugged.

"Is she infected?" Will whispered.

"No," Natalia said firmly. "I don't know what they're doing. We'll just have to wait and see what happens."

"I'm going to talk to someone," Alec said, getting angry. "They have no right and no reason to hold her against her will. She should be out here with us."

"Don't," Natalia said, clutching his arm. "Just leave it. I'm sure she's fine and she'll be in here with us soon. Please don't bring it up to anyone."

"I'm sure it doesn't hurt to ask," Will said. "There's guards all over the place. We can see when she's being released."

"Stay out of it," Natalia shouted at him. "Can we all just go to the cafeteria? I think we'd all feel better if we had something to eat and drink."

Alec wasn't particularly hungry, but he followed the girl. Will followed close behind, extremely interested in Natalia.

It was nearly two in the afternoon, and the few other residents of the quarantine had already had their lunch.

Natalia grabbed a plate and loaded it with leftover sandwiches and chips. Alec grabbed a few handfuls of dry carrots and floppy celery. Will grabbed everything he could get his hands on.

"If there's something you know and you're not telling me, I want you to know that I won't let anything bad happen to you guys. You can trust me."

Natalia looked at her plate and frowned, not touching her food.

"What happened to Lainey?"

"You need to understand that it's not her fault," Natalia whispered. "She's completely innocent and is being falsely accused of doing something she hasn't done."

"What are you talking about?"

"I can't say. It's too bad."

"It can't possibly be that bad. You're talking like she's being accused of killing someone."

Natalia bit her lip. "When we said we had never met before this, that was not entirely true."

"You knew each other before the virus?"

"Hardly. My dad's a virologist. They worked in the same lab. I met her once, years ago."

Alec sat still for a moment as he connected the dots. "Lainey was only a nickname," he muttered to himself.

Natalia nodded, and her eyes welled up with tears. "She didn't want to tell you about this because you're a cop. She didn't think you would believe her. She didn't know whom to trust."

Alec was furious. It was one thing to be lied to, but another to have protected the person who'd released the virus on the world in the first place. If he knew who she was, he could have turned her in to the military much earlier. He was just thankful that they had all been brought in.

Perhaps the worst of all was that he'd completely misjudged her character. He thought she was really cool. He felt incredibly stupid for having a crush on a criminal mastermind.

"Well," he said tersely, getting up from his seat, "I'm going to my bunk. It's been a long day, and I'd like to be alone now."

He kept walking as both Will and Natalia protested and pleaded for him to come back. He kept walking, even though he wanted to find an officer and tell them everything he knew about her. He wanted to find Elaina Morgan and scream in her face for tricking him into helping her.

He was much too exhausted for all of those things. Instead, he tucked himself into his assigned bunk and tried to pretend that none of it had even happened.

Chapter Twenty-Seven

"Doctor Vincent," an assistant called after he got off the phone, "we have someone here that you're going to want to see."

"Okay, send them in," he said without looking up from his microscope.

"Um, I think it's best if you meet them somewhere other than a laboratory. This is unrelated to your current assignment."

Dr. Vincent finally looked up. "I'm not sure if I follow."

"It's your daughter, Natalia," the assistant said. "She was picked up by some of the patrol team this morning and is being held in protective custody. She's not allowed to leave the quarantine area, so you're going to have to go to her."

Bretton felt as though he may faint. He sat down hard on his stool. "Is she okay?"

"As far as we know, she hasn't been infected.

However, due to protocol, we can't release her until she's passed the quarantine period. It's just standard procedure. But you're more than welcome to see her. I'm sure she's excited to see you."

Bretton was silent. He didn't know what to do or say.

"Well, when you're ready, we'll have someone escort you over there. Just let us know."

"Okay," he said weakly. "Give me just one more moment to finish up."

Bretton panicked. He didn't think he was ever going to see his daughter again, let alone see her completely unscathed.

Since she had survived without becoming infected, it meant that he probably could have pulled her back into the car or fought off the kidnappers without being killed. He felt cowardly that his tiny daughter could live in such a hostile environment when he hardly could.

He wasn't sure how she would react to seeing him after all that time. He hadn't even tried to look for her or send help because he thought she was dead. He hoped she would be so relieved that she was safe that she would forget about everything that had happened in that period. Maybe she would understand that there was little that he could do and even be proud of his new accomplishments.

Once she was cleared to go, she would return to her mother, of course. With his new job, Bretton wouldn't be a suitable parent. But she would be pleased with his new income. He could make up for all the fear that he'd caused her in those weeks. She would be fine, but he needed to get this initial meeting finished so he could make amends and return to work.

"I'm ready to see my daughter now," he said to one of the guards and was led to the quarantine tent.

He had spent so much time in the lab that he didn't even realize that this makeshift shelter had been constructed so close to the base. As he rode in an all-terrain vehicle, he realized that he hadn't been outside in the sunlight for days.

He was led through a door and instructed to close his eyes for twenty seconds as a disinfecting mist blew onto every surface of his body. Once that was over, the next set of doors opened and he entered into an open recreation area.

In the center, sitting at a plastic table with a newspaper in hand, was his daughter.

"Natalia," he said softly, tears coming to his eyes. "I thought I'd never see you again."

She looked up at the sound of her name. Her eyes widened, then narrowed as her mouth turned into a scowl.

"What are you doing here?" she hissed.

"It's a long story. I was picked up by the military shortly after you were taken from me. I've been working with the virus at the lab here. I was brought here to make a vaccine."

"Oh," she said coldly. "And how's that going for you?"

"Fine," he lied, not wanting to tell his daughter that he'd failed at his original task. Plus, secrecy bound him to keep quiet about what he was really working on.

He could sense that something was not right about her. She was quiet and especially moody.

"Is something wrong?" he asked. "I'm really happy to see you. Aren't you excited to see me at all?"

"Nope," she said shortly.

He sighed. "Natalia, I'm so sorry about what happened when we left the city. I tried everything I could, but there was no getting you back. There were just too many of them and not enough of me to fight them all off. I was devastated, Natalia. I thought you had been killed or infected. You have no idea how horrible it's been for me, not knowing what happened to you but fearing the worst."

"That's rich," she scoffed. "I've been running for my life. I've seen some of the most horrific things known to man, but I should be more understanding of your situation," she said sarcastically. "You suffered so much in your cushy little laboratory while I fought off infected people and slept on the streets."

Bretton bit his lip. She wasn't hearing his apology.

"I don't think you're listening to me, Natalia. I'm sorry. There was nothing I could do."

"See, I don't think that's true," she said softly.

"What do you mean? You know what happened. They took you away from me. You were gone so fast."

"I watched you drive away. If you would have waited just another minute, I could have jumped back into the car and then none of this would have ever happened. You didn't even try."

Bretton had been caught in a lie. He hadn't realized

that Natalia had a chance to free herself from her captors.

"Oh, and not to mention, you didn't try to get help. Why didn't you have your new military friends come looking for me the second you got to the lab?"

"I–I did what I could. You don't understand what these people are like. They have a very strict agenda, and I didn't have enough power to call the shots."

"I can't believe you," she said, shaking her head.

Bretton thought she seemed a lot older and more mature than the last time he saw her. She didn't act like a little girl anymore. She had grown up a lot in the few weeks since he'd left her on the side of the road.

"I need you to accept my apology," Bretton said plainly.

"No," she replied. "You don't deserve to be forgiven. I can't wait to get on the phone with Mom and tell her about everything that happened. Let me guess, she thinks I'm dead too?"

"I haven't talked to her."

"You what?" she barked, raising her voice much louder than Bretton felt comfortable with.

"I haven't had the time."

"My mom has probably been worried sick about me. Even if you did think I had died, didn't you think it was worth telling her?"

"I was afraid," Bretton said wearily. "I didn't want her to blame me for what happened."

"She should blame you for what happened. It's your fault. I need to call her."

"Wait," he said, reaching for her hand. "We don't

have to do this. Just tell her that we're both fine. She doesn't need to know the specifics."

"You're a horrible person." She scowled.

This angered Bretton. He had been in a laboratory, working for his life for the past two weeks. She was being ungrateful for everything he could offer her in the future. Once she told his ex-wife about what happened, that would be the last he would see of her. In fact, he was worried that he would somehow be sued for negligence.

"You're being a stubborn brat right now," Bretton said, squeezing her wrist. "I've done too much for you to ruin my life. Sit down and listen to me."

With her free hand, Natalia slapped her father's face with all the strength she could muster. He fell back into his seat, a red hand-shaped welt forming on his face.

The soldiers assigned to guard him raced in and held Natalia back. He watched her struggle against them, his hand pressed to his stinging face.

"What do you want us to do with her?" a guard asked.

"Take her to her barracks. She can wait out the rest of her quarantine in isolation if she's going to be difficult. It's not up to me anymore. She doesn't want to be my daughter, so I'm not going to tell her what to do."

Bretton crossed his arms and watched Natalia struggle to break free. She seemed furious, and there was nothing more he could do to change her mind about him.

"You're a real bastard, do you know that?" a voice yelled from across the room.

"Alec——" Natalia protested.

"No, he needs to know that he put you in so much danger," he said to his traveling companion. "You're a coward for leaving her alone like that. I want you to understand what she went through after you ditched her."

"Doctor?" a guard asked, wondering if he should restrain the police officer too.

"I'm not going to touch him," Alec said, raising his hands to prove his point. "Your daughter was kidnapped by two armed men who were going to keep her in their bunker and repopulate with her against her will. Then, she escaped and was chased after by infected people for days. She had to sleep in a shipping container and drink rainwater to survive. She ran for days, only stopping to search for food and water. Now, she has to see her piece of work father again. Give the girl a break."

"Really?" Bretton asked, going pale. He hated to imagine his daughter in any of those situations.

She nodded. "I had some help, though," she said, looking at Alec. "Get this——the person who kept me alive was your work rival."

"What?"

Natalia grinned, making Bretton feel uneasy. "I owe my life to Elaina Morgan. If she can get us out of the mess that was never her fault, I think you owe your life to her too."

Natalia walked away, but Bretton ran over to her to catch up.

"You're not making any sense, Natalia. What's this about Elaina Morgan?"

"She's here, Dad. She saved my ass on more than one occasion and was brought in with me."

"She's dangerous," Bretton said loudly, trying to reestablish this belief.

"She's not, and you know that. I know she never said anything to me about it, but I think you have more to do with this epidemic than she does."

Bretton swallowed hard. "You don't know what you're talking about."

"Elaina didn't do this. I believe her. But if it wasn't her and it came from your lab, it just makes me wonder what really happened. I don't know if we'll ever know the truth, but you need to make sure that Elaina gets whatever she needs to finish her work. I'm sure she's done much more to save this planet than you have."

With that, she was gone. She ran back to her barracks, and Bretton didn't have the energy to chase after her.

If his own daughter suspected that he was involved with the outbreak, then Elaina certainly knew what was going on. He needed to get to her before she told anyone else what she knew. He needed to convince her that whatever happened was a mistake, but her fault, nonetheless.

"Hey," Bretton shouted at one of his assistants, "I need someone to explain why the hell I wasn't told that Elaina Morgan was on the premises."

"I don't know, Doctor Vincent," he said, looking sheepish. "Do you want me to figure out who was responsible for briefing you?"

"No. I need to see her," he said weakly. "I need to speak with Elaina Morgan."

Bretton was far more nervous to see Elaina than he was to see his own daughter. If he couldn't explain to Elaina what had happened, then everything he'd worked for was at stake.

Chapter Twenty-Eight

B retton was extremely nervous about seeing Elaina, but he was doing his best to hide it. He strode down the hall with purpose, giving demands to his assistants.

"Oh, and somebody find Elaina Morgan for me," he barked as they rounded the hallway toward his lab. "I've been waiting to give her a piece of my mind for quite some time, and I don't want this to be delayed any longer."

"Don't worry, it won't be," Elaina responded quietly from her seat in the laboratory. She had one wrist hand-cuffed to the lab bench.

Bretton stopped in his tracks. He had been hoping to buy a little more time before having to come face to face with her. He wanted to fabricate some good excuses as to why the virus left the lab and why it looked so different from hers. He also wanted to lay some groundwork and accuse her of all sorts of terrible things to build some reasonable doubt in the base.

He was out of time. He had to face the woman who had made his career more difficult for years. She had been the one person in the way of his fame and fortune, and he figured she was returning to steal the limelight once again.

"Can we speak alone, please?" he said to his staff.

"I don't think that's a good idea," a guard said.

"I'm not going anywhere," Elaina replied, jangling the chain on her arm. "I'm not a threat."

Elaina stared directly at him. He looked at the floor.

"We'll be waiting outside if you need us," his guard said, motioning the rest of the staff outside.

Elaina waited until the door was shut before she began speaking.

"Did you have a chance to speak with your daughter?"

Bretton winced. It didn't help him to know that Elaina had some dirt against him.

"I did. I was very happy to find out that she's just fine. She's a little tired and shaken up, but she should make a full recovery. I heard that you spent some time with her."

"You could say that." Elaina smirked. "I'm not sure how much you had to do with raising her, but I'm quite fond of Natalia. She's a very smart girl."

"I know. She's really something. She said that you helped her out of a few bad situations. Thanks for that."

"Of course," she replied. "I had the opportunity to

help her, so I did. I think anyone would in that situation."

Bretton knew that she was making a dig at him, but he couldn't fight back on that comment. He decided to let that point go and move on.

"Let me ask you this, Elaina—what do you think you know about the epidemic?"

She knew he wasn't asking for his own information —he wanted a heads up about what he needed to deny if he were ever accused of the crimes she attributed to him. She had proof, and any virologist worth a damn could look at their samples and understand that something was fishy.

Once she could show her evidence to the world, he wouldn't stand a chance. He would have no proof for which he could use to frame her. She decided to tell him what she believed to be true just so she could see the look on his face when she revealed that she knew what he was up to.

"Where shall we begin? I must say, I was truly horrified when I thought there was a chance that my virus was making everybody horribly sick. I hadn't seen any symptoms like that in my research, so it didn't make sense to me why they would present in humans. Then, the mutations happened, and the rage symptom threw me for a major loop. It was so frustrating not having any idea why it was happening. There was no lab for me to go to study—the police heard that I was in charge and were planning to arrest me. I think you know more about that bit than I do."

Bretton shook his head. "They only ever asked me

who was working on that kind of virus. I told them what I knew about the Morgan Strain."

"Which was very little," she interjected. "I don't think I shared the purpose of my virus with anyone. I think people just heard rumors and filled in the gaps. It's strange how imaginations will create the craziest truths."

"But you ran. You could have talked to the police and cleared things up," Bretton replied.

"At that time, I still thought it was a possibility that it was my fault. Not only would it be extremely dangerous to be caught, but if I were locked up, I couldn't do anything to fix this. While on the run, I managed to do quite a bit of work. It was then that I collected a sample of the virus from an infected person and compared it to mine. And guess what? The killer virus is a cheap imitation of mine. That led me to figure out that someone had been meddling with my work in an attempt to improve upon what I was working on. Am I getting close?"

"You're not that sneaky," Bretton said. "I knew what your virus was for, but it had a lot of flaws."

"Minor ones, yes, but I was still working on it. Oh, I was so close to having it right. My guess is that you threw something together in hopes that it would be better than mine, so then you could take the credit."

She watched his body tense up and knew that her hypothesis was right on.

"Why?" she asked simply. "That was my life's work."

"Your life's work," he spat. "When I was your age, I didn't even have my doctorate yet. You have no idea how it feels to work with an overrated colleague.

Everyone thinks you're some shining star, but you just seem impressive because you're young and beautiful. No one else in our field gets the same treatment as you, and there are some of us who have accomplished much more."

Elaina sat quietly and thought about what he said. She was offended that he was suggesting that she didn't work hard for what she'd accomplished and her praise was undue. She'd never really liked Bretton, but now, she had a solid reason to hate him.

"You don't have anything to say for yourself? You set me up. First, you ripped off my work and contaminated people. Then, you pointed your finger at me as this epidemic raged on. Then, you decided to hide out here and work for the government to make a cure for the horror you created? Let me guess—you haven't been able to figure it out, have you?"

"This is why I don't feel any remorse about what happened to you," he said, getting angry. His face turned bright red. "You're a child. You may be advanced for your age, but you're still naïve in the ways of the world. Do you really think that everyone is just going to pat you on the back for everything you do? Do you think that you'll never be expected to compete with someone better than you? Get real. We're just trying to get our discoveries out there before the next guy. You have to work quicker and be smarter. If I didn't feel pressured to improve upon your work, do you think any of this would have happened?"

Elaina couldn't believe what he was saying. He was practically admitting guilt but still putting blame on her.

If she weren't chained to the table, she would have gotten up and walked away. She didn't need this—she had more important things to do.

"You don't think I can do this? Why, because I'm young? Because I'm a female? You underestimate your daughter, too, and she's ten times braver than you could ever be. You're nothing but a coward. You're selfish and weak."

This struck a nerve with Bretton. Channeling his daughter's fury from earlier, he raised his hand and struck Elaina across the face. She took her blow and blinked back tears as she stared him in the eye.

Bretton wondered if he had gone too far, but there was no going back now. Elaina Morgan had done her best to ruin his career, and he wasn't going to sit down and listen to her hurl insults at him.

"I shouldn't have hit you, but you've brought out the worst of me. I wasn't always this way. I was competitive, sure, but in a healthy way. I just wanted to be the best, to discover and create things that would change the course of history. I wanted to be remembered for my advances in the field. I didn't expect for some spoiled brat to come into my lab and take my resources from me."

"What did I take from you? Besides, if you were so threatened by my skill, why didn't I make you a better scientist? That's what healthy competition is supposed to do."

Bretton clenched his teeth. "You forced me to take drastic measures," he spat. "If you would have just let me do my work without trying to be a superstar, then I wouldn't have had to work so quickly and recklessly. I'm sure you tell yourself whatever you need to so you can sleep at night, but you need to know that you're responsible for what has happened to this city. As thousands of people die, know that this is a direct result of your actions."

Elaina took a deep breath. She wasn't sure if Bretton was ever a rational person, but he certainly took a dive off the deep end. She wanted to make sure that justice was served. Even if it meant that she had to put her virus studies on the backburner. She could not work in a field where Dr. Vincent could carry on as he pleased.

Elaina had had enough of his insane accusations. She just wanted to get to work. She had been in a holding cell, trying to convince the military police that she was innocent and that she wanted to try to fix things. She wasn't sure if they believed her that she didn't commit the original crime, but they seemed convinced that she wanted to find a cure.

She was, quite frankly, surprised when the colonel asked her what it would take to correctly get the job done. She quickly found out that he didn't mean compensation either. She quickly told him that she had already started working on an antidote and that she just needed a little more time to perfect it. She was fairly certain it worked for her strain, but she needed to make sure that it worked for Bretton's strain.

The fact that the military would even suggest torturing their own citizens in order to motivate them to do work for them was horrifying. Elaina didn't want to work for an employer who treated their employees poorly, but she didn't think of working on the cure in their labs as actually working for them. She was working for herself and the rest of humanity. What the military wanted to do with her cure once it left the lab was beyond her concern as long as everyone who needed it could get it.

"Doctor Vincent," she said softly, hoping he'd calm down enough to end their conversation. She wanted to get back to her lab. "Is there anything else you want to discuss? Otherwise, I would like to go back to my holding cell. I'm supposed to have a meeting with the colonel," she lied to get her out of the uncomfortable situation.

He stared, unblinking, at her. "You're not working on the cure, are you?"

"No," she lied again. "I thought you said you had it covered."

He glared at her. "You little bitch, you're working on this behind my back."

"This is beyond your expertise, Vincent," she retorted. "What difference does it make if the cure is finished soon? Do you want me to tell everyone that you figured it out? I'll do that if that's what it takes."

"You can't be trusted. Maybe I should just keep you here."

"Is anyone out there?" Elaina yelled toward the door. "It's time for me to go."

"You're not going to take me down, Elaina Morgan. I won't stand for it."

"Please hurry," she yelled, feeling nervous.

The guard walked in and unlocked the handcuffs. Elaina rubbed her sore wrist.

"You've become unstable," she said, turning back to him. "You're a good scientist, but you'll never be great if you don't learn how to control yourself."

"Good?" he scoffed, reaching into his lab coat pocket. "I think I'm on the verge of genius."

When the guard turned his back, Bretton lunged at Elaina, sticking her in the belly with a syringe. It happened so quickly and unexpectedly that she couldn't react quickly enough to stop him.

"What was that?" she cried, holding her stomach. He hadn't been gentle with the needle, and a tiny drop of blood appeared on her shirt at the site of the sharp pain.

His only response was a sly smirk. His silence was telling, and she feared the worst. In a lab full of deadly viruses, there was a good chance that there was something sinister coursing through her veins. She wasn't sure whether the guard had seen what had happened, or he just didn't care.

Bretton was quickly ushered away, and Elaina was left to figure out how she was going to survive this infection without a sure-fire antidote.

Elaina wasn't sure if her sudden dizziness was from the virus or from fear, but she sat down on the cool concrete floor before she fainted. She needed to get up and do something about the injection, but her legs felt numb. She wanted Natalia or Alec—anybody—to come calm her down. She wasn't sure if she could go on in the state she was in. What would happen if the infection took over her mind? There would be no one left on Earth who knew the virus like Elaina did.

She closed her eyes and thought about her sister before her early death. She was so sweet and calm, even in terrible situations. When Lily was diagnosed with cancer, Elaina remembered that she was the one who comforted her family members when it should have been the other way around. Lily had a way of assuring everyone that they would be fine, even when she couldn't be sure of it. Even on her deathbed, Elaina didn't fear for her sister because Lily had convinced her that everything would be okay.

Elaina pretended that her sister was in the room with her, telling her to get up and save herself.

"Okay, Lily," she said, pulling the familiar vial from its safe spot in her jacket, "Let's see what you can do."

Chapter Twenty-Nine

Alec watched from his bunk as the armed guards performed their security checks. They would not be bringing any more residents into the quarantine, so all of the doors had to be sealed and locked. Alec rolled over on his back, quietly waiting for night to fall.

He had almost completed his first day in the decontamination camp, and it had gone slowly. After being on the run in the city, on high alert at all hours of the day, being in a blank, sterile environment was incredibly boring. He couldn't stand having nothing productive to do.

It was strange watching the soldiers mill about, something that he had experience doing in his line of work. But there was something he didn't trust about them. They gave him limited information and strict orders. He had tried to calmly ask if he would get his gun back when he left the camp, but he was only met with noncommittal answers.

When he spoke louder, with more authority, he was ordered to return to his bunk. If he could not comply with orders, he would be segregated from the group and placed in a solitary cell, as opposed to the group cells their bunks were in. He obeyed, annoyed and defeated. He didn't want to fight with anyone—he just wanted answers and he wanted his concerns to be listened to.

He thought that, as a cop, his profession would gain him a little more respect around the camp, but to the soldiers, he was just another civilian who had committed no crime except for staying alive under present circumstances. Instead of fleeing the city or illegally bribing officers, he had done his duty to serve and protect. His repayment was to be treated like a criminal.

Alec felt like he needed to talk to Natalia, but she was currently sitting on her bed, crying and throwing expletives wherever they seemed to stick. Will was next to her, a reassuring arm around her shoulders, nodding along with her story. There wasn't room for Alec over there. He had pieced together what had happened to Natalia, so there was nothing left to learn.

What he really wanted was for Natalia to tell him that she had made a mistake, and that the girl he knew as Lainey was not Elaina Morgan, mass murderer, after all.

He once had a girlfriend who'd lied about all sorts of stupid things. She would tell him that he couldn't go over to her place because they were in the middle of fumigating and it would be too dangerous to go in. In reality, she was hiding the fact that she would have other men over at late hours of the night. She'd tell him that she was deathly allergic to leafy greens and to make sure that none of her food contained any. Later, he found out that she was just a picky eater and didn't want to have to pretend to like vegetables.

The list of petty lies went on, but even then, Alec struggled to part ways with her. He knew that she was no good for him, but he couldn't help but hang on to every word and try to keep up. When she eventually dumped him because he worked too much and couldn't devote enough time to her, he was devastated, but with time, he felt great relief. He was relieved that there was nothing keeping him in a toxic relationship and that he no longer felt the desire to be with someone who made him feel terrible.

Alec hoped that he would soon feel that way about Elaina. He hated the fact that he had grown attached to her in the first place, but he despised himself for continuing to have feelings for her that he just couldn't shake. As he waited out his time in quarantine, he waited for time to heal the wounds left by her lies.

Natalia seemed sure that Elaina hadn't done anything wrong. Natalia was a child, though, so he wasn't convinced that he could trust her judgment. She was a bright girl, but she had gone through a lot with Elaina. It would make sense that she would side with the person who saved her from a few scary situations.

What he really needed was to hear Elaina tell him the truth. It probably wouldn't change his current perception of her, but it would give him the closure he needed. He needed to know why she would do something so careless and dangerous because the Elaina he knew wasn't like that at all. She was intelligent, independent, and caring. He saw the way she'd cared for a girl that she didn't know very well and wondered why there was such a disconnect between the girl he'd tried to protect and the one on the news.

Alec got up to walk around as he was starting to go stir crazy in the confinements of the bunks. But there was really nowhere for him to go. The cafeteria had closed until breakfast, the tiny recreation room had been sealed, and even the bathrooms only had two tiny stalls and a shower. There was nowhere to go but his own bed.

After stretching out, he returned to his bunk and tried to will himself to sleep. But rest didn't come for Alec, who had spent the last few days in and out of consciousness. It was much to early in the evening to go to bed, and Natalia and Will's discussions from the corner weren't helping.

"Alec Lawrence," a voice over the loudspeaker said. "Please report to the recreation hall immediately."

Natalia's and Will's heads turned his direction. He shrugged his shoulders at them and left his bunk. He didn't know what they wanted with him, but he was a little relieved to have a reason to leave the bunk.

An officer met him in the open space and escorted him to a small office off the side of the decontamination unit. He gestured to a short chair, and Alec sat down, his knees rising above his waist.

The man, who later introduced himself as the

colonel, peered down at him from his elevated seat behind the desk. Alec felt small, but he wouldn't let them play mind games with him.

"Officer Lawrence," the colonel boomed. "I understand that you are one of Elaina Morgan's accomplices."

"Accomplices?" he interrupted. "Hell no. I didn't even know she was Elaina Morgan until I got here. I thought she was just some woman who got left behind in the virus and needed a little help."

"So you weren't helping her escape?"

"I only wanted to help her escape the virus, not the law. You know it's part of my job description to capture criminals. If I knew what I know now, I would have never let her get away. I was on duty when things really got bad. I could have arrested her and brought her down to the station days ago. I just didn't know."

The colonel studied Alec's face, searching for a hint of a lie. When he seemed satisfied with his answer, he continued.

"We need all the information you have about Elaina. I understand that you were made to believe that she was someone else, but there's a good chance she let some information about herself slip out along the way. What do you know about her?"

Alec thought hard. They'd had a few long discussions, but they didn't have anything to say about personal details. When he thought about it, Elaina had been very careful to conceal anything that could identify her.

"I didn't learn much about her, to be honest. She

seemed like a very nice, normal person. She met up with Natalia when she saved her from being attacked. I thought they were sisters. Elaina just seemed so protective of her and wanted to make sure she was okay. I remember her being very anxious to move on from our shelters. She came from a school but wanted to get to a hospital. I didn't think that was a good idea, so we stayed in a shipping container instead."

"I see," the colonel said, writing down a few notes. "How else might you describe Ms. Morgan?"

From the back of his mind, words like quiet, sweet, and beautiful came to the forefront, as did liar and traitor.

"I don't know. She never gave me any reason to doubt her during the time we spent together. She was a fine person and a good travel companion. I was just trying to do my job and save as many innocent lives as possible."

"And did you engage in a romantic or physical relationship with Ms. Morgan in this time?"

Alec blushed hard. "No," he said quickly. "It was strictly cordial."

"Thank you for your honesty," the colonel said, shutting his notebook. "Now, I'd like to ask you a question from one professional to another."

"Sure."

"Given everything you know about Elaina Morgan now, what do you think should be done with her? You've seen a lot of criminals in your line of work—she's got to be the most dangerous of them all. We have a lot of people out there who want justice, and it'll be impossible to get her in a courtroom for a very long time to come. What, in your opinion, would be a reasonable punishment for her until then?"

Alec knew where he was going with this and felt sick. He hated Elaina, but he didn't want to think about the cruel and unusual punishment that would probably be inflicted upon her. If she were found guilty of her crimes, it seemed reasonable for her to sit in jail for the next few decades. But he didn't want her to get hurt. If the Elaina he met was even remotely her genuine self, she didn't deserve poor treatment.

"I'm afraid I'm not qualified to speak on these manners," Alec answered, standing up from his chair. "Is that all you need from me?"

The colonel looked back at his notes, disappointed that he couldn't get more from Alec. "Yes, that is all. Thank you for your cooperation."

Before Alec left, he made one last request.

"Can I talk to her?"

"To Elaina? I don't think so. If you want her to know you're disappointed in her, I'm sure she's already figured that out. Besides, she's meeting with our head of the research department. She'll have to be back in her cell soon. There are reports of infected citizens moving closer to the area. Of course, it's nothing that we can't handle, but we'll be under lockdown, just to be safe."

"Really?"

"It's nothing to worry about. Just sit tight and keep our conversation between us. I know I can trust you to keep the others calm in case things get noisy out there."

"Sure," Alec said softly. "Let me know if I can be of further service to you."

He walked back to the bunks, shaking. He needed to get out of captivity. He didn't want to know the dark and dirty secrets behind the people who ran the country. It was too much for him to bear.

"What was that about?" Will asked once he returned.

"Nothing. Just some simple questions."

"About Elaina?" Natalia asked.

He nodded.

"What did they say?" Natalia sat up a little straighter and balled up her fists.

"Not much. I told them the very little I knew about her, and that was it."

"She's innocent, you know," Will said.

"Stay out of it," Alec warned. "You don't know anything about this."

Natalia frowned. "There's no use, Will," she said softly. "Just leave him alone. He will never understand."

Alec felt like everyone had turned against him. First, Elaina had deceived him. Then, Natalia convinced Will of her lies and was trying to act like he was the unreasonable one. He'd had enough. Alec pulled the covers over his head to block out the dim light and placed the pillow over his ears. He wanted to have some peace and quiet for once.

In the distance, sirens blared. The others stood at attention, fearful expressions on their faces. Alec was prepared for a potential situation, so he didn't feel concerned with the ruckus happening outside their cell.

"What was that?" Will squeaked, grabbing Natalia's arm.

"I'm sure it's nothing," Alec replied. "We're safe here."

The noises got louder. One crash from the outside of the cell even startled Alec. Gunfire rang out, and Alec could only imagine the carnage beyond their building.

Alec listened closely to the voices outside the cell to figure out exactly what was going on out there. He held a finger to his lips, prompting the other two to fall silent.

"—more than we were prepared for," a voice said.

"What do we do with the civilians under quarantine?"

"We have strict orders to leave them," the first voice said. "If we abandon the base, they must be left behind. It's too risky to take them."

Alec's stomach dropped. After everything they had been through, they were just going to be left in their cage like bait. He was done helping them. At the first chance he had, he was getting out.

"Listen," he whispered to Natalia and Will, who looked absolutely horrified. "Things could get bad here. When the time is right, we're going to escape."

"How?" Natalia cried.

He searched his brain for any rational thought, but nothing came to mind. He didn't know exactly where they were, nor did he know what resources would be at his disposal.

"We'll figure it out as we go. Be prepared."

The three sat huddled together and waited for any sign that their situation was about to change. Without warning, a vehicle crashed into the side of their building and infected people started pouring in. Now, Alec understood the soldiers' concern—they had become organized and were battling by the hundreds.

"Now," Alec yelled, and they crept through the building, waiting for the infected to stop pouring in so they could get out through the hole in the building.

"We have to get Elaina," Natalia cried.

"We don't even know where she is," Alec said. "Absolutely not."

"Guilty or not, she's still the only hope we have of stopping this virus," Natalia reasoned. "No one here is going to protect her. We have to help her."

As much as Alec hated to admit it, he knew that she was right. "Fine, let's find the lab and see if we can find Elaina," he ordered. "If it's too risky, we get the hell out of here."

They nodded, and the three of them took off toward the main building in search of their long-lost companion. The once pristine and hidden military base now looked like the heart of Seattle. Cars were on fire, rubble was scattered underneath their feet, and the smell of burning chemicals and infection filled the air.

"There." Will pointed at a rectangular building. "That door is open. Let's go."

Dodging bullets from both sides, they ducked their way into the laboratory. The power had been cut, but the emergency lights cast a white, fluorescent glow over everything.

"Elaina," Natalia called, searching for her friend. "Are you in here?"

"Hey," Will yelled, pushing tables and chairs to the side, "I see someone over here."

Alec's heart skipped a beat. Sitting on the ground with bottles and syringes surrounding her was Elaina. Her eyes were red and full of tears. For a moment, all anger dissipated and he wanted nothing more than to hold her in his arms and make sure everything was okay.

"What happened, Elaina?" he said softly.

"He injected me with something," she blubbered. "I don't know what it was, but he's gone now."

"Who's gone, Elaina?" Natalia asked, her voice shaking.

"Doctor Vincent."

"What's going on?" Will asked, his eyes darting back and forth. "What's wrong with her?"

"I didn't know what to do. I don't know if it works yet," Elaina said, a small object gripped tightly in her hand.

"Elaina," Alec said firmly, squatting down to her level. "You're not making any sense. What do you have that may or may not work?"

"LILY," she said, her big eyes looking straight into Alec's.

Outside, it sounded like the world was ending. The only organization that Alec figured could keep him safe was losing their battle. There was no law, no protection. All he had was his gang of unlikely characters working together to stay alive. It was all he had left.

"Okay," he said softly, helping her up from the floor. "Let's get out of here."

Chapter Thirty

Elaina wouldn't budge. Even Will tried lifting her up, but her body fell back to the ground like dead weight.

"Come on, Elaina," Alec urged. "We have to go now if we want to survive."

"You don't understand," she sniffled. "It's not safe."

Elaina had seen the progression of the virus in a reasonably healthy person. She knew that the incubation period was short, and symptoms progressed rapidly. Even if she did escape with the others, she would be sure to infect the others. Then, if she couldn't separate herself quickly enough, she may even turn against them. She cared about them too much to give them a death sentence. They needed to go on without her.

"Listen," Alec said, holding her face so she was looking him in the eyes, "this base is being taken over by the infected. If you stay here, you will certainly be killed.

I don't care about what you did. I just need you to come with me."

Elaina didn't know how to admit the fact that she may very well be a loaded weapon. She so desperately wanted to go with them and escape the military base, but she would be putting herself and others at risk if she went on the run again. She was stuck.

"I'm sorry," she started, getting ready to tell them about what she believed she was injected with.

"You can save your apologies," Alec interrupted, swooping her up into his arms. "We need to get out of here."

The blood from her injection sites left tiny dots on Alec's sweatshirt, though he didn't notice. He was too busy dodging gunfire.

"Can you run?" he asked.

"I think so," Elaina replied.

"Then I'm going to put you down. Just follow me, okay?"

She nodded, and he gently set her on her feet. Her legs were shaky to start, then her strides fell long and even.

Dr. Vincent, surrounded by a team of armored soldiers, ran past the four as they hid behind an overturned truck.

"Should we follow them?" Alec asked.

"Why?" Will hissed. "They're not helping us."

"They're headed toward the quarantine unit. If he's taking them to save Natalia, then maybe they'll be of some worth to the rest of us."

"Not me," Elaina spoke up. The others looked at her with pity. She was probably right about that. Not only did the military have little motivation to save her, but Bretton certainly wouldn't want to waste his security detail on her.

"Let's follow them," Elaina said. "At the very least, Natalia will be safe."

Alec led them in the direction of Bretton's entourage, being careful not to follow too closely behind them. He wanted to place themselves at the right place at the right time.

Elaina hoped that their plan would work. Having Bretton reject her would be the perfect excuse for her to stay behind. He could inform them that he had infected her. That way, she wouldn't have to break the horrible news, and Bretton could face the fallout that would be sure to happen afterward. The others could go to safety, and she could remain at the base and do her best to stay alive.

"Where are they going?" Alec asked as they neared the quarantine unit. Bretton and his guards showed no sign of slowing down to look for Natalia. Before anyone could answer him, Bretton was being hoisted into a tank, the door slamming shut behind them. The group watched in awe as the humongous vehicle slowly rolled away.

They looked at Natalia, worried about how she would react to being left behind by her father for the second time. Instead of complete despair, she looked unsurprised.

"We need a car," Natalia said. "There's a open

garage full of military vehicles. Let's pick one and get the hell out of here."

They ran toward a truck and piled inside, Alec in the driver's seat and Natalia and Will in the back. A vehicle was coming straight for them, and it wasn't clear if the occupants were military personnel or infected civilians. Either way, everyone was an enemy.

Elaina knew that she couldn't go with them. They were smart and resourceful. They would make it to safety with no problem. They were all so young still and had so much life ahead of them. She couldn't hold them back.

Even if her serum worked and fought off the virus as she had hoped, she was still in a lot of trouble. Everyone knew her secret, and she wasn't sure anyone would be willing to help her.

Alec started the truck and put it into drive. He nearly pulled away before he realized that they were short one passenger.

"Get in," he shouted over the roar of the engine. "Someone's coming."

"I'm not going with you," Elaina said, tears forming in her eyes.

Alec sighed, getting fed up with Elaina's theatrics. "Then don't, I guess. We're just trying to help you."

Natalia rolled down her window and extended her head outside.

"Elaina," she pleaded. "I know that you didn't cause any of this. I've suspected that my dad had something to do with this for a while. We want you to be safe. Just get in the car, and we can all have the chance to get the truth out there. We can't know unless you get in the car and tell your side of the story."

"It's more complicated than that," Elaina said, watching the vehicles come closer.

Alec reached his hand toward her through the open passenger door. "Take my hand," he shouted.

She knew she should run in the other direction, but Elaina couldn't control herself. She had longed for human contact for a while now. She was so lonely and just wanted to belong to people for once. Her family was broken, her workplace was shattered, and the closest thing she had to friends were getting ready to leave. She couldn't go on by herself. She needed people.

Elaina gently placed her hand in Alec's, feeling the warmth from his body flow through hers. Then, with a firm yank, he pulled her up into the seat and Natalia shut the door behind her.

Alec dropped her hand and gripped the steering wheel. He stomped on the gas, sending them lurching forward.

"You'd better put your seatbelts on," Alec said, his face changing from warm and inviting to stony and serious.

Alec, Elaina, Natalia, and Will rode through the gravel and mud, past the battle that was going on at the base and onto the highway. As far as they could tell, their car was the only one on the road. Usually a curious bunch, no one had even asked Alec where he was driving—everyone was just relieved to be on the move again.

Alec, typically protective and tactical, was cold and

distant, not wanting to make eye contact with anyone. Natalia, usually curious and concerned, had yet to ask a single question regarding their location or plans. Will, full of optimism and eager to speak, had yet to say a word, let alone crack a joke.

Then there was Elaina, harboring a secret that she tried to let out but just couldn't. As hard as she'd tried to back in the lab, the words just wouldn't come out. It was as if the second she admitted to herself that she was likely infected, she would succumb to the virus. She wasn't ready to give up—not yet, anyway.

As they drove through the sunset, Elaina kept her mouth shut, positive that she was already in too deep.

It will be okay, Lily's voice in her head reassured her.

But what if it's not? her conscience whispered, the temporary calm evaporating as the hum of the truck's engine quieted her racing mind.

About Max Lockwood

Max Lockwood writes suspenseful, post-apocalyptic thriller and dystopian fiction while living in New York.

Growing up with parents who were preppers and always planning for the worst, but hoping for the best, got him interested in writing in the first place. "What would happen if the world were to change?" is something he asked himself his whole life. Until one day he decided to put it down on paper.

His stories will have you reading on the edge of your seats…you have been warned!

Sign up for Max's mailing list and find out about his latest releases, giveaways, and more.

For more information, be sure to check out the links below!
max@maxlockwood.com

Also by Max Lockwood

The Morgan Strain Series

Point Of Transmission (Book 1)

Point Of Proximity (Book 2)

Zero Power Series

It Began (Book 1)

Trying To Survive (Book 2)

They Invaded (Book 3)

Fending Them Off (Book 4)

Excerpt From It Began

Chapter One

S chool was annoying, even when she was the one standing at the front.

Clara was rethinking a lot of life choices, and not for the first time. In fact, she thought of it often and wondered why she'd thought it would be a good idea to become a teacher, and a high school teacher at that.

"Now, if you would all just pay attention..."

She threw the words out there not expecting much and sighed because nothing changed anyway. It was a particularly trying class, one of the hardest in a long time. Usually, she could get at least one or two students to pay attention, but that wasn't even the case.

"Please turn to page fifteen in your textbooks," she tried again, but got nothing.

Still, she couldn't just stop teaching. So she went on. If anyone caught even part of the lessons, she could take it and—well, not be happy, but at the very least content. She couldn't even blame them, she remembered what it was like, being a teenager. Few cared about school; she just happened to be among the few, and even she had been impatient for high school to be over.

She was attempting to teach the freshmen about the importance of grammar, but they were all preoccupied with passing notes and giggling amongst one another. It was pretty common, actually, which was why she disliked sitting in first year classes, especially so close to the beginning of the school year.

These kids were fresh from junior high and still thinking like kids, in their mind, school wasn't so important. That, or they were thinking they could breeze through it like they did junior high. They didn't know yet that the grades they came out with would pretty much determine their futures. It wasn't her job to tell them, and would they care about that anyway, even if she did?

Usually she would do something, at least discourage them from such blatant disrespect, but she was tired. She had a specific job description; go in, teach her class, then leave. She was giving them all the materials they would need for their tests. If they didn't take advantage of it and failed, well… she couldn't say it wasn't entirely her problem, since as the teacher, if her students failed she would be held accountable, but she couldn't even care about it just then.

Clara was just that *tired*.

When the bell rang, it felt like she hadn't made any progress. It was likely true, but she couldn't help feeling partly relieved to be done with the day. But largely, she just felt dissatisfied.

"Do you kids know the meaning of discipline? Because if you don't, I'm going to introduce you to it," she threatened, but their laughter drowned out her voice.

Not that any of them heard her, or if they did, they didn't seem to care. They were too busy running for the door, about as eager as she was to get out of the room. She knew her attempts at punishment were futile. These kids didn't take her seriously, and they likely wouldn't any time soon. She let herself sigh when the last one was out the door and felt a heavy weight settle on her shoulders. Not that she was dying to punish them, anyway. It would be best in the long run, but then she'd have to put up with her students pretending to pay attention while secretly hating on her. She didn't think she could survive pranks being thrown her way, not again, no matter how weak or seemingly harmless.

Clara gathered her things so she could leave. Thankfully, it was her last class of the day, so she had no reason to stick around. She'd collected assignments and a short quiz, though, so she had too much on her hands, literally, and she could only curse herself for the miscalculation. She could have asked one of the students, she'd done it before, but she had a fear of freshmen while they were still so green. It left her anxious at the start of every school year since she taught them English.

She struggled to carry her paperwork out to the car, feeling ridiculous as she tried to juggle everything in her arms with her jacket and the strap of her bag slipping off every now and then. The heels of her shoes weren't helping, but then she'd been in a rush this morning and ended up with a pair with longer heels than she liked for standing around and teaching. She could only curse herself for the mistake.

Then a kid rushed past her and made her drop it all. It could have been by accident, or not, but she lost her balance and watched everything fall to the ground. There wasn't much of a breeze to blow the numerous papers too far, so small mercies. Still, she felt the weight on her shoulders grow heavier, knowing she'd have to pick them all up, but wishing for a second that she could just leave it all and go home. Only to sigh, because she knew that would be irresponsible.

She might not like her job, but she needed it.

Close to tears, Clara bent down to pick up her things, grabbing for the papers first before they could flutter away. Her feet ached in her shoes and in her frustration, she wished she could toss them off and lob them at the kid that did this and didn't even bother to help, though she hadn't even seen who it was.

Dammit!

"Hey!"

Cooper, a friend and fellow teacher rushed over to her. She looked up, startled to see someone else kneeling beside her to help her out. She was surprised, and could only gape at him for a moment. He looked up and winked as he grabbed papers in his hands. She just felt overwhelmed at the nice gesture, Clara couldn't remember the last time someone had stopped to think about her.

"What?"

She blinked. "Um…"

He rolled his eyes, handing over her hand bag and jacket and taking the papers already in her possession. "Just thought I should remind you I'm here to help—after all, we are carpooling together. So get that look off your face."

She wasn't sure what face he meant. But after blinking a couple of times, her eyesight went blurry, and she could feel her expression crumple.

No.

She didn't want to cry, not now—not here, of all places. If any of the kids saw they'd just make fun of her for it later. Kids were cruel, after all, she remembered that much from her high school years, even when they simply thought they were having fun. If she'd ever hurt someone so carelessly, and if she had the opportunity, she'd apologize profusely for being such a little shit.

Cooper saw her crying and his expression softened immediately, a hand raising to wipe a tear away. She wouldn't let more fall, though. It would only worsen the humiliation. Then his hand tapped her chin lightly.

"Keep your chin up, Clara. I know it's hard, but you don't have to let yourself be so overwhelmed. If you need any help, you can ask for it. No one would think you're weak for it."

She gave a huff of laughter, and it sounded a little wet, but she swallowed back the lump in her throat.

No crying.

Cooper Hewett was two years older than her, with dark hair, olive skin and green eyes that always seemed to twinkle with hidden laughter. He was fit and muscular, he looked every part the physical instructor at the school. He was also Clara's best friend—nearly her only friend, really, since she hardly talked to the others as much. He was the only bright spot in most of her days, always looking to make her laugh with his good sense of humor, or give her a pick-me-up when she looked down.

They finished picking up her stuff and he gave her a hand up. She appreciated the help, but knew he wasn't entirely correct. There were people that would look down on her if she gave in and broke down, they couldn't help themselves. But she wouldn't tell him that.

"I'm sorry. I just had a difficult day."

She scoffed internally. What an understatement.

Another kid ran past, and Clara knew before she even opened her mouth that she was going to shout something immature aimed at them.

"I didn't know Ms. Thomas and Mr. Hewett were in *love*."

Clara just rolled her eyes without bothering to turn back. The kid could have been sneering at them instead of making light fun, but she didn't want to see to know which. Not that she had to, because Cooper did.

"Hey, keep running your mouth and I'm gonna give you bad grades as revenge," he mock threatened, making Clara smile as she heard a light laugh behind them, getting further away.

He was better at joking with the students than she was. Hell, he was better at a lot of things. She knew if it had been him in that classroom instead of her, he would have gotten the students to behave while getting their respect in the process. He wouldn't have the kind of problems she did. Of course, he actually loved what he was doing, when it was just a replacement of her dreams for her.

Of all things about him, she couldn't understand that. There were times when teaching teenagers actually brought him joy. It helped that he had a positive attitude, and a general outlook towards life. Clara envied him that, just a little.

Cooper led the way to the car, unlocking the door and letting her get in first as he put her paperwork in the backseat with his own smaller workload holding them down, then got in the driver's seat. Finally, they were on their way home, and she couldn't help feeling relieved, and a little guilty for doing so.

"So, care to tell me what that was all about?" Cooper asked, voice gentle.

Clara knew he meant her almost breakdown. She didn't want to talk about it, but if there was someone she trusted to tell about her problems, it was him. He'd helped her out more times than she could count, all to be a good friend, acting offended when she even mentioned paying him back for all of it. Besides, maybe it would help lessen her burden a little if she could vent about it.

"I wasn't in the best place today," she sighed, rolling her head on the headrest to look outside. "I haven't been for a long time, really."

She caught his glances in her peripheral, but wouldn't meet his eyes.

"What does that mean?"

She sighed again, feeling heavier. "I don't know, just... I guess my expectations for the job crashed and burned. A while back, I just didn't want to think about it, and now it's *all* that I can think about."

"You had expectations in this job?" he joked, and she cracked another smile, only for it to disappear as she sighed again, suddenly feeling older than her years.

"It wasn't anything realistic, I don't think. I just didn't expect to be this..." she floundered, waving her hand, only to let it drop in her lap when she couldn't find the word.

It wasn't quite hate, but it was definitely discontent. But that would be stupid to voice out loud, because a lot of people ended up doing what they didn't like. Complaining would only make her a hypocrite.

"I just wish I could quit," she said suddenly, turning to look at him. He glanced over and caught her eyes for a moment before turning back to the road. "I can't say I entirely hate it, but I did not see this for my life. I hated high school, so like... why the hell did I think becoming a teacher was even a good idea?" she clenched her fists together, looking down at them in her lap. "But no matter how badly I want to. To just quit and look for whatever other job there is out there to tide me over. I know I can't because I'm the only source of income for the family."

She had plenty enough qualifications to attempt it, and she was sure she would find a job, eventually. But with the current economy, it was hard to say when, and where would she get money before that? Besides, of all positions she could take, teaching had some permanence, and even if she lost her job, she could get into another school with little fuss. But that wouldn't exactly help the problem.

Even if she couldn't stand her job, she knew she had to, and it was what had carried her forward all this time. Her family needed her. She didn't mind occasionally going without a meal, but when she had the means to, she wouldn't let them suffer more than they had to. She was all they had and vice versa, after they lost her parents a while back.

She could complain and cry all she wanted, but she knew she wasn't the only one hurting. Breaking down on her own would mean being selfish.

"Hey," Cooper murmured, catching her attention and making her turn to him. His voice was low, serious, and so different from his usually happy personality. "I know it's hard. I can't say I fully understand your situation, as you are dealing with things I can't even begin to imagine. But you don't have to keep it all in. I'm here for you if you ever need anything. And you have to know how I admire you for your hard work. In your position, I would have broken down a lot sooner, believe me. I just can't handle pressure like that."

Not so surprisingly, Clara felt more than just a bit better. Having Cooper around was always good for an ego boost. He was always encouraging her, helping her go on when all she wanted to do was give up. She didn't believe he wouldn't be okay in a similar situation, though. He didn't like too much pressure, but Cooper was reliable. He'd run himself to the ground without complaint to help someone else, as he was already doing with her.

The car slowed down as they got to her house, then parked at the curb. He was out the car before she could stop him, reaching into the back to take her things out for her. She circled around, pulling on her jacket with her bag's strap over her shoulder so she had her arms free to take her things.

"Thank you, Cooper. For… well, everything." There were too many to list them, after all.

He just smiled and leaned closer to give her a kiss on the cheek.

"Don't worry about it. It was my pleasure, believe me."

She gave him a skeptical look, but didn't argue. She held her things tight to her chest with one arm, holding out the other to pull him into a quick hug, reciprocating the kiss on his cheek, and then he was getting into the car and driving away.

Chapter Two

C lara stood, watching the car drive off until it was out of sight. She hesitated before going into the house, not really wanting to be home.

She loved her family, truly, but with the way she was feeling, being home wasn't going to be helpful for her, or anyone. If school was frustrating, being at home was about twice as much. She wondered if she could call Cooper back and do something with him that evening instead. Another reason she'd stuck with school so long, it was another reason to stay away from the usually oppressive atmosphere at home. But she knew she couldn't just turn back around and leave, knew she had responsibilities to attend to. It wouldn't be fair to escape, thinking only of herself.

She sighed and entered the house.

Almost immediately, she wanted to step outside and pretend to be peaceful a moment longer. The grocery delivery bags were strewn in the hallway, probably from when they were dropped off hours ago. Since she didn't have the time and no one else left the house, it was necessary. But it was becoming a common occurrence to come home to find unattended deliveries, and it never grew less annoying.

Her grandmother, Viola, was dozing on the couch. She slept more than anything these days, but usually she was in her room. Clara didn't like her being by herself. Even if something happened and she was awake, the possibility that she could defend herself was low, but Clara didn't care about the logistics when it was dangerous either way.

Clara wondered where her sister could be. She knew Tessa would never leave the house alone because of her phobias, though, so she decided it was likely she was in her 'den.' She rolled her eyes and set her things aside to lighten her load. Sure enough, when she went upstairs, she found her sister in her bedroom.

She was meditating, surrounded by scented candles that made Clara's nose twitch, and her tarot cards laid out in front of her. It was another common sight that never grew less annoying, and she couldn't help the loud sigh that ruined her sister's concentration, eyes snapping open. She shot a glare at Clara that was returned in kind, only fiercer. She was used to her sister's moods already. If only they would stop.

Dark eyes, with bags underlining them, glared at her from under a dark mane of unkempt hair. They looked a lot alike, but Tessa wasn't big on looking after herself. Clara had to look in a mirror, make herself presentable for her job, but her sister didn't have that need and she rarely bothered. Clara considered it a small miracle she occasionally remembered to at least shower on her own. Though, Clara would have been glad if Tessa looked after their aging grandmother some more, she knew the dynamics when she left home were usually the reverse.

"You ruined my meditative state."

Clara just rolled her eyes at the bland accusation, not even the least bit guilty.

"You've had all day to meditate," she snapped back, a little more harshly than intended, but she wouldn't take it back. "But since you've stopped for now, anyway, you should come and help with unpacking the groceries."

Tessa crossed her arms over her chest, scowling sullenly as she huffed. "I don't want to right now, just let me finish what I was doing."

"No excuses," she narrowed her eyes threateningly.

"But I was doing something important," she insisted, and Clara rolled her eyes.

"You can come back after you help me."

But of course, it couldn't just be that easy. Tessa was hard to deal with. She hadn't always been that way, but after their parents died and she grew older, she grew a fascination with weird things. Clara blamed herself, she had let it fester, thinking it was her sibling's way of coping with what had happened. She had responsibilities falling on her she didn't have before, either, but Clara still took the bulk. She didn't blame her sister, but she would have appreciated some cooperation, at least.

Tessa was acting childishly, protesting as they bickered back and forth like they were both years younger than their actual ages. Times like this, it was hard to remember Tessa was actually older, twenty nine to Clara's twenty five years. But they had been living together long enough to know how to deal with each other, since they'd pretty much always been stuck at home. Eventually, she agreed, getting up grudgingly and slinking out of her room.

It startled Clara, like it always did, how thin her sister was. She was four years older and an inch taller, but she always looked so frail, like a light breeze could blow her away. Clara calmed down as she followed her downstairs and they picked up the grocery bags, taking them over to the kitchen and started unpacking.

"So, how was your day," she started conversationally, glancing over at Tessa as she arranged things in the fridge.

"I had a premonition."

She wasn't even fazed by that statement, it no longer threw her. She was always skeptical of her sister's predictions, and found it hard not to roll her eyes. That was something else that had changed after their parents' death. Since Tessa had felt uneasy just before it happened, she'd convinced herself she could see the future.

"Whatever you say, Tessa," she answered calmly, putting away some cans in a cupboard.

She wouldn't consider her sister crazy, but she did get tired of the topic. She couldn't fight against it because it would only start another argument. They were both stubborn and a fight meant that being at home would be unbearable for as long as they kept up the argument. More often than not, Clara was the one backing down, more for the sake of her own sanity than anything else.

When the sounds behind her suddenly stopped, she turned around to see her sister standing still with her back to Clara. She was about to ask if there was a problem, when the other woman suddenly spoke.

"A terrible event is coming our way, and we should prepare for the world's end."

Her voice, her words, were serious. She didn't turn around, and in that moment, Clara was so glad, because she wasn't sure she wanted to see what expression her sister had on her face just then. She felt a shiver work its way down her back, feeling uneasy.

Cut it out.

She shook her head, shook away the uneasiness. It was foolish to take something so paranoid so seriously. Her sister was wrong. Even though she didn't feel as calm as before, she ignored her sister and the light churning in her stomach.

Putting the rest of the groceries away, sans what they'd need for their dinner, she moved to the stove, setting out a couple of pots but not turning anything on at the moment. She just suddenly needed to be out of that room, by herself. She told herself sternly that she was, in no uncertain terms, running away.

"Would you cut the vegetables for dinner? I'm going to go check on grandmother."

Tessa didn't argue, just moved to do as told. As Clara left the room, she heard what her sister muttered to herself but ignored it as well.

"You'll be sorry when my predictions come true."

Chapter Three

I gnoring the irregular beating of her heart, Clara moved to the couch where her grandmother was still sleeping and shook her awake. It took a bit more shaking, and Clara would have been worried, but then she was moving, her eyes fluttering open. They glanced around before falling on her. She was confused for a few moments, looking unsure of where she was.

Before she could grow frantic, Clara took her hand and made her focus on herself instead of looking around the room.

"You're home, remember?" she murmured, keeping her tone soothing as she brought her other hand up to brush back some of the older woman's hair. "And I'm your granddaughter, Clara. Your name is Viola. Do you remember that?"

She waited with her breath held, feeling relieved when she got a nod. When Viola came to properly and looked like she was trying to sit up, Clara helped her, resettling the blanket around her shoulders. Then she sat back on her heels.

"Clara, did you just get back?"

She smiled wanly. "No, I was here a while ago."

"You could have woken me up sooner," Viola chastised.

"It's fine, I didn't want to bother you. I saved you some dinner so you could continue your nap." She went to push herself up. "I'll go get something for you."

But a hand on her shoulder stopped her. "No, thank you, dear."

She sighed. "You need to eat."

"But I'm not hungry," her grandmother insisted.

"Grandma, I insist. You should eat before you go up to bed."

It was entirely possible she hadn't eaten at all the whole day. Clara trusted her sister, but she could get distracted, and their grandmother was growing forgetful. Clara always made sure she had a meal before she went to bed, though.

At least she didn't argue, allowing Clara to get up and go bring her back a plate of food. Back in the living room, the plate went to the coffee table, and then she sat beside her grandmother. She got a disapproving look, but then her grandmother sighed and reached for the plate. She didn't eat, though. Actually, she looked bone-tired, and Clara didn't think it was physical exhaustion because she looked like Clara felt.

"I'm sorry, Clara."

She arched an eyebrow in surprise. "For what?"

Grandmother gave her a sad smile. "I'm sorry you have to take on so much work at the moment."

Ah. She must have noticed Clara's condition. It made sense, when she could remember who Clara was, she was sharp. She'd been taking care of the both of them for years so she was used to the sisters' moods and reading their emotions even while they tried to keep them hidden.

But Clara didn't blame her grandmother—or her sister—for leaving most of the work to her.

Grandmother could hardly help her condition. The onset of Alzheimer's was a surprise, one they were not properly equipped to deal with. They'd only managed to see a doctor once, to diagnose her, and that was it. But Clara had been doing her research and they'd been surviving. Her grandmother also had arthritis, which meant she couldn't do much. Even if she had a job, she would be hard-pressed to actually do it.

It meant it was more up to Clara to care for the family, but she didn't mind it, no matter how tired she felt. Even though she hated her job, someone had to take care of the family, and Clara wasn't just going to back away from the responsibility.

So Clara forced her facial muscles into a smile, placing a hand on top of her grandmother's, gripping tight when she turned it around to clasp her hand properly.

"It's okay."

Grandmother didn't believe her, but she blinked a few times, firming her lips in a way that meant she was trying not to cry. Clara leaned in to give her a quick hug before sitting back so she could eat.

They sat in silence and Clara watched as her grandmother ate without another complaint, until she finished her meal. Clara took the plate with her back to the kitchen, and then came back with a glass of water for the older woman to drink.

"Could you do one thing for me?"

Grandmother smiled. "Of course. Name it."

Clara could feel warmth spread in her chest. She knew she was lucky to have had their grandmother when their parents passed away, or who knows where they would have ended up, with Clara being a minor and Tessa and her special conditions. No matter what she asked, Grandmother would do her best to accomplish it. It lifted her burden every time she reminded herself the situation wasn't as bad as it could have been, that there was still so much good in it. She had her grandmother, her sister—her best friend.

It wasn't always enough, but Clara could move forward with that alone. This time, though, she'd need something extra. She took a breath.

"Can you handle Tessa for the evening so I can go out with Cooper?"

Grandmother suddenly looked delighted. Clara knew she adored Cooper, and she was a little jealous he knew how to handle her grandmother better than she did on the bad days.

"Of course, I can. Anything for my granddaughter."

Clara leaned forward to kiss Viola goodbye. "I won't

take long, okay? And neither of you have to wait up, I think Tessa's already gone back to her room."

She gave a last wave before leaving the house and dropping her fake cheery demeanor. Tessa would have heard her, hopefully, and do what she needed to, so Clara would have the time for herself.

Clara, however, didn't go to meet Cooper. He lived a bit far off, though she could have walked over to his place if she wanted to, or called him to come pick her up. But even though it was what she really wanted to do, she wouldn't. Because what she needed wasn't her best friend trying to comfort her. Instead, she headed over next door and knocked quietly, checking the street in case anyone had noticed her.

These visits had to be kept under wraps, for both their sakes. Besides, the last thing she wanted were rumors starting and getting back home. Her family had enough to deal with as it was.

Her neighbor, Dante, answered the door with a baby strapped to his chest. It was a regular occurrence, one that no longer surprised her. It was still strange to see him and realize he was actually a good father. He was bouncing the baby girl as he let Clara into the house, glancing quickly around the street before closing the door and locking it.

"I'm just putting the baby to bed and then I'll be with you," he promised, but he was looking down at the baby and not her.

She didn't bother with a reply and he didn't wait for one. He headed up the stairs as she sat down on the couch and waited for him to return. He could take anywhere from a few minutes to an hour when the baby was extremely fussy. She sat awkwardly, looking around and trying not to move too much, though with how restless she felt, it was nearly impossible. She'd been coming here for a while, but what she couldn't get used to was the waiting when she had all the time and space to think and she was trying not to. Because when she stopped to let herself think, her thoughts went down all the wrong paths.

Her eyes bounced around the room, trying to distract herself as she sat on her hands to stop them from twitching, spotting a picture of Dante and his wife. It made her wince and glance away, take a breath and try to center herself again.

Why did she even do this?

He was married, and Clara, when she thought about it, was annoyed about how low she'd fallen. Besides, it wasn't like she felt anything for him. Several times, she'd thought of stopping, and when she did, she kept wondering how it had all started in the first place. She hadn't set out to seduce a married man, hadn't expected to end up in an affair she didn't even want and found unsatisfying.

But it was a good outlet, so much better than other dangerous ones she could have found. He could make her forget, at least for a moment, and that was all she wanted.

When Dante returned, he leaned down and planted a wet kiss on her mouth, before pulling back so he could sprawl on the couch beside her and took a moment to catch his breath. She resisted the urge to wipe her lips.

"So, how was your day?"

He leaned closer, and again she resisted, this time the urge to pull away, or push him away. She skimmed over the details, knowing neither of them were there for small talk.

"It was a day. I had a test and had to collect assignments, so it was a little livelier than usual."

His wide palms touched her shoulders, then slid slowly down her arms, making her body shiver. She wasn't sure if it was the good kind or not.

"What about you? How's your baby been?" she asked in return as he unbuttoned her blouse.

His smile was wry, his eyes focused on what he was doing.

"She was a little ill this morning so it's been hectic for a while, but she's doing fine now."

With small talk out of the way, he leaned closer to kiss and nip on her neck, and she dropped her head back so he had more room. Once he ran out of buttons, he reached inside her blouse to place his hands on her waist. He ran his hands up as he licked a trail down her throat, cupping her breasts through her bra and giving a light squeeze.

Whatever she truly felt about these meetings, her body responded as it was supposed to. Her back arched, pushing her breasts farther into his palms, goose bumps appearing on her skin at the bare contact. She rubbed her thighs together, wishing he'd just get on with it.

Like he read her mind, or just took her cues, he pulled away and stood up, holding a hand out to her. She pushed away all the thoughts that told her she should slap his hand away, get up off the couch and button up her blouse then run out. Because then she'd have to face her problems and deal with them instead of running away. But running from her issues was such an easy thing to do, painless for the most part. She took his hand and he pulled her up.

"Come upstairs with me," he murmured, already tugging her behind him as he headed for the stairs again.

"Okay," she agreed, going along with him, though without much enthusiasm.

He didn't call her out on it. This was all about mutual gratification, not what they were feeling, and that was why it worked for her, why she'd fallen to it in the first place and why it was so hard to stop.

She tried to ignore the heavy feeling in her chest as she followed him up the steps, her hand still held in his.

She was ignoring a lot of things for her peace of mind, lately.

YOU CAN CONTINUE READING this story here.

Made in the USA
Middletown, DE
03 September 2017